I0594260

Published July 2025
Published by Indies United Publishing House, LLC

Cover art by Leslie A. Piggott
Edited by: Jennie Rosenblum

Paperback: 978-1-64456-816-3
Kindle: 978-1-64456-817-0
ePub: 978-1-64456-818-7
AudioBook: 978-1-64456-819-4

Library of Congress Control Number: 2025906936

INDIES UNITED PUBLISHING HOUSE, LLC
P.O. BOX 3071
QUINCY, IL 62305-3071

www.indiesunited.net

IDENTITY UNVEILED

IDENTITY UNVEILED

The Cari Turnlyle Series, Book 7

by Leslie A. Piggott

INDIES UNITED PUBLISHING HOUSE, LLC

Dedication

To Brad: much like Bob, you are ever so patient. I'm so glad
you're my forever love.

Table of Contents

Chapter 1

E lizabeth Marino pressed her fingers to her eyes. Maybe she should have taken her mother-in-law up on her offer to pay for a maid. She tried to fan the smoke away from the smoke detector as she hurried past it to the baby's room. Her sister was flying in that evening and she'd been cooking and cleaning while Baby Whitney napped.

"I'm coming, sweet girl!" she called out from the hallway in response to the six-month-old's cries.

The smoke alarm continued to wail from downstairs. Elizabeth gritted her teeth. She'd been so focused on cleaning up the living room that she had forgotten she'd started browning the ground beef for the meat sauce. She was planning on making lasagna for dinner and wanted to get it assembled before she left for the airport. Her husband could put it in to bake while she picked up her sister. Whitney howled louder. She needed to comfort her baby and then she could get the alarm to reset. Maybe she needed to open a window. It was pretty cold outside, so that seemed like a last-ditch effort. She opened the nursery door and scooped up a distraught Whitney.

"You're okay, baby. That's right. Mommy's here. Mommy's here," she repeated to her trembling baby.

The smoke alarm finally quit beeping when she was halfway down the stairs. No sooner did that noise stop than her cell phone burst out into song. Her sister's ringtone. She'd kept it active so she wouldn't miss any calls during her travel day.

"Rebecca! Did you make it to New York?" she asked as she returned with the baby to the kitchen.

Her sister's image smiled back at her from the video call. "Yeah, it says my connection is on time too. I have a little less than an hour before the short flight to Cleveland. I can't wait to meet Whitney!"

Whitney reached toward the phone in response to her name. "She's excited to meet you too," Elizabeth responded.

The image bounced and then went dark as her sister bumped into another traveler. Elizabeth realized she must have dropped her phone, so they were staring at the floor.

"Oh! Sorry!" Rebecca exclaimed. Her face returned to the screen as she retrieved the device. "Uh, Elizabeth, I gotta use the restroom. I'll check in with you later."

Elizabeth started to respond, but the call had ended. She was surprised her sister had been so abrupt, but she didn't have time to dwell on it. "Well, duty calls, Miss Whitney. We have a lot to do before Auntie Rebecca gets here."

The baby's lip started to quiver.

"Oh, silly me! I didn't change you or feed you yet. Poor Whitney. Let's fix that," she said and turned around to the stairs. The dinner was already ruined. She could call her husband later and ask him to pick up something on his way home in place of the lasagna.

* * * * *

Detective Alex Runimoss cleared his throat. "Tell me you aren't looking at Stenoway's accounts again," he said with a sigh.

"Why does it bother you so much that I'm still working this case?" Detective Genevieve Viacorte asked as she entered the login information into the fields on the screen.

"Because there isn't a case anymore. It's closed!" he said and threw his hands up in the air. "You have to let it go. The FBI signed off. Grusky signed off. You. Signed. Off."

"Because I had to. Besides. It only takes a minute of my time to look at his account every now and then," she argued.

"Every now and then? More like three times a day," Alex scoffed. "This isn't healthy."

"I know Stenoway didn't act alone. He's not an outdoorsy guy. He wears loafers and dress pants. I bet that night he ran from you was the first time he'd run in years," she challenged him.

"Maybe so, but he confessed," Alex reminded her. "And no one else has died—"

"Been *killed*," she emphasized.

"Been killed," he said with an eye roll. "We did a good job. We locked up the criminal, Gen."

"Why is no money being spent?" she asked him for what felt like the one-hundredth time.

"They locked that account once they tied it to him," Alex repeated his argument from their earlier discussions.

"What about his other accounts? He's only spending money on his rent and utilities. He never paid the lawyer. Your argument is that the guy is on retainer. How come he never pays him?" she asked pointedly. "And who is paying him $2000 every month? You proposed that was the blackmail money, but it didn't start until he was in prison."

"I don't know, Gen. Maybe we missed one of his accounts. Maybe he only pays the lawyer a yearly fee," Alex hypothesized.

"Why does a low-level city employee have a high dollar attorney on retainer? Does that make any sense to you?" she asked.

"Clearly, he needs one," Alex countered. "And how do you know he's high dollar?"

"You saw the tailored suit and the Lexus, just like me."

Alex shrugged.

She rolled her eyes. "Clearly, we're not on the same page about this. I'm taking a personal day tomorrow. I'll have my cell if you need to reach me."

Alex spun his chair to face hers. "You never take personal days. You even work for free on the weekend. What are you up to?"

She squared her jaw. "I need to talk to a few people. We don't have a case right now, so who cares?"

"Who are you talking to?" Alex pressed her.

"You said you didn't want to be involved, so don't be involved," she told him flippantly. "And I take personal days sometimes. Like on Friday, I'm leaving early for Cari's wedding rehearsal."

"Yeah, that's the same," Alex said and sighed. "Be careful, Gen. Don't get on the wrong side of the department. You're a good detective, but you've got to color inside the lines."

"Even if it means the wrong person is in jail for *multiple* murders?" she asked, her hazel eyes flaring.

"Stenoway isn't innocent," he reminded her.

"I never said he was," she argued. "He's not *the* guy, though, Alex. I know he isn't."

"And you've done a more than thorough job trying to find his accomplice. You've gone through his phone records, pored over his financials like a stalker for literally months, and nothing has turned up. It's possible he acted alone," Alex told her.

"He didn't act alone. I'm certain of it. Just because his phone records didn't implicate anyone else in this scheme doesn't mean they aren't out there. He probably used a burner," Genevieve said and smoothed her dark hair back into place.

"We searched his house. The FBI searched his house. No one found a burner phone," Alex repeated the argument he'd made multiple times over the last six months.

Genevieve held her ground. "Maybe he gave it to his lawyer to hide for him."

Alex tossed his head back and rolled his eyes. She felt the same frustration. They were just not going to see eye to eye on this.

"At least tell me which hornet's nest you're going to be kicking tomorrow," he asked in a gentler tone.

"I'm going to find Shelly. Maybe it's a waste of time, but it's an avenue I've ignored so far."

* * * * *

"I'm taking off for the airport!" Elizabeth called out to her husband.

He stepped into the family room. "Did Rebecca finally call you back? Did her flight land?"

"Uh, no, I didn't hear from her again, but her flight landed. I'm sure she just got caught up with something or maybe her phone died before she could text about being on the next flight," Elizabeth proposed. "I need to get going, though, or it's going to be crazy late when we eat dinner. Have fun with our sweet baby while I'm gone. I love you, Tony."

"Love you too, babe," he said and waved goodbye.

She grabbed her keys and went out the front door. The brisk January air cut through her parka and she pulled the zipper up to her chin. She clicked the button on the door handle of the SUV and slid into the seat. The leather was cold against her jeans. She was definitely using the SUV's seat warmers tonight. It was usually Tony's work car, but the other car had the car seat in it. She didn't want to move it and didn't know how much luggage her sister was traveling with. She put the vehicle in reverse and backed out of the driveway.

The airport was less than twenty minutes away. Her GPS showed almost no traffic. She pulled up her contacts on the vehicle's Bluetooth function. Her sister was one of her 'favorite' contacts. She selected Rebecca's name and hit the button to place the call. The line rang once and then disconnected.

"Ugh, that stupid dead spot got me again," she grumbled to herself and repeated the action to call Rebecca.

The call connected and rang once before someone picked up.

"This Rebecca. Leave me a message. Byeeee."

"C'mon, Rebecca. Don't send me to your voicemail. Talk to me," she said and hit the redial button.

Again, the call connected, rang once and then played her voicemail message.

"Uh, rude. Call me when you're off the plane. I'm on my way to pick you up," Elizabeth said feigning annoyance.

Maybe Rebecca was getting off the plane and couldn't talk at that moment. Elizabeth turned the radio on and started singing along. She tapped her thumbs on the steering wheel to the beat. This was the first time Rebecca would see their new house and meet Whitney. She was so excited for her visit and couldn't wait to have her in the car. The two sisters were seven years apart, but had grown to be close when Elizabeth was in college. Rebecca had been a gracious older sister when they were growing up. Sure, she got annoyed with Elizabeth when she snooped in her room, but Rebecca had made space for Elizabeth in her life. She'd take her for ice cream if she had a bad day. She gave great advice and was such a good listener. An incoming call pulled Elizabeth from her thoughts. *Mom?*

"Hey, Mom. What's up?" Elizabeth asked as she exited off the freeway for the airport.

"I saw Rebecca's flight landed. Is she with you now?" her mom asked in an excited voice.

"Not yet. I'm almost to the airport now. Did she call you?" Elizabeth asked her mom.

"No, I'm just wishing I could be there with both of you," she responded. "Give me a call once you're together. Send me photos!"

Elizabeth laughed. "For sure, Mom. I'll talk to you soon. I love you."

"Love you too. Have the best time together."

The call ended. Elizabeth decided to try to get Rebecca on the phone again. She highlighted her name from the list and hit the call button. The line rang twice and finally clicked.

"Hello?" a male voice said.

Elizabeth's hand went to her mouth. Who was answering Rebecca's phone? "Uh, who is this?"

"The JFK airport lost and found. Did you lose your phone?" the man asked.

"What? No, I'm trying to reach my sister. Her name is Rebecca Davenport. Can you page her or something?" Elizabeth asked. *How could Rebecca lose her phone?*

"Sure, what was the name again?" the man asked.

Elizabeth's hands went cold. She was replaying the man's earlier words. *JFK airport?!* "Did you say the JFK airport?"

"Yes, ma'am. We're over by the baggage claim. What was the name you wanted me to page?" he repeated.

"Baggage claim? Where was the phone found?" Elizabeth asked, panic welling in her throat.

"The bathroom just down the way, also in baggage claim," the man informed her.

"This must be a mistake. I must have somehow connected to the wrong phone or something. My sister had a connection at JFK. She wouldn't have been in baggage claim. She would have stayed up at the gates. I talked to her earlier. Her flight was on time. She's supposed to be in Cleveland," Elizabeth explained.

"There are some cards in the back here. Want me to check the name on them?" he offered.

"Yes, please," Elizabeth responded.

"Let's see. Rebecca Davenport. Is that who you're looking for?" he asked.

Elizabeth's heart sank. "Yes, but why would her phone be there? Maybe she set it down and someone picked it up by mistake. I bet that's it. That's why she hasn't called me to tell me where she is. How do we go about getting her phone back to her?"

"She can either come to the lost and found and retrieve it *or* I can send her a form to fill out and she can pay to have it shipped back to her," he said.

"We're going to need the form. Let me give you her email address," Elizabeth replied. "It's Rebecca Davenport at Gmail dot com."

"All one word?" he asked.

"Yep. Thanks so much for your help. I need to go. I'm picking her up here in Cleveland. Without a phone, it's going to be a bit more challenging," Elizabeth told him.

"I understand. I'm sending her the form now," he paused. "The Gmail icon just popped up on the phone, so it seems like it went through. Good luck finding your sister," he said and ended the call.

"Thanks," Elizabeth muttered.

She drove along the passenger pick-up line and scanned the people for her sister. About twenty people were waiting along the curb; most of them had a cell phone up to their ear. The only ones who didn't were either children or the apparent spouse of someone else who did. She reached the end of the row without seeing Rebecca.

"I guess I'll make another lap," she said to herself.

Her phone rang again and she clicked the answer button. "Hey, Tony. I don't have her yet. She seems to have lost her phone at the New York airport."

Elizabeth could hear Whitney crying in the background. "Whitney was wondering if you'll be home soon. She thinks parent number two is not cutting it."

"Hopefully, soon. I'm making another lap through passenger pick-up," she told him.

"Good luck," her husband said. "We'll be here, anxiously awaiting your return."

The call ended. Elizabeth entered the pick-up line again and searched the crowds for Rebecca. She wasn't there. Elizabeth felt the uneasiness start to creep back in.

Oh, maybe she went to the drop-off line instead. If she didn't check a bag, she might have just walked straight outside. Elizabeth changed lanes and entered the drop-off line instead. It was mostly deserted. No one was waiting at the curb. One lonely vehicle was stopped. Two people got out and retrieved luggage from the trunk. Elizabeth bit her lip. *Back to pick-up, I guess.*

She made three more laps through the pick-up line. Rebecca was nowhere to be seen. Elizabeth parked in the parking garage and pulled on a pair of gloves. She didn't know why her sister wasn't coming outside. She braced herself for the cold air and locked her car doors. The wind had picked up and her face felt frozen as she crossed the walkway into the airport. She should have gone up a floor and used the enclosed catwalk instead.

Inside the airport, she looked at the overhead signs for directions to customer service. The line wasn't too long. She hoped it would move quickly.

"Attention travelers from JFK. If you haven't retrieved your bag from baggage claim, please come to the window for United to claim your luggage," a voice said over the airport intercom. "We're moving the unclaimed bags now."

Elizabeth looked over her shoulder toward the baggage claim carousels. A worker was walking toward carousel three, where one bright orange suitcase was rotating. Her heart sank. That had to be Rebecca's bag. She recognized it from their family trip about a year ago. She'd teased her that it was traffic cone orange.

"Excuse me, Miss?" a woman said.

Elizabeth turned back to the customer service line. The woman behind the desk was looking at her. "Oh, sorry! I didn't expect the line to move so quickly."

"How can we help you this evening?" she asked.

"I'm here to pick up my sister, but she somehow lost her phone at the connecting airport. I haven't been able to find her," Elizabeth told the woman.

"Name?" she asked.

"Rebecca Davenport. Do you need me to describe her?" Elizabeth asked.

The woman shook her head no and pressed a button on the microphone. "Rebecca Davenport. Please come to baggage claim to meet your party. Rebecca Davenport to baggage claim, please. Your party is waiting," the woman said into the intercom microphone. The message repeated loudly across the airport.

"Anything else?" the woman asked Elizabeth.

"Uh, no. If she doesn't come, what do I do?" Elizabeth asked uncertainly.

"I guess you keep waiting," the woman said with a shrug.

Elizabeth stepped away from the counter and walked to the baggage claim carousels. The United window was near carousel three. She waved at the employee through the glass. He slid it open.

"Name?" he asked.

"Uh, Rebecca Davenport," Elizabeth replied.

"I need to see the claim receipt or some ID," he told her.

"Oh, um, huh. It's my sister's bag and I can't find her," Elizabeth replied.

"She'll have to come get it herself," the man said and started to close the window.

"No. You don't understand. She's not here. She's supposed to be here, but I can't find her. They just paged her, but she hasn't come. Her flight landed forty-five minutes ago. Something isn't right," Elizabeth said frantically.

"She's probably in the bathroom. Give her some time. She'll come out," the man said and slid the window closed.

Elizabeth took out her phone and called Tony. He answered immediately.

"Hey, I don't want to jinx it, but we're doing okay. How is Rebecca?" he asked.

"Tony, I can't find her. I don't think she's here. She never claimed her bag. I asked them to page her and she didn't come. I don't know what to do," Elizabeth said with tears in her eyes.

"Whoa. How long ago did they page her?" he asked calmly.

"I don't know. Maybe three minutes ago," Elizabeth told him.

"Maybe she's in the bathroom?" he said, echoing the employee's response.

"She's not here," Elizabeth said more emphatically. "Something's wrong, Tony. Her phone is still in New York. I don't think she got on the flight at all."

"Give her a few more minutes to respond to the page, babe. Why would she have not gotten on the flight?" Tony asked her.

"I don't know. I can just feel it. As soon as they told me her phone was in New York, I knew something was off. She never loses things. She's incredibly responsible," Elizabeth argued.

"Things happen. Why don't you ask them to page her again? If she hasn't shown up in ten minutes, then maybe something is wrong. Or maybe she just missed her flight and doesn't have a way to contact you," Tony said.

"You're always so calm and rational. I'm losing my mind over here," Elizabeth said, feeling somewhat ridiculous. Of course there were reasonable explanations for what was happening. "I'll call you with an update soon."

She got back in the customer service line. Three people were ahead of her. She kept checking the baggage claim area and the escalators for signs of Rebecca while she waited. The person ahead of her stepped up to the counter.

"I left my e-reader in the seatback pocket," he explained. "How can I get it back?"

Elizabeth could see on the woman's face she didn't think he would. "Go talk to the baggage claim attendant for your airline. They might have found it, but don't get your hopes up. It's pretty rare to have those returned."

The man's shoulders slumped and he walked away. Elizabeth stepped up to the counter again.

"I take it you didn't find who you were looking for?" the woman asked. "Let me page her again. What was the name?"

"Rebecca Davenport."

The woman repeated the message from before into her microphone. Elizabeth waited for it to echo through the airport.

"What do I do if she doesn't turn up?" Elizabeth asked with a tremble in her voice.

The woman grimaced. "Let's hope you don't need to worry about that."

"Do I come back here? Or go to a security person?" Elizabeth asked.

"You'd need to request a flight manifest from the airline," the woman told her. "Come back here and I'll help you get connected with the right people. Next!"

Elizabeth backed away from the counter and turned in a circle. Rebecca wasn't at baggage claim and she wasn't on the escalator. Elizabeth gulped. Her sister was missing.

Chapter 2

Genevieve tapped her pencil impatiently on the desk. Randall Pierce was in a minimum-security facility. It shouldn't take this long for them to bring him out for an interview. A few months ago, she and Alex had arrested Pierce for fraud. He'd intentionally put in low bids for landscaping jobs in the city in response to being blackmailed by Anderson Stenoway. His actions were connected to a convoluted scheme which led to the deaths of five people. The door finally opened and a guard escorted the man to the table. He pulled out a key.

"Ah, man. Do you really have to cuff me to the table?" Pierce whined.

Genevieve had forgotten how much she disliked this man. The guard ignored his protests and secured his handcuffs to the bar across the table. Pierce slumped as much as he could in the chair.

"Thanks," Genevieve said to the guard before he left the room. "Now, Mr. Pierce—"

"I thought we agreed on Randy," he interrupted.

"My apologies. Randy, I've been trying to track down your friend, Shelly," she said as she pulled the photos from the envelope he'd given the police during his initial interview. "This is Shelly, correct?"

Pierce reddened and looked away from the photos. They were proof of an extramarital affair between him and the mysterious Shelly. "Do we have to do this?" he whined some more.

"You told us you first met 'Shelly' when she jogged past your job site. Then, wonder of wonders, she appeared a few days later at your favorite coffee shop. Which coffee shop, Randy?" Genevieve asked him as she shuffled through the photos to one of them sitting together drinking coffee.

"It's on the way to the warehouse district. Forever Grounds or something like that," Pierce told her.

Genevieve made a note. "And the hotel you frequented? None of the photos show any distinguishing characteristics, so I need your help with that too."

"It's down the street from the coffee place. It's like the only dive over there. It's a motel," he said in embarrassment.

"Did you pay for the room, or did Miss…uh, Shelly?" Genevieve asked him.

Pierce reddened again. "Ugh. She paid for it. It was already paid for. I got the feeling she was living there, but I don't know that for sure."

"Did she drive there or ride with you?" Genevieve asked.

"Uh, she walked and I drove," he said with more embarrassment.

Genevieve leaned forward. "You wouldn't let her ride in the car with you?"

"That was her idea, so we wouldn't be seen in the car together," Pierce explained.

"After drinking coffee together in public, she was worried about being seen in the same vehicle? Or was it you who was worried about being seen in a car with her?" she asked in surprise.

"I never claimed that this was an intelligent time in my life," Pierce grumbled. "I actually never saw her in a car. She was always jogging or walking. Again, it was her idea. Maybe she didn't want to be seen in the car with me either."

Genevieve felt a spark of adrenaline. Maybe she'd finally gotten a lead on the woman she could use: the coffee shop. She'd been tracking Anderson Stenoway's financials for months, but nothing was convincing her superiors the case deserved a second look. She was certain Stenoway hadn't acted alone. In fact, she didn't think he was the mastermind at all. She stood up and pressed the button on the wall for the intercom.

"We're finished in here," she said quickly. "Thanks for the insight, Randy."

The man's head dropped to his chest. The guard returned and opened the door. Genevieve nodded her thanks and made her way to the exit to retrieve her belongings. She was anxious to look up the motel on her phone, but first she needed a full name. Pierce didn't know anything more than 'Shelly' and Genevieve wasn't going to get very far with that.

She grabbed her phone and signed out of the visitor log. She'd visited Pierce as a civilian rather than a law enforcement officer, so her badge and gun were in the glove compartment of her Expedition. Her visit wasn't exactly sanctioned by her boss, Lieutenant Grusky. She'd gone to visit Pierce after her shift ended and was taking a personal day the following day in hopes of finding this mystery woman. Genevieve hurried out to the vehicle and unlocked it. She was going to talk to the coffee shop first. Hopefully, the barista would remember the woman and have some sort of record of her real name. She had a little over an hour's drive back to her apartment.

* * * * *

The fitting room felt claustrophobic to Cari. Her sister, Bea, was behind her lacing up the corset of Cari's wedding dress.

Cari'd found it in a bridal shop chain and it only needed a few alterations to fit her perfectly. The white, spaghetti-strap dress had small white flowers with pearl centers embroidered on the bodice. The long, full skirt fell within an inch of the floor and showed off her narrow waist. It had a train in the back with delicate lace overlaid onto the white silk. This was her final fitting before the wedding on Saturday. She stared at her reflection in the mirror. Her curls were a little frizzy within the ponytail she'd forced them into that morning. Her mom and her grandmother were in the sitting area with the tailor, waiting for her to come out.

"Do you need help with your shoes?" Bea asked her as she tightened the ribbons into a bow.

"No, I fastened them before I stepped into the dress, remember?" Cari replied.

"Okay, all set," Bea said and took a step back. "Oh, Cari. It looks amazing on you! I'm not sure I'll ever stop being jealous of your green eyes. Ready to show Grandmother and Mom?"

Cari smiled at her older sister. "Let's do it. Thanks for your help."

She twisted the doorknob and pulled the door open. She felt Bea lift the back of the gown so it wouldn't drag on the floor. They walked down the corridor to the waiting area.

"Wow, Cari! Does putting the dress on make everything seem that much more real?" Grandmother asked with a big grin. "You are stunning. I'm so…so…"

Grandmother put her right hand up and then coughed into her elbow. "Sorry. Got a little choked up there seeing my youngest granddaughter in her wedding dress."

"Do you think they hemmed it enough?" her mom asked. "It looks a little tight at the waist. Bea, did you pull the ribbon cording too much?"

"Mom, it's just how it's supposed to be," Bea said waving her off.

The tailor cleared his throat. "I have to agree. I think this dress was made for you, Miss Turnlyle. How does it feel?"

Cari looked down at the dress. It felt like she was living in a dream. *Was she really getting married in a few days?* "Uh, it feels great. A little heavy. I don't think I've ever worn a dress with this much fabric before."

He smiled. "Well, I think it looks fantastic. If you're happy, I'm happy."

She returned the smile. "I'm happy. Thanks, Aiden."

"Whenever you're ready, you can change out of the dress and I'll help you get it packaged up for Saturday," Aiden told her. "Do we want any photos before our beautiful bride turns back into a journalist?"

"Yes!" Grandmother exclaimed and then coughed again.

"Are you sure you're okay, Grandmother?" Cari asked with concern.

She cleared her throat. "I'm fine. Let's get a photo together."

Bea pulled out her cell phone and gave it to the tailor. Grandmother pushed herself out of her chair and joined Cari near the pedestal she'd stepped onto. She sounded winded and Cari started to ask if she was really okay again. Her grandmother grabbed her hand and squeezed it. It felt like a signal to just let her be, so she stayed silent. The four women posed for a photo.

"Perfect. What a lovely group of ladies," he said and returned Bea's phone.

"You'll text those to the rest of us, right, Bea?" Grandmother asked.

"Doing it right now, Grandmother," Bea replied.

The two older women took their seats and Bea followed Cari back to the fitting room. She unlaced the back while Cari went through her checklist.

"Okay, so we need to check in with the florist and make sure everything is set for pick up on Friday afternoon," Cari reminded Bea.

"I called the bakery this morning. They assured me the cake would be ready for pick up on Saturday morning and that it was okay for Robby to get it," Bea told her. "There you go. Ready to step out of it?"

Bea helped Cari out of the dress and then slipped it back onto the hanger. Cari grabbed her sweater and pulled it over her head. She heard a buzzing sound and looked at her watch. She accepted the call as she undid her shoes.

"Is this Cari Turnlyle?" a vaguely familiar voice said after Cari answered.

"Marjorie? I didn't expect to hear from you ever again. How have you been?" Cari asked.

"Do you have a few minutes?" Marjorie asked. Cari could hear panic in her voice.

"What's going on?" Cari asked as she pulled on her jeans.

Bea mouthed that she was going to take the dress out to Aiden. Cari nodded her understanding.

"I need your help. My cousin Rebecca has gone missing and we didn't know who else to call," Marjorie explained. "Can you meet me today? Like right now?"

Cari's eyes widened. "Oh, wow, Marjorie. This sounds urgent; I'm not really an investigator. Shouldn't you call the police?"

Marjorie sighed. "My cousin Elizabeth already did that…uh, Elizabeth is Rebecca's sister. She doesn't think they're taking it seriously. Please, you have connections. Rebecca has two kids. They need their mom."

Cari bit her lip. She felt completely inadequate at finding a missing person on her own. "Um, I'm actually right in the middle of my final fitting for my wedding on Saturday. Could I call you back in a bit? I might be able to ask—"

"Wedding. Oh. I mean, congratulations, of course. Forget I called. We'll figure something out," Marjorie said and the call ended.

"Wait!" Cari said too late.

She pulled on her boots and stuck her dress shoes into the shoe bag. Bea knocked slightly as she reentered the room.

"Who was that on the phone?" she asked.

"It was a college student I met a couple years ago. Her name is Marjorie. Do you remember the scandal at the university?" Cari asked.

"Oh, with the sports medicine guy and the athletes?" Bea asked.

"Yes. Well, Marjorie was key to figuring all of that out," Cari explained.

Bea's face saddened. "Wait, wasn't she the girlfriend of the kid who died?"

Cari nodded. "Yeah, it was awful."

"What did she want?" Bea asked.

"She said her cousin is missing. When I told her I was getting fitted for the wedding, she clammed up and ended the call," Cari told her.

"What are you going to do?" Bea asked with wide eyes. "There's so much going on this week."

"I know, but I have to call her back. Maybe there's just been a miscommunication," Cari suggested.

"It's never that easy, but suit yourself," Bea said. "Aiden has your dress and is getting it bagged up. What else do you have planned today?"

"I need to pick up the programs from the printer, but other than that, I'm pretty free," Cari replied.

Bea picked up Cari's shoe bag and tucked it under her arm. "Ready to go?"

Cari looked around the changing room to make sure they had everything. "Yeah. Let's go see if they've made a decision about dinner tonight."

"Daddy was talking about barbecue. I told him it wasn't the south, but he's pretty insistent," Bea said knowingly.

They walked down the corridor to the other two women. Grandmother smiled when she saw them.

"There they are. What's next on our to-do list, girls?" Grandmother asked and then started coughing.

Cari's mom grabbed a bottle of water off the table and twisted the lid off. "Here, drink this."

Grandmother started to reach for the water, but another coughing fit came on first. Cari and Bea rushed to her side. Cari took the water from her mom.

"Here, Grandmother. Here's the water," she said. "Are you sure you're okay?"

"I'm fine. I'm fine," Grandmother repeated. She took the water, but waved them away. "No need to hover."

"Cari, why don't Mom and I go get your programs and you take Grandmother back to the hotel? We can meet you there later," Bea suggested.

"Sure, Mom knows where the hotel is, but I'll text you the address just in case," Cari said and pulled out her phone. "Done."

"Got it. Everyone ready?" Bea asked the group.

Grandmother pushed herself to her feet. Cari grabbed her hand. "Let me just get the dress from Aiden and we can take it out to my car."

Grandmother took a deep breath. "Sounds great, sweetheart."

Cari looked down at her grandmother's feet. The navy blue support shoes looked stretched and tight. She decided not to say anything. She could tell Grandmother was tired of them worrying over her. Maybe she would talk about it once they were back in her hotel room.

* * * * *

Genevieve removed the photo of Shelly and Pierce sharing coffee from the envelope. It had the clearest shot of both their faces. It was almost lunch time, so there wasn't a line. She walked up to the counter. A young man whose nametag read "Ralph" smiled.

"What can we get for you today?" he asked.

Genevieve placed the photo on the counter. "I'm trying to locate this woman. Do you recognize her?"

Ralph picked up the photo and studied it. "Oh, right! She came here pretty often like a year or so ago. I haven't seen her in forever. Is she okay?"

Genevieve shrugged. "As far as I know. I need to speak with her. Do you remember her name?"

Ralph gave her a big smile. "You're probably going to think I'm crazy, but I do remember her name. You see, I'm a chemistry student at Onore University and she has a really unique name. I'd never seen it before...well, except in my chemistry classes."

Genevieve tried to give him an encouraging smile that she hoped didn't look like a grimace. She waited for him to continue.

"Anyway. Her last name is Palladium! Isn't that crazy? Like, I'd never really seen that anywhere except the periodic table and then, wham! There it was on her credit card. I didn't want to come off as a creeper, so I didn't say anything, but man, that's the coolest last name I've ever seen. Palladium," he chuckled at the memory. "I told all my chem buddies about it."

Genevieve gave him a real smile this time. "It's been a while since I've taken chemistry. Does Palladium have two ls or one?"

Ralph grinned and bobbed his head. "Two. P-A-L-L-A-D-I-U-M. Palladium. It's number forty-six on the table and it's—"

"Thanks, but I don't really need to know about the chemical," Genevieve reminded him. "I appreciate it, Ralph."

She turned to walk away and heard him mutter something about it being an element, not a chemical.

The motel Pierce described was only a couple blocks away. Genevieve got back into her Expedition and drove to the motel. Pierce had called it a dive and he wasn't lying. The stucco walls had cracks and vines running up and down them. The windows had a thin layer of dust coating them. It looked like it had been there for decades. Their roadside sign was missing the L and just read "MOTE" with the street number below it. She parked and exited her car.

The glass door to the office creaked loudly as she pulled it open. She wondered if it was more effective than the tingling bells connected to the structure. The clerk's head popped up in response to her entrance. His long, shaggy hair covered some of the wording on his faded t-shirt. Genevieve tried not to flinch when she spotted the piercing in his eyebrow. She wondered how that didn't constantly hurt.

"Good afternoon. Welcome to the no-tell-motel," he said with a grin. "My name's Ricky."

She set her photo on the counter. "Hi, Ricky. I'm looking for a woman who might be staying here. Her last name is Palladium."

He jiggled the computer mouse. "Is she staying here now? Or is this from the past?"

"Possibly both?" Genevieve said hesitantly.

"I'll just search the history," Ricky responded. Genevieve wondered why he'd asked the question at all if the answer was irrelevant.

"Zero results for Paladin," Ricky said.

"Uh, it's Palladium," Genevieve enunciated the word. "I wrote it down for you."

She turned her notebook toward him and pointed at the name.

"Ah, I see," he remarked. His punched the letters in with his two index fingers one at a time. "Still zero."

Genevieve frowned and pointed at the photo. "Do you recognize her?"

"For sure. I mean, it's been a while since she's been here. She used to come once or twice a week," he raised his eyebrows.

So much for no-tell, Genevieve thought. "Can you remember anything else about her?"

He nodded. "She always paid in cash and never stayed the night. She'd pay for the room in the morning and then leave. She and her *friend* would show up separately an hour or two later. And then the other *friend* used the room next door."

Genevieve ignored his vulgar facial expression. "The other *friend* was there at the same time?"

She didn't think Follard and Pierce knew each other. She was surprised Stenoway would have had Shelly bring them to the same motel on the same days.

"Yeah, you know, the guy with the huge camera around his neck. He got here before her and would book the adjacent room," he said with a shrug.

Genevieve realized her assumption was wrong. She found a photo of Stenoway on her phone and showed it to Ricky.

"Was this the man with the camera?" she asked him.

He leaned in and looked at the screen. "I actually have no idea. He wore huge sunglasses and a hat. I can tell you he was white. That's all I've got."

"What was his name?" Genevieve asked.

"Beats me. He paid in cash too," Ricky explained.

Genevieve made a note. "Do you remember what kind of car the woman drove?"

"She wasn't a driver. I'm pretty sure she walked here every time," Ricky told her. "She was really into…exercising."

Genevieve raised her eyebrows. "Which direction did she come from?"

Ricky shrugged. "Uh…maybe the Microtel that's down the road a bit?"

She looked out the window. "On this road or a different one?"

"Oh, it's about five or six blocks down this street. Away from Brenington," Ricky replied.

"Perfect," Genevieve said and picked up the photo.

"Anything else?" Ricky asked.

"That's all I need. Here's my card in case you remember anything else about her or any of her friends," she said as she slid her card across the counter.

She pushed open the squeaky glass door and got hit in the face with a strong gust of wind. She crossed her arms and hurried back to her car. She'd never really paid much attention to the lodging options in Brenington as she had a place to live and her family rarely came to visit. Just as Ricky told her, the Microtel was a handful of blocks down the street. She pulled into the parking lot and found a spot near the entrance. The Microtel was much cleaner and looked like it had been recently painted. The flower beds were well-maintained too. She stepped toward the automatic doors, but they didn't register her presence. She rolled her eyes. She was just an inch or two too short to get picked up by the sensor until she was right underneath it sometimes. She lifted one hand over her head and the doors slid open.

"Good afternoon. Checking in?" the young woman at the front desk asked her.

"Hi, Marcy," Genevieve said as she read the woman's nametag. "I'm trying to find this woman and heard she might be a resident here. Do you recognize her?"

She placed the photo on the counter for her to see. Marcy barely glanced at it.

"I just started working here on January 1st. Let me get Deena for you," she said and pressed a button on her headset. "Deena, could you come to the front desk for me? Great, thank you...she'll just be a moment."

Genevieve started to take the photo back, but Marcy had her hand on it. She looked around the lobby. It couldn't have been more different from the motel. She thought she might still smell like stale cigarette smoke from her brief encounter in their lobby. Hopefully, she was just imagining it. She didn't want to have to get her suit dry cleaned again so soon. The door labeled "Employees Only" opened and a tall woman with long, brunette hair came over to the desk. She had on bright red lipstick that stood in stark contrast to her pale, white skin. Genevieve noticed her nails were painted the same shade.

"Hi, I'm Deena," she said and extended her hand.

"Hi, Deena, I'm Detective Viacorte with the Brenington PD. I'm trying to find this young woman. Her last name is Palladium. Do you recognize her?" Genevieve asked. She felt a little guilty using her badge when she wasn't really there in an official capacity.

"Oh yes. She was a resident here for several months, almost a year maybe," Deena said after looking at the photo.

Genevieve tried to keep her shoulders from drooping. "Did you say 'was' a resident?"

Deena nodded. "She moved out quite a while ago."

"Rats," Genevieve said in disappointment.

"Is she in some sort of trouble?" Deena asked.

"She's not in any trouble. I need to speak with her in regards to an investigation," Genevieve said vaguely. "Is there any chance she left a forwarding address?"

Marcy frowned and gave Deena a look. "We aren't supposed to give out guests' information. Don't you need a warrant or something?"

Genevieve knew she wasn't going to be able to get a warrant. She couldn't even get them to keep the investigation open. "I don't have a warrant. Like I said, she's not in any trouble. She's a potential witness and I need to speak with her."

She started to grab the photo when Deena spoke again.

"Well, I don't see what the harm is. She left something behind and I had to send it to her. I should be able to find the address from our shipping system. Just a sec," Deena looked at Marcy who took the hint and stepped away from the computer.

Genevieve tried not to get her hopes up. Stenoway had discouraged them from looking for Shelly. Initially, she hadn't even considered it. She wasn't sure what the woman could offer to the narrative that she didn't already know. When tracking his financials hadn't produced enough weight to warrant a visit to the supposed mastermind, she'd looked through her notes of their interview again. It could be possible that he was trying to obfuscate and make her seem insignificant.

"Here it is!" Deena exclaimed, breaking into Genevieve's thoughts. "Do you need it electronically or can I just write it down for you?"

"Writing it down is fine," Genevieve said with a big smile.

Deena tore a page from the notepad near the computer and carefully wrote down the address. "She actually isn't too far away, but she said she couldn't return for the item. I can't promise you she's still there, but here's where I shipped it."

Genevieve took the paper from her and looked at it. "Interesting. It's barely over an hour from here. Before I go, is there anything you can tell me about her time here?"

Deena looked lost in thought for a moment before she responded. "Well, not really. I don't know what she was in town for, but she seemed to do a lot of exercising in the mornings. Some days, she never left. Other times, she'd get back here right before lunch. I always wondered if she had a remote job and if so, why didn't she just work from her real home?"

"It does seem a little odd. Did anyone ever join her here?" Genevieve asked.

"Not that I saw, but I wasn't here every day," Deena replied.

"Okay, well, thanks for your help. Have a nice day," Genevieve said as she picked up the photo.

"Any time!" the two women said in unison.

Genevieve checked her watch after getting back in her car. It was close to two o'clock. Palladium's new address was west of Brenington in Vermont. She definitely didn't have jurisdiction there, but that hadn't stopped her yet today. She plugged the address into her maps app and then turned on the Expedition. Palladium might not be home, but she had to at least try.

Chapter 3

The route to Vermont was desolate. Genevieve was glad she'd stopped for gas before leaving Brenington. It seemed like the filling stations were few and far between. She was only a few miles from her destination. Normally, Alex was with her when she was going to interview a witness. He had fifteen years of experience on her and they usually bounced ideas off each other enroute to the person's home or business. She was on her own for the first time and wasn't sure what to expect. She needed to gain Shelly's trust, if Shelly was her real name. She exited the freeway. The address she'd gotten from the Microtel was just a few blocks away. She reviewed the questions she wanted to ask. She wanted information on who hired Shelly. Was it Stenoway? Genevieve had a copy of the video from his interview on her phone. Were other people involved? Had she been paid to seduce anyone else?

She made the final turn to Palladium's address. Her GPS said it was the third house on her right. The house had tan siding and dark green shutters. An old Kia sedan sat in the driveway. She pulled alongside the curb and turned her car off.

"Here goes nothing," she said as she climbed out of the SUV.

She rang the doorbell and saw there was a camera attached to it. She hoped her small stature made her seem less intimidating. She tapped her notebook against her leg as she waited for someone to answer the door. She heard the deadbolt flip and then the door slowly opened. The blonde woman from Pierce's photos stared back at her.

"Ms. Palladium?" Genevieve asked hopefully.

"Who are you?" the woman asked. Her eyes darted from Genevieve to the Expedition and back.

"I'm Genevieve Viacorte. I..." Genevieve paused. She hadn't come up with a cover story. Usually, she just said she was a detective investigating a case. "I'm looking into—"

"You're a cop," Palladium said and started to close the door.

Genevieve put her hand up to stop her. "Please. I just want to talk. I think you can help me."

Palladium shook her head and pushed harder on the door. "You shouldn't be here. If he finds out..."

"You know Stenoway's in prison, right?" Genevieve said as she braced her arm against the door.

"Who the hell is that?" Palladium said and pushed some more.

"Look. You're not stronger than me. I'm trying to get some answers. You aren't in any trouble, but I could use your help," Genevieve said and positioned her foot against the base of the door.

Palladium relented. "Fine, but you can't stay long. I can't risk him finding out."

Genevieve stepped inside and the woman locked the door behind her. "Can't risk who finding out?"

"I don't know his name. I only talked to him on the phone," she responded. "Let's sit in the kitchen. It's away from the windows."

Genevieve followed the woman to the kitchen. She was starting to regret not telling Alex where she was. There was a reason you worked with a partner.

"Have a seat," Palladium offered as she sat down at the kitchen table.

Genevieve held up her notebook. "Is it okay if I take a few notes while we talk?"

"Suit yourself," she said with a shrug.

"You said you don't know Stenoway. Can I show you a video and see if maybe he went by a different name with you?" Genevieve requested.

"First of all, he never gave me his name. That should have been a red flag, but I ignored it," the young woman said angrily.

"Okay, but maybe you'll recognize his voice?" Genevieve suggested.

Palladium put her hand out. "Let's see it."

Genevieve pulled out her phone and cued up the video. "This is from his interrogation back in July of last year."

She watched the woman's face as the video played. Genevieve had the volume up so you could hear Stenoway's voice. Palladium didn't seem to recognize him at all.

"I've never heard that voice nor seen that man in my life," Palladium told her. "I take it that's your Stenoway?"

"Yes. His name is Anderson Stenoway. He confessed to murdering five people as part of a larger scheme involving blackmail and..." she paused and looked at Palladium. "Seduction."

Palladium's face went white. "Did you say murder?"

"Yes. He claims to have been the mastermind and murderer of five people in the tri-county area," Genevieve responded.

Palladium raised a shaky hand to her face. "I had no idea. I...I thought he was...well, *just* blackmailing..."

"I want to make sure we're on the same page. Are you Shelly? Or was that just a nickname for your role as the seductress?" Genevieve asked her pointedly.

The woman blushed. "I'm not proud of it, but yes. That's me. My name really is Shelly and it's not short for anything. I'm just Shelly, not Michelle."

"Tell me how it happened. Who put you up to this?" Genevieve asked gently.

"I lost my job and couldn't find another one. I had to apply for unemployment. I went to one of those job resource centers to look for temporary work. They added my name and number to some list and told me to upload a resume to their site. A few days later, I got a phone call," Palladium told her.

"From the temp site?" Genevieve asked for clarification.

"That's what I thought initially. I mean, it was just a random number, but they said something about me looking for work, so that's what I tied it to," Palladium explained.

"Okay, go on," Genevieve replied.

"Let's see. This guy on the phone said he had a job for me. There was a man named Pierce who ran some construction site. I was supposed to jog past the work site a few times and catch his eye. Then, he told me to start going to this coffee shop to have a 'chance' meeting with him," Palladium looked at the floor as she spoke. "I didn't know anything about the guy, but I needed the money. I was already behind on my rent and the utility company was threatening to turn off my water. I was facing homelessness. This guy on the phone said he'd pay me in cash and would cover six to twelve months of lodging and food. He left one of those check cards in my car and said I could get a room at the Microtel. Every month, I got a new card and paid for the room. I'm single, so I told myself I wasn't cheating on anyone. It was his choice if some man wanted to be a dirtbag."

Genevieve nodded. She didn't want to interrupt the woman's story, so she stayed quiet and let her tell it at her pace.

"The guy was a complete pushover. The first time he ran into me in the coffee shop, I knew I had him. He was so full of himself. I was instructed to rent a room at this dive motel down the street," Palladium paused and looked at Genevieve. "I'm so ashamed of this next part. I mean, I needed the money to survive, but I should

31

have just gotten a job at a retail store or something. You must think I'm such white trash."

Genevieve put her hand on the table, palm up. "No judgment. I'm sorry this happened to you."

The woman sniffled. "Thanks. Anyway, the guy on the phone told me which room to rent and to pay in cash. He'd leave the cash in my car the night before. I don't know how. I always locked it. I feel like an idiot. I didn't know he was taking pictures. He somehow had a camera in the room. I don't know. It makes me feel gross."

Genevieve felt guilty making Palladium recount the ordeal; she decided to hold off asking about Follard for the time being. She wanted to know if the man from the phone had contacted her again since she left Pierce high and dry.

"Have you heard from the man again? The one who called you to offer you this…job?" she asked Palladium.

"No, and I hope to never hear his voice again. He told me to get out of town and forget I was ever there. The first six months I lived here, I constantly looked over my shoulder. I didn't realize this was all connected to a bunch of murders, but the guy gave me the creeps. He told me if I went to the police, he'd plaster the photos of me all over the internet. I wish I'd never taken his call," Palladium said and hung her head.

"He shared the photos with you?" Genevieve asked.

Palladium blushed. "He left an envelope…one of those big ones with a brad to keep it closed…it was waiting for me at the front desk when I checked out of the Microtel. Inside were all the photos he had of me…well, you know."

"How did it end? Did he just call you up and say the job was complete?" Genevieve asked.

"Basically. The guy on the phone told me it was done. I'd met my part of the deal and now I needed to leave town," she replied. "I had to be out of the room by the end of the week, but I wasn't about to let him change his mind and make me stay longer. I started packing immediately."

"You just packed up and left that day?" Genevieve asked her.

"Yeah. I didn't have much. I'd sold all my furniture from my apartment to cover my rent before the guy called with this 'job' offer. I only had some clothing and toiletries," she told Genevieve.

"And something else," Genevieve surmised. "A piece of jewelry maybe? A bracelet or a necklace?"

The woman's eyes widened. "How did you know?"

"The Microtel staff told me you left something behind and they had to ship it to you," Genevieve informed her. "That's how I got here."

"But how does any of this help you?" Palladium asked.

"It confirms my theory that someone else is. involved," Genevieve told her. "Do you have the man's phone number? The one who called you?"

Palladium shook her head. "No, but it wasn't just one number. It changed every month or two. I think he must have used burner phones."

"That's okay. I appreciate your help," Genevieve said.

"If you found me this easily, am I safe? He has to know my real name. I moved out of state because I thought that would help, but clearly, I'm not as stealth as I thought I was," Palladium said with big eyes.

"I'll call the Microtel and ask them to delete your address from their system," Genevieve offered. "And I'll ask them to let me know if anyone comes in looking for you."

She pulled out one of her business cards. "If you need anything, or feel unsafe, just call me."

Shelly took the card. "Thanks. I'm hoping to never see anyone from New York again. Not the happiest time in my life."

"If you don't mind my asking, do you own this house?" Genevieve asked.

"I'm renting," Shelly told her. "I swallowed my pride and I work shifts at a local grocery store. I have a degree in graphic design, so I'm still trying to get hired somewhere with that. For now, I'm just playing it safe and getting by. Something will turn up one of these days."

"Good luck. Thanks for your help," Genevieve said and stood up from the table. "I'll see myself out."

She unlocked the front door and closed it behind her. She heard the deadbolt click back into place when she was a few steps away. Genevieve picked up her phone and unlocked it. She opened her email app and typed out a quick message to Alex. He refused to text unless he absolutely had to, so she chose email to keep him happy this time.

I found Shelly. Lots of updates. I'll be in touch. -Gen

This reinforced her theory. Stenoway hadn't acted alone. He was just another player, so who had called the shots?

* * * * *

Cari took a drink from her water bottle and set it back on the side table. Grandmother had decided to take a nap and was fast asleep in the bedroom of the suite. Her parents had rented rooms for both her grandmother and themselves at a nearby hotel for the week of the wedding. She pulled out her phone. Time to call Marjorie back.

"Cari? I didn't expect you to call me back. Please, don't interrupt your wedding plans for me," Marjorie begged.

"The wedding isn't until Saturday, girl. Plus, my mom and my sister are much more into planning and doing. I have the whole week off. Tell me about your cousin," Cari requested.

"Okay, if you're sure," Marjorie replied. "I have these two older cousins...well. They aren't *old*. They're older than me, uh, but, well, one of them might be older than you..."

"Marjorie, I'm completely comfortable with my age. Please continue," Cari encouraged her.

"Sorry. Okay. My cousin Elizabeth called me in a panic last night. I'm the only person she knows in New York. Her older sister Rebecca was supposed to fly into Cleveland last night, but she wasn't on the plane," Marjorie said quickly.

"She missed her flight?" Cari asked.

"Maybe?" Marjorie said it as a question. "She lost her phone in the JFK airport and then she never showed up in Cleveland. Her bag did, but not her. Elizabeth begged and pleaded with all the security people and airport people...I don't even know how she managed to get this information, but it turns out Rebecca didn't get on the plane for Cleveland. And she isn't in the JFK airport. It closes down for the night, of course. They searched it and no one was there. It's like she disappeared."

"She didn't disappear. She has to be somewhere," Cari said emphatically.

"Of course, but where? And why would she leave her phone behind?" Marjorie asked.

Cari felt a shiver go up her spine, but kept the theory that popped in her head to herself. "What do you need from me? I don't really have access to the airport any more than anyone else does."

"Oh, I know, but you're a good investigator and you *know* people who can make things happen," Marjorie buttered her up. "The police aren't being helpful at all. They said Rebecca must have decided to leave the airport voluntarily."

"Did they review the video footage? Have they actually seen her leaving the airport?" Cari asked.

"Elizabeth said they promised to review the footage and get back to her, but she doesn't think they're making it a priority. Her sister would have called her by now. They'd both been looking forward to this trip for months!" Marjorie told her.

"That is weird," Cari agreed.

"Elizabeth is flying out here with her six-month-old daughter today. Rebecca's husband is flying in too, but he had to make arrangements for their kids with his mom first. I'm not sure when he lands. He said he wasn't going to leave without answers," Marjorie said slowly.

"Well, hopefully, he keeps his cool and doesn't get arrested," Cari remarked. "Let me make a few calls and I'll get back to you, okay?"

"Thanks, Cari. You're truly a life saver!" Marjorie exclaimed.

"Well, I haven't done anything yet. I'll be in touch. Take care, Marjorie," Cari said and ended the call.

She decided to check in with Bob next. He was only taking half a week off as his parents weren't arriving until Thursday. He answered immediately.

"How is my beautiful bride-to-be?" he asked jovially.

"Pretty good. I feel like I'm juggling a lot of plates, but my sister is managing to catch all the ones I'm dropping, so it's good," she said with a laugh.

"How did the fitting go?" he asked.

Cari paused, remembering Grandmother's coughing fits. "Uh, the dress is fine, I mean, it's perfect."

"But…" he encouraged her to continue.

"Something is wrong with Grandmother. She's tired and out of breath. She had a couple coughing fits. I'm worried about her," Cari said and felt tears in her eyes.

"Oh no! That sounds concerning. What did she say?" Bob asked.

"She waved us off and said not to hover. She's resting now and has been for over half an hour," Cari told him.

"Well, she is pretty old. She probably takes a nap most days," Bob surmised.

"I guess so. It just feels more serious," Cari said sadly.

"I'll keep my eye on her on Thursday when we have our pre-rehearsal, pre-wedding, pre-family dinner thing," he said pausing between words.

"Ugh," she groaned. "I hope it isn't as awkward as it sounds coming out of your mouth."

He laughed. "It's going to be great. Or it's not, but we'll be together, so that's all that matters."

"I love you, Bob Hursley," she said with a smile.

"I love you, too. Now, what other plates can I take off your hands?" he asked.

"You'll never guess who called me today," she said.

"I can hear the sleuth peeking out from behind those words. Who called?" he asked with a laugh.

"Marjorie Pryor!" Cari exclaimed.

"Wow. Is she still at Onore?" Bob asked.

"She didn't say. She is still in New York, though. Her cousin has gone missing...from the airport and she asked me for help," Cari explained.

"Ah, there's my sleuth. How does she propose you find her missing cousin?" Bob teased.

"She said the police aren't taking it seriously. They promised to review the footage in the airport and get back to her sister or husband, but they haven't heard anything," Cari told him.

"From the missing cousin? Or the police?" Bob asked.

"Either. It's odd that the cousin hasn't contacted anyone, right? She was traveling to Ohio to see her sister and new niece and then poof! She's gone," Cari said and snapped her fingers.

"Yeah, that seems off. I might be able to look at the traffic cams outside the airport. Do you know what the cousin looks like?" Bob offered. "I'll have to get Green to approve it, though."

"Oh right. I always forget you can't just do whatever you want," she grumbled. "I could ask Marjorie to text us a photo. What about inside the airport?"

"That's way out of my zone of control. Maybe Genevieve knows someone, though," Bob suggested.

"She's next on my list! Thanks so much, Bob. Hopefully, she can help me out. Love you."

"Love you more," he said and ended the call.

Cari thumbed off a quick text to Marjorie and then scrolled to Genevieve's name. She wasn't sure what time her friend got off shift today, but she hoped she'd answer her phone. It seemed like finding Rebecca wasn't going to be a simple task.

* * * * *

Genevieve bobbed her head along to the music from the radio. She wasn't sure what she'd expected to learn from Shelly, but her not knowing or recognizing Stenoway was big. Obviously, Stenoway was involved, but right now, he was playing the fall guy. His job within the city governments had made him a key player in the scheme, but she wanted to know who was in charge.

She kept coming back to the bank account. They hadn't gotten access to it initially because of some sort of struggle connecting his name to the account. No withdrawals had been made from the account since they linked Stenoway to Elaine Frobish's murder back in July. In reality, the amount of money transferred between Pierce and Follard's companies to Stenoway wasn't that substantial; it was less than $50,000. A monthly deposit of $2,000 had begun after his incarceration. Before they caught up with Stenoway, varying amounts were withdrawn from the account at irregular times.

She'd been over his accounts multiple times. Alex theorized the monthly $2000 deposit was half of the blackmail money he got from Pierce and Follard. He'd made regular weekly cash deposits of $500 in another account weekly before they arrested him in July. It didn't make sense for him to split the money up, but she was sure he had a reason. She supposed he could have saved half of it and was having it deposited now, but why? Now that she knew he couldn't be the mastermind, she was starting to question her theory. None of this added up, but hopefully, she could convince Grusky to let her interview Stenoway again. How was he still able to make the $2000 deposit each month if he was in prison? He wasn't able to blackmail Pierce or Follard anymore, so who was paying the man?

She started to call Alex on her Bluetooth when another call came in first. *Cari. She probably has another wedding task for me.*

"Hey, Cari. What's up?" she asked.

"I'm so glad you answered. I got a call today from Marjorie Pryor…remember her? She's the girlfriend…" Cari trailed off.

"Right. The case with the athletes at Onore. I remember," Genevieve confirmed.

"Well, her cousin has gone missing and she asked for my help," Cari explained.

"A child?" Genevieve asked with concern.

"No, uh, I don't know how old the cousin is, but she's an adult—a mom actually. She was flying from Charleston to Cleveland and had a stop at JFK. She made it to JFK, but never showed up in Cleveland," Cari told her. "She hasn't called anyone since right after she got off the plane at JFK."

Genevieve listened to Cari recount the details she'd learned from Marjorie. "That is concerning, but why are you calling me? I don't have any jurisdiction over the airport."

"But you know people, right? They've asked the police to review the security footage and find where Rebecca—did I say the cousin's name? Rebecca Davenport is the missing woman. Maybe you could talk to your FBI buddy and get access to those video feeds?" Cari asked.

Genevieve cringed. She did not want to ask a favor of Dureski right now. She was probably going to anger him by going to visit

Stenoway. "I might know someone I can call. Give me a few hours and I'll get back to you."

"It sounds like you're driving. Did I catch you in the middle of something?" Cari asked.

"Uh, I took a personal day today. I'm just on my way home from an appointment," Genevieve told her.

"Oh, okay. Well, keep me posted," Cari said and ended the call.

Genevieve drummed her fingers on the steering wheel. She did know some officers who worked at JFK. She hated to bother them. If someone called her and told her she wasn't treating a case seriously enough, she'd be annoyed. Still, it *did* sound like the woman was missing. She had kids; it seemed unlikely she'd just walk away from her family.

"Siri, call Officer Lochaven," Genevieve commanded.

Calling Officer Lochaven.

The line rang a few times before he answered. "Viacorte. What can I do for you?"

"Hey, Loch. I need a favor," she replied and retold Marjorie's story.

"Not you too," Loch complained. "The sister is calling; the husband is calling. I think I even got a call from her cousin! Everyone is on my back about this woman."

"Is it really such a big deal? I know you have a job to do separate from tracking down a missing person," Genevieve commiserated.

"*Possible* missing person," he corrected.

"Possible missing person," she repeated. "I know you're busy, but something feels off about this. How many moms would walk away from their kids without saying goodbye?"

"Ugh," Loch groaned. "Fine, but when we see her exit the airport of her own accord, you're buying me a round or two of drinks."

"Deal," Genevieve said. "Thanks, Loch. Sorry to be a thorn in your side."

"You owe me one, Viacorte," he responded and ended the call.

She smiled, but her mind immediately returned to Stenoway and his money. She was almost back to Brenington. Grusky couldn't say no to her this time.

Chapter 4

C ari pulled up the checklist their wedding planner, Aspen, had sent her to stay organized. Grandmother was still resting and she didn't have anything else to do. Aspen had a tab for each portion of the wedding: Catering, Florist, Bride's attire, Groom's attire, Bridesmaids' duties, and so on. She opened the timeline to make sure she wasn't missing anything.

Bob's family was arriving the next day. She was possibly meeting them for lunch, but definitely joining everyone for dinner. His Aunt Lydia wasn't arriving until Friday as she didn't want to leave her bed and breakfast business for longer than necessary. Cari had a few cousins and aunts and uncles coming to town on Friday as well.

"Always working," Grandmother said as she entered the room. "How long was I asleep?"

Cari looked at her watch. "Less than an hour. Did you have a nice nap?"

"When you get to be my age, it feels good to sleep at all," Grandmother said with a smile and sat down next to her on the sofa. "What's next on our list today?"

"I was just looking at the list," Cari said. "I think we've met all our duties for today."

Her grandmother took a breath and coughed. Cari reached for a bottle of water and twisted the lid off.

"I'm okay. I just get these little coughing fits now and then," Grandmother said and took a drink of water. "I heard Bea and Robby asked you and Bob to be the kids' guardians if anything were to happen to them."

Cari gulped. "Yeah, I was really surprised. I'm not very motherly."

"Oh, don't be silly. You're good at everything you do," Grandmother said and patted her cheek.

"It feels so morbid to think about anything like that ever happening," Cari said.

"Yes, but it is always a good idea to have a living will. Don't you have one?" Grandmother asked her.

A light knock sounded at the door. Cari got up to see who it was.

"We got the programs and lunch," Bea said and held up a bag. "Oh, Grandmother, you're awake!"

"I'm ready to tackle the next thing on the list, but Cari said we've met all our obligations today," she responded. "We were just talking about you and the kids."

Bea raised her eyebrows.

"All good things my dear," Grandmother assured her. "I was telling Cari she needed to have a living will like you and Robby do. Also, I think it's wonderful that you named Cari and Bob as guardians..."

Grandmother started to cough again. Cari grabbed water and handed it to her. She took a few sips and smiled.

Bea looked at her watch. "Speaking of the kids, Dad is ready to get the kids off the bus, right?"

Their mom nodded. "He is. He even went by the convenience store and got them each a candy bar to surprise them."

"Ugh. They are going to eat so much sugar this week," Bea groaned. "Anyway, I brought the programs up here along with the ribbon we're going to use to make bows."

Cari gave her a blank look. "Bows for the programs?"

Bea laughed. "No. Bows for the ends of each pew. We have white ribbon to tie into bows. Those will attach onto little brackets and be along the aisle side of each pew. Then, for the reception—"

Cari's phone buzzed with a call. *Marjorie again.* "I'm sorry. I need to take this. I'll be right back."

She exited the suite into the hallway, but flipped the deadbolt on the door so it couldn't latch behind her. "Hi, Marjorie. Any news on Rebecca?"

"Elizabeth called and said the officer at JFK has agreed to go through the security footage with them. She is at the airport now. Rebecca's husband won't arrive for another hour. Is it okay if I give Elizabeth your phone number? She was hoping you could help go through the video with them. I know you're getting ready for your wedding, so please, say no if we're asking too much," Marjorie said quickly.

"I have some time this afternoon. I'll drive over to the airport now," Cari offered. "And, feel free to share my number with Elizabeth…I have to ask a kind of awkward question."

"What is it?" Marjorie asked quietly.

"Is Rebecca in a safe marriage?" Cari asked gently.

"Of course!" Marjorie exclaimed. "Do you really think if she wasn't, she'd leave her kids behind to fend for themselves?"

"I'm sorry, Marjorie, but the police are going to ask these questions too," Cari informed her.

"It feels so icky to say something like that about Keith. You're right. They probably already asked Elizabeth that," Marjorie relented.

"More than likely. Please let Elizabeth know I'll be on my way shortly. I'm not sure what the traffic is like. I'll probably get there around the same time as the husband," Cari surmised.

"I'll call her next," Marjorie promised. "Thank you, Cari!"

Cari pushed the hotel door open again. "I'm sorry to leave when you're all here for me, but I need to go help a friend with something. It might take a while."

"At least eat your lunch first," Bea said and handed her a sandwich. "You still like egg salad, right?"

Cari smiled and took the wrapped sandwich from her. "Yes, but I need to eat it in the car."

Her mom frowned. "You'll still join us for dinner, right?"

"I'll do my best, Mom," she said and smiled.

She picked up her messenger bag and slid her phone into it. "Thanks for being so understanding. I'll be in touch. Love you all. Thanks for making the bows. I'm sorry I can't stay and help."

She waved goodbye and left the hotel suite again. Her car was in the parking garage below. She felt bad leaving her grandmother. She had more than a little cough. It seemed like she was out of breath too. Cari wondered if she had pneumonia and that's why she was so tired. She rubbed the locket that hung around her neck. Her grandmother had gifted it to her when she graduated from high school. The locket held a photo of the two of them and Cari wore it every day. Normally, she'd call her grandmother when she recognized she was rubbing the locket for comfort. She released the charm from her hand and sighed.

* * * * *

"Alex, is Grusky in his office?" Genevieve asked on her way past their desks.

"I thought you were taking the day off," Alex said in a surprised tone.

She stopped and turned back to him. "I am, but I have some new information I need to run by him."

"Hold up. I saw your email. Let's talk it through before you burst in there with your pants on fire," Alex suggested.

"Fine," she said and walked back to her desk. "I found Shelly. She's never heard of Stenoway. I showed her the video of his interrogation and she didn't recognize him or his voice."

"Did she claim to have met the person? Does she know what he looks like?" Alex challenged.

"Well, no. She only talked to him on the phone, but I believe her one-hundred-percent. She did not recognize his voice," Genevieve argued.

"Maybe he altered his voice on the phone," Alex hypothesized.

"Oh my gosh. Why do you have to shoot every one of my theories down?" Genevieve said, her hazel eyes flaring.

"Chill. Grusky is going to ask the same things," Alex told her.

"What about the money? I was going over all of it in my head again on my way here. We guessed that the two-k he's depositing every month was half of his blackmail money, but who is still being blackmailed? Those payments are still getting deposited," Genevieve asked with her hands up.

"Okay, so maybe we were wrong about that being the blackmail money," Alex agreed.

Finally. "If it isn't blackmail money, then what is it?" Genevieve asked him. "He definitely isn't earning a salary anymore."

"Also true," Alex relented.

"Okay, so come with me to convince Grusky," she said and stood up.

"Fine," he said and rose from his seat somewhat reluctantly.

She knocked impatiently on their lieutenant's door.

"Come in!" he hollered from inside the office. "Viacorte, I thought you took the day off?"

"As you know, I've been reluctant to move on from the Stenoway case," she began and saw his shoulders slump.

"Not this again, Viacorte. How many times do I have to say no?" he asked her.

"I took the day off to look for Shelly, the woman who seduced Pierce and Follard," she explained. "Stenoway said we wouldn't find her as she was long gone, but it only took me a few hours to locate her. She's in Vermont."

"Okay, great," Grusky said with a shrug.

"She never met Stenoway in person; she only talked to someone on the phone. The name Stenoway meant nothing to her, but admittedly, the person never gave her a name. She did hear their voice, so I played part of the interrogation for her. She said it wasn't him. That isn't the person she talked to on the phone about her role in all this," Genevieve told her boss.

He ran a hand over his bald head. "That is a bit off-putting, though, he could have altered his voice for a phone call."

"Agreed, but combined with the inconsistencies with his finances, it confirms my theory that he did not act alone," Genevieve said assertively. "I want to interview him again."

"What are you going to gain from that?" Grusky asked.

"He's protecting someone or he's afraid of someone," Genevieve explained. "We can offer him a better deal if he gives us their name."

Grusky frowned and rubbed his head some more.

"Lieutenant, with all due respect, I think it is clear he did not act alone. If we don't find who his partner or leader was, then we are letting a murderer walk free," she pressured him.

Grusky let out a long sigh. "Fine, I'll call the prison, but you're taking Runimoss with you."

She felt the hair on her arms start to tingle. She'd finally done it. "Thank you, LT."

"Let me make a call and get it set up," he said and looked at the door.

Alex pulled the door open and held it for her. She smirked at him even though it irritated her when he played the gentleman with the door. She was getting her way where it mattered.

"I can't believe you're dragging me back into this," he grumbled when they got back to their desks.

"You know it's the right move. We closed this case too soon. There's more to the story and I'm going to get to the bottom of it," she told him turning on her computer.

"What are you doing now?" he asked with a groan.

"I want to look at his accounts again," she said and pretended not to see him roll his eyes.

"How much blood are you going to squeeze from that rock?" he asked.

"Until it has nothing left to give," she responded as she logged in.

She opened a browser window and navigated to the different bank accounts linked to Stenoway. His personal savings account was the one that got the cash deposits each week when he was still blackmailing people. He had a checking account too; regular withdrawals were made for utilities and rent before he went to prison. Now those came from the savings account. She wasn't sure if he'd given his lawyer power of attorney to make the payments for him or what. The third account was the one she'd gotten access to last. It was the one they couldn't initially connect to the criminal. She clicked on one of the $2000 deposits. The line item expanded to show the transaction ID number and the account the money transferred from.

"Look," she said and pointed at the screen. "This isn't a cash deposit. He said he got cash as blackmail payments. And the account from which the money transferred isn't either of his accounts."

"Well, it does seem ridiculous and a waste of time to move your money from one account to another," Alex remarked.

"I don't think this is his account," Genevieve argued. "I think they put his name on it so we'd think it was his and let the investigation end."

"Okay, I'll entertain your theory for a moment. If the money isn't coming from his account, whose account is it coming from?" Alex asked.

"That's what we need to figure out or get him to tell us," she said as her desk phone rang.

"Detective Viacorte," she said. "You're on speaker, LT."

"I got you a meeting time with Stenoway for tomorrow morning. Don't make me regret this," Grusky said.

"Can we request a copy of his visitor log?" she asked.

"One step ahead of you," Grusky responded. "It's in your inbox now."

"Thanks, sir," she said and heard the line click.

She replaced the receiver and opened her email application. The first email was a forwarded message from Grusky. She clicked on it to open it.

"Well, that's even more interesting," she said to Alex.

"I'm afraid to ask..." Alex mumbled.

"The only visitor he's had is his lawyer: Salzer," Genevieve said with satisfaction.

"And this is pleasing to you because...?" he asked.

"It goes back to the money again. This man is driving out to the prison once a week to visit his client, but not getting paid for it?" she questioned Alex's memory.

"I'm not making the retainer argument with you again. I agree. There is a lot of circumstantial...evidence...I use that word loosely...to suggest we might have missed something," Alex said. "Happy?"

"No. I'll be happy when we find the other guy," she said and closed the browser windows.

* * * * *

49

The caller ID on the incoming call showed the name Aspen Wilson. Cari sighed and wondered what she'd forgotten to do now. She pushed the answer button.

"Hi, Aspen. How are you today?" Cari asked in what she hoped was an enthusiastic voice.

"Cari! I'm glad I caught you. How did the final fitting go?" Aspen asked.

"I think it went really well. The dress fits great and it's in its travel bag all ready to go for Saturday," Cari replied.

"Oh, you should get it out of that bag before it gets wrinkled. Wait. I can't remember. Do you have pets?" Aspen rattled off question after question.

"No. No pets for me. I'm not home enough to be a good pet mom," Cari told her.

"Oh, good. So, it sounds like you're driving, but when you get home, get your dress out of that bag. I'm sure the tailor packaged it as well as he could, but you don't want to walk down the aisle in a wrinkly dress," Aspen coached her.

The horror! "Of course not," Cari agreed. If she had to spend over a thousand dollars on a dress, she probably should make sure it wasn't wrinkled. "I'll call Bea and ask her to remove it from the bag after we hang up."

"Perfect. Your sister is the best. I'm glad she lives close by. Okay, so everything is confirmed with the florist. I'll be at the church on Friday morning as soon as they'll let me in to start decorating. What time do you plan to arrive?"

"Uhhh...I'll ask Bea and have her call you," Cari said uncertainly. "She was talking about making the bows earlier this afternoon.

"Okay, great. Talk to you soon, Cari," Aspen responded and ended the call.

As she approached the parking options for JFK, she debated about spending more money by parking in the closest garage or being thriftier and choosing one further away. The wedding costs loomed in her mind and she chose the lane with the far-out parking option. She didn't know how long she'd be at the airport, but the cost could really multiply fast. Her phone rang again just as she turned off her vehicle. It said the call was coming from Ohio.

"Hello?" Cari answered as she pulled her messenger bag from the passenger seat.

"Is this Ms. Turnlyle?" a woman's voice asked.

"Yes, is this Elizabeth? Please, call me Cari."

"Oh, what a relief. Yes, I'm Elizabeth. Marjorie told me how great you were when all that stuff happened at her school two years ago. We could really use your help," Elizabeth said quickly. "Marjorie said you'd be coming to the airport."

"I just parked. I'm waiting for the train to pick me up. Do you have any updates about Rebecca?" Cari asked. She needed to get on the AirTrain to get to the airport, but wasn't sure which terminal to go to.

"I got a call from someone named Officer Lochaven. He's going to let us view the video from yesterday," Elizabeth explained.

"Right, Marjorie mentioned that. Where should I meet you?" Cari asked.

"Does the train bring you to level three? I think it does," Elizabeth said, answering her own question. "Oh, but this airport is huge. Um, we're in terminal four. There's a place called the Welcome Center. I'll meet you there."

"Here comes the train now. It should only take me a few minutes to get there," Cari informed her.

"Marjorie told me you have curly hair and big, green eyes. She didn't mention if you were tall or short. Are you wearing anything recognizable?" Elizabeth wondered.

Cari looked down at her coat and scarf. "I have on a grey peacoat with a rather bright orange scarf."

"Orange scarf, got it. See you shortly," Elizabeth confirmed and ended the call.

Cari stepped onto the train as she slid her phone into her messenger bag. Elizabeth sounded surprisingly calm for someone whose sister was missing, but maybe she was one of those steady-under-pressure people. She hadn't mentioned Rebecca's husband; Cari wondered if he'd arrived yet. She remembered she had promised to call Bea about taking her dress out of its bag, so she pulled out her phone again.

"Hey, Cari. Did you get to the airport okay?" Bea asked. "Oh, by the way, I took your dress out of its bag and hung it up in Grandmother's suite. I didn't want it to get wrinkled."

"You're on top of everything, Bea. That's exactly what I was calling about," Cari said and laughed. "I'm also supposed to ask what time we're getting to the church on Friday to decorate…"

"I'll give Aspen a call and we'll make a plan. Is that okay?" Bea offered.

"That is perfect. Again. I'm sorry I was such a terrible maid of honor for you. You're taking care of so much for me," Cari said gratefully. "How is Grandmother doing?"

"Uhh, yeah," Bea's voice grew quieter and Cari heard a door click closed in the background. "You noticed her coughing fits too? She keeps saying it's nothing, but I'm kind of worried about her."

"Me too. You know, maybe she's allergic to Mom's perfume or something," Cari suggested. "They don't usually spend this much time together."

"Oh, that's a good thought. Grandmother would never say anything to Mom about it either," Bea agreed. "It seems like whatever it is, it's making it hard for her to breathe."

"I guess I wasn't aware she had asthma. Isn't that a symptom of people with asthma?" Cari asked.

"Yeah, Hilary has mild asthma, so I should maybe talk to Mom about cutting back. Maybe it's a new habit she picked up on their cruise from last fall," Bea hypothesized.

"Who knows?" Cari said with a shrug. "Well, I'm about to get off this train. Thanks for taking care of me this week, Bea. You're the best big sister a girl could ask for."

"Love you, Care-Bear," Bea responded.

Cari felt herself blush. "Love you, Queen Bee."

Their childhood nicknames had been points of contention when they were young, but now they used them endearingly. The train came to a stop at terminal four and Cari waited her turn to exit. She looked at the overhead signs and scanned them for directions to the Welcome Center. She needed to ride the escalator down to the first floor. The sign indicated she should take the longer escalator down which would bypass level two and go straight to level one. She stepped onto the escalator and stayed to the right in case anyone needed to pass her. Not surprisingly, the airport was crowded with travelers coming and going. She watched several families with small children struggling to stay in line. She wondered how much busier the airport was during the holidays compared to a random week day in January.

"Cari? Cari Turnlyle?" A woman's voice called out.

Cari looked in the direction she heard her name and saw a tall woman with a baby strapped to her chest waving. The woman had straight brown hair and was wearing a Browns' sweatshirt with jeans. Cari smiled and waved back.

"Thank you so much for coming all the way out here. This is such a nightmare. I probably shouldn't have come with Whitney, but my husband has to work and we don't really have a sitter..." she trailed off.

"Whitney is your baby?" Cari asked trying to keep up.

"Yes! This is Whitney!" She cooed and then rotated ninety degrees so Cari could see the sleeping baby better. "She's been such a trooper. Anyway, Officer Lochaven is getting the video set up. It's right this way."

Elizabeth had on a visitor ID sticker. She'd stuck it to the baby wrap. Cari wondered if they'd give her one too.

"The officer asked me repeatedly if I'd been contacted about a ransom demand, but no one has called me," Elizabeth told Cari.

"What about her husband? Wouldn't they call him first?" Cari asked.

"Keith swears he didn't get any calls either. I don't think Officer Lochaven believes us," Elizabeth said quietly. "Keith was only here for a little bit and after he left, the officer asked me if Keith was abusive. He thought maybe Rebecca came out here to run away from him."

Cari had wondered the same thing. She waited for Elizabeth to continue.

"I was so shocked to hear him suggest that! Keith would never. He's a very loving husband and father. They've been married for a long time. I would know if she wasn't safe. She'd say something or I'd see something," Elizabeth said adamantly. Cari wondered if she was trying to convince herself as much as Cari.

They reached the welcome center and Elizabeth knocked on a door to the side. A few seconds later, the door swung open. A middle-aged Black man in an airport police uniform looked from Elizabeth to Cari. He was about six feet tall and had closely cropped hair.

"Ms. Turnlyle, I presume?" he asked.

"Yes, I'm Cari," she said and extended her hand.

"Officer Lochaven, though a lot of people just call me Loch. I'm going to need to see some ID. Sorry. It's rather irregular that you're being let into this room at all," he explained.

"No problem," Cari responded and pulled out her driver's license.

He looked it over and passed it back. "Let me get you a visitor badge."

Loch opened a drawer and pulled out a sheet of stickers with the word "visitor" printed on them. He handed one to her.

"Stick this on your shirt where it can easily be seen," Loch instructed her. "Okay, I've got the videos paused at just before Mrs. Davenport's arrival. Mrs. Marino, will anyone else be joining us?"

Cari could tell the officer was irritated. She wondered where Rebecca's husband was, but figured she could ask later.

"Uh, Keith is off getting us hotel rooms and hopefully taking a shower," Elizabeth told them. "Poor guy, he stinks of stress and fear and...life. I don't think he's slept in over a day. I guess I haven't either. Whitney has been prepping me for today, who knew?"

Officer Lochaven stared at the woman as she rambled on. "Okay. Let's get this started."

He sat down in front of a computer screen. Four images were frozen in a two-by-two grid. He moved the mouse over the first one. "This is just outside the gate where her flight landed yesterday. It takes almost fifteen minutes for everyone to deplane. I'm going to put it on two-x speed. Tell me when you see her."

The people entered the gate area from the door to the jetway at a rapid pace. It was almost comical. Cari watched as the passengers dragged their bags along behind them, some in pairs and some traveling solo. She had no idea what Rebecca looked like, so she paid attention to the other people in the gate area. One person was staring intently at everyone who came off the plane.

"There," Elizabeth's voice startled Cari. "That's Rebecca. This is right around when I was talking to her on the phone. We did a video call, see? She's holding her phone away from her face."

Elizabeth pointed at the screen. Cari saw a blonde woman with pale skin smiling as she talked to the phone in front of her. She was dragging a roller bag behind her with her left hand and held the phone with her right. After a few seconds, she stepped out of frame of the camera. Officer Lochaven paused the video.

"Okay, so we should be able to pick her up on this feed," he commented and clicked on the screen below the one he'd just paused. "Let me just get it to the correct time…okay, there she is."

Cari looked at the screen and saw the blonde woman cross from the left to the right again. She'd only moved four or five steps when another person bumped into her. Cari realized it was the woman she'd been watching earlier. The collision had made Rebecca drop her phone. Another phone landed next to Rebecca's. She picked up one phone while she apologized to the other woman. The woman picked up the other phone and held it out to Rebecca. She ended the video call and took the phone from the other woman.

"Wait, why would she take that phone?" Elizabeth asked. "I heard someone say 'you dropped something' or something like that while I was talking to her, but that's not her phone. Wait. Why is she giving the woman her cell phone?!"

Cari watched as Rebecca passed the phone she'd been talking on over to the other woman. Rebecca nodded to the woman and they both continued walking together.

"They're probably headed to the bathroom. Ms. Marino, do you recognize this other woman?" he asked.

"I've never seen her before in my life," Elizabeth replied. "But they traded phones. I don't understand."

"Are you sure? The two phones looked a lot alike. Maybe your sister picked up the other woman's phone by mistake," Officer Lochaven suggested.

"No, I was on the phone with her. A *video* call. I saw her face again. Didn't you see her end the phone call before she took that woman's phone?!" Elizabeth's voice was starting to get screechy.

Cari saw the baby's foot twitch and wondered if she was going to wake up soon.

"Let's watch it again," Loch suggested.

He moved the cursor back to the same starting position and clicked play. Cari watched the two women collide. It almost looked like the other woman intentionally ran into Rebecca. Cari kept her eye on the cell phones. Elizabeth was right. They definitely switched phones.

"Well, good catch. It does seem strange that they'd swap phones," he said thoughtfully. "Let's see where your sister goes next. The video in the top right has the women's restroom in frame. We'll be able to see who goes in and out."

Officer Lochaven clicked on the video in the top right and adjusted the time to match the previous one. As he predicted, Rebecca went into the restroom while the other woman kept moving. They watched the door to the restroom for several minutes, but Rebecca never came out. Cari could feel Loch growing more impatient by the minute. She knew he probably felt like they were wasting his time.

"Okay, I've seen ten other women go in that restroom and come back out since she went in. We must have missed her. I'm going to rewind it," Loch said and adjusted the time again.

Elizabeth and Cari leaned toward the screen as Rebecca entered the bathroom again. Women and children entered and exited one after another, but Rebecca didn't come out. Cari knew the bathrooms had been searched, so she couldn't still be inside.

"Wait. Can you roll this other video back to where Rebecca is almost out of frame?" Cari asked Officer Lochaven.

"Sure," he said and shrugged. He moved the cursor to the correct time and hit play.

"Okay, Rebecca has a bright turquoise suitcase. Let's watch for that," Cari directed them.

Officer Loch raised his eyebrows. "Good idea, Ms. Turnlyle."

He adjusted the third video again and hit play. Cari stopped looking for a woman with long blonde hair and watched for the brightly colored suitcase instead.

"There. She has on a hat and sunglasses and her hair is tucked inside the hat. She looks completely different," Cari pointed out. "The hair I can see looks like it's black now too. Did she put on a wig?"

"That's definitely her. I recognize the birthmark on her right hand. Why would she put on a disguise?" Elizabeth asked with tears in her eyes.

Chapter 5

The white satin ribbon had a thin gold border that sparkled in the light. Bea admired the bow she'd just finished. *Not too bad.* Grandmother was dozing on the sofa while she and her mom constructed wedding decorations.

"Typical Cari to just rush off and leave us here to do all of this for her," her mom grumbled.

"She's very busy, Mom. She took the whole week off from work. No one expected that, right?" Bea defended her little sister. "Besides, she was never going to make a respectable bow. She doesn't do crafty things."

"It seems like she has zero domestic skills. Maybe we babied her too much," their mom lamented.

"We all have different strengths, Mom. You tell us that all the time. We only need to make twenty. It's not a large sanctuary. We're already halfway finished," Bea encouraged her.

"Speaking of domestic skills..." she said and set the ribbon down.

Here it comes.

"Since when did you and Robby swap Cari and Bob in for your dad and me?" Mom pressed her. "They aren't even married yet!"

"But they're much closer to us than you and Daddy *and* they see the kids a lot more often," Bea explained. "The kids wouldn't have to switch schools, which is preferential. I mean, it's all a formality, right, Mom? It's just something you need to have in writing. It's not like we lead dangerous lives or anything."

Her mom pursed her lips. "Well, I don't think Cari is made out to be a mother."

"She has changed so much in the year we've lived here. And Bob is fantastic with the kids. They adore him," Bea said and smiled. "We aren't demoting you, Mom. We're just making a logical change. You can understand that, right?"

Grandmother let out a snort from the sofa. Bea quickly looked her way, but it seemed like she was only snoring in her sleep. She felt her mom's hand on her own.

"She's getting older. It's natural for people to rest more when they get over eighty-five," she assured her and picked up the ribbon again.

"Has Daddy said anything about her health? It seems like she's having a hard time just breathing," Bea said.

Her mom shook her head. "He hasn't mentioned anything to me."

Bea tied another bow and set it aside. "Do we have a plan for dinner? The kids are used to eating around 5:30, so they're going to get grumpy if we make them wait too long."

"Let me give your dad a call and see if he's found a place. You know he's been looking." Her mom finished the bow she was working on and took out her cell phone. "I can't remember, will your kids eat Tex-Mex now?"

"Hilary will. Joel is hit or miss, but they almost always have a kids' menu. I thought Dad was trying to push for barbecue," Bea reminded her mom.

"It isn't a good week for barbecue. I vetoed that. He'll get over it," she said and pressed a button on her phone.

Bea went back to tying the ribbon into bows. The guardianship conversation hadn't been as terrible as she'd imagined it to be. Hopefully, it wouldn't get brought up again.

* * * * *

Officer Lochaven paused the video feed. "Okay, so now we know your sister left the restroom dressed in a hat and dark glasses. Let's see where she goes next. I just need to find the right camera feed."

They waited while he opened a folder on the computer and scrolled through a list. He referred to his cell phone a couple times before selecting another file within the folder.

"This should be it," he said and clicked play after the video loaded. "There she is."

Cari watched Rebecca pull her suitcase through the airport. The newest camera angle was wider or zoomed in less, so they could follow her further than with the previous three cameras. She reached the security exit and kept walking.

"Where could she be going? Why would she just leave?" Elizabeth asked, her voice barely above a whisper.

Baby Whitney started to whimper, so Elizabeth swayed side to side to try to soothe the baby back to sleep. She quieted back down for a moment and then let out a wail.

"I'm sorry. I probably need to change her and then feed her again. Cari, can you keep watching? I'll be back as soon as she's finished," Elizabeth assured her.

"Of course," Cari replied. She was invested in finding Rebecca now.

"I've got the next video queued up when you're ready," Officer Lochaven said as Elizabeth left the room with Whitney.

"I'm ready," Cari told him.

His hand hovered over the mouse. "Before I start this video…how well do you know these people?"

Cari blinked. "Not at all. I know Mrs. Marino's cousin."

"I think it's weird that the husband isn't here trying to tear the place apart to find his wife. He got off his flight, checked in with his sister-in-law, and left," Officer Loch explained. "If it was my wife, I'd be knocking on every door and talking to every person here until I found her. It feels like he's going through the motions."

She nodded in understanding. "It is a little odd, but Mrs. Marino said he hasn't slept in over a day. Maybe he's in survival mode."

He frowned, but didn't object. He jiggled the mouse and then clicked the play button on the video.

"Okay, there she is. Looks like she's heading for the AirTrain," he observed.

"Do you have cameras on those?" Cari asked.

"They do, but I'm hoping to catch her exiting the train. It's pretty rare for people to drive and park at the airport. It's cheaper to park at one of the metro lots and ride the subway to the AirTrain," he explained. "Okay, we've got her entering the AirTrain. Let's go to the stop for the changeover to the subway."

He took a moment to find the next video file and then confirmed the time stamp from where they stopped the previous one. Cari hadn't realized how easy it was to track one person through the airport. She was thankful Rebecca had a brightly colored bag as they could find her quickly within a crowd.

"This should be her train," Loch stated and pointed at the screen.

"Oh, I see her," Cari exclaimed. "She's going toward the E-line."

"Once she's on the subway, I'm not going to be any more help to you," he explained. "I don't have access to the subway's cameras."

"Who can we contact about those?" Cari asked. "We've made it this far and it feels like we're so close to figuring out where she went."

"Let's see which train she gets on first," Loch replied. "Between you and me, something feels off about this. We haven't been contacted about a ransom, unless the sister and the husband are both lying to me."

Cari bit her lip. "But why would they lie? I agree, we don't know the whole story, but I feel like Elizabeth is just as much in the dark as you and me."

Loch grimaced. "It seems like she willingly left the airport and...there she is, getting on the E-line."

He paused the video before speaking again. "The time stamp says 5:37 p.m. You'll need to tell that to metro."

"Metro police?" Cari asked for confirmation. "Can't you connect us with someone? Surely, you know someone in that department."

Officer Lochaven looked at the closed door. Cari wondered if he was thinking about Rebecca's sister and husband. She pleaded with him with her eyes.

"I'll make a call, but I'm not promising they'll help you," Loch told her.

He pulled out his phone and moved to the other side of the room. Cari gave him space. She wanted to stay on his good side. A quiet knock sounded at the door. She looked through the window and saw Elizabeth holding her baby girl out of the baby carrier.

"Hey, Officer Lochaven is trying to get us in touch with someone in metro. Your sister got on the E-line at 5:37 p.m. That's as far as we can track her from here," Cari explained quickly.

"I still can't wrap my mind around this. Why wouldn't she call? Doesn't she know we're all worried out of our minds?" Elizabeth asked. "And her kids? She wouldn't abandon those kids. She loves them."

Cari looked at her watch. She was going to need to leave soon if she was going to meet her family for dinner. She didn't even know where they were planning to meet yet. Officer Loch rejoined them.

"Okay, it took a little begging and I'll probably have to pick up his bar tab for a year, but my friend over in metro will meet you tomorrow morning to look at the subway footage," Officer Lochaven told them. "I'll write the address down on my card for you. You'll need to be there at eight o'clock sharp."

"Tomorrow?" Elizabeth said, her eyes wide. Cari put a hand on her shoulder.

"Thank you for your help. Can we get your friend's phone number?" Cari asked, not wanting to offend him. "Or would you give him mine?"

Loch unlocked his phone. "I'll text him your number. He can call you if he wants."

Cari recited her phone number for him. "We really appreciate your help. Please let us know if you hear anything else from the airline or otherwise."

He nodded. "Here's my card if you need to reach me again. I hope you find your sister."

Elizabeth gave him a smile, but there were tears on her cheeks and her lips were quivering. Cari felt bad for her. She couldn't imagine what she'd be like if Bea ever disappeared like this.

* * * * *

O'Zook's, the Tex-Mex restaurant their mom selected for dinner looked more like a bar than a restaurant, but Bea decided to let it go. The week was not about her; she was there to keep the peace and make sure things ran smoothly. In its defense, it did have a kids' menu, so maybe she shouldn't feel so awkward about bringing two children there.

They had a round booth near the back, which Joel was thrilled about. He'd scooted all the way to the back position and was happily swinging his legs under the table. His grandparents sandwiched him in place, blissfully unaware one of them would have to get out of the way when he inevitably asked to go use the bathroom mid-meal. Cari had called to say she was running a bit late, but was at least on her way. At least Robby was on time. Ever since Cari and Genevieve had exposed his boss in the blackmail scheme, his hours had improved drastically. She had been surprised Robby wanted to continue working there, but he'd explained his boss was just as much a victim as anyone else. Robby wasn't going to bring it up and hoped everyone would forget it ever happened.

"What can I get everyone to drink this evening?" the waitress asked.

"Mommy, can I get a soda?" Joel begged.

She exchanged a glance with Robby. "Uh, sure, Joel. What would you like?"

"A coke!" he squealed with delight.

"Is Pepsi okay?" the waitress asked him.

"It's fine," Bea responded for him.

"Bea, you have to try their margaritas! They're *so* good," her mother suggested and then turned to the waitress. "I'd like a house marg, frozen with sugar."

The waitress made a note and then looked at Hilary who sat on the opposite side of her grandma. Hilary looked at her mom with pleading eyes and Bea nodded in encouragement.

"Um, I'd like a lemonade, please," Hilary said almost audibly.

Bea knew what she would order without actually hearing her words. The waitress leaned in and put a hand to her ear.

"I'm sorry?" she asked.

"Lemonade, please," Hilary repeated, slightly louder.

They'd saved a seat for Cari on Hilary's left, which was the edge seat for that side of the table. The waitress turned to Robby.

"Just water for me, please," he requested.

"Same for me, thanks," Bea echoed.

Her mother made a tsk sound from across the booth. Bea ignored it.

"Another vote for water," Grandmother said. "They tell me I can't drink enough of that."

"I guess I'm last then," her dad observed. "Let's see. I'll have an iced tea."

"I'll have those right out," the waitress informed them. "Any apps before I put in your drink order?"

"Chips and queso!" Joel shouted with his eyebrows raised.

Robby put his hands up. "Sure, bud. One large order of queso, please."

"Sorry I'm late! I forgot about the traffic getting out of the city. I should have parked further out and taken the subway all the way to the airport. Live and learn. Oh, um, can I get a strawberry margarita on the rocks with salt and a water, please?" Cari asked the waitress.

The waitress added the items to the tab. "I'll be back with your drinks in just a moment."

"How did it go at the airport?" their mother asked.

"Well, we made some progress. It does kind of seem like the woman left the airport by choice, but I don't know why," Cari explained. "We're meeting with the metro police tomorrow to see if we can figure out where she went from the airport's AirTrain."

"You're leaving us again tomorrow?" their mother asked with a disappointed look.

"I'm sorry, Mom. I'm kind of invested now. Hopefully, we'll locate her quickly and it will all be easily cleared up before lunch," Cari said and smiled.

"Well, we got all of your bows made today. You owe your sister a big thank you for that," she remarked.

Bea cringed. "I had fun making the bows with you, Mom," she paused and pulled out her phone. "Here's a photo of our finished product."

Cari took the phone from her and opened her mouth to speak, but their mom beat her to it.

"Tomorrow, we're eating dinner with Bob's family too, right? His parents and siblings and so forth? You need to be on time for that. Make a good impression on your in-laws," their mother instructed Cari.

"Patricia, they're both adults," their dad reminded her quietly.

"Thank you both so much. I think the bows look amazing. I'm sorry I wasn't here to help tie any of them. I really do appreciate it," Cari said and smiled. "Did you get everything squared away with Aspen for Friday? What time do we need to be there?"

"Yes, I talked to the church secretary and they'll have the doors unlocked for us at nine o'clock. The head custodian will have the tables and chairs out of the closet for us to arrange as we'd like. Aspen is bringing the backdrop you selected along with some fake greenery...I think she said ivy...to decorate it. The florist will drop the flowers off around ten and we can put the corsages and boutonnieres and your bouquet in the refrigerator in the church kitchen. I also printed some QR codes for people to scan; they link to your online photo album. Guests will be able to add any photos to it during the reception. I think that's it," Bea recounted from memory.

"Maybe you should start a side hustle as a wedding planner, Bea. That was impressive," their dad said with a chuckle.

Bea laughed. "It's all part of my duties as the matron of honor. I'm *honored* to get to do it."

"I'm excited for you and Bob, Cari," Grandmother said. "It's going to be a lovely day. I'm glad we all get to be here together to see it."

Bea smiled at her grandmother and squeezed her hand under the table. "Me too," she agreed.

"I'm STARVING," Joel interrupted. "Are we ever going to order?"

Cari laughed. "I think I see our waitress headed our way right now. Lucky for you, they have endless chips here, so there's no way you'll starve."

The waitress had a tray of beverages and her colleague had a second tray with the chips and queso. He placed the items on the table while she distributed their drinks.

"Darren, did you want to say something?" Patricia asked.

Their dad looked confused for a moment. "Oh! Yes. One check please and I'll get it."

"Daddy, you don't have to buy us all dinner," Cari interjected.

"My treat. How often do we all get to eat together like this?" he asked.

"Fair enough. Thank you," Cari responded.

They quickly placed their orders. Joel began devouring all the chips in the bowl nearest him without any queso. Grandmother clinked her knife against her water glass and they all looked her way.

"You beat me to the dinner tonight, Darren. I'll let it slide this one time," she said with a sparkle in her eye. "This is a special week. Let's all remember how happy we are and how blessed we are to be together. I'm so proud of each of you and I love you very much."

"Cheers." The adults responded in unison. Hilary and Joel raised their glasses and joined in clinking them with the others around the table. Bea smiled. It was good to be together.

* * * * *

Cari put her car in park and hurried around the other side to help her grandmother get out. She was relieved she hadn't heard her cough all evening. The temperature had dropped below freezing while they were eating dinner, but thankfully, the sidewalks were clear and dry.

"I'm perfectly capable of getting out of this car on my own, sweet girl," her grandmother admonished her.

"I know, I just wanted to be ready to assist if needed," Cari told her.

"Oh, here come your parents to fuss over me too," Grandmother lamented.

"It sure is cold here in January," her dad said when he reached them. "Ready to go inside, Mom?"

"I'm ready. We'll see you tomorrow, Cari. Sleep well," Grandmother said and gave her a hug.

"Love you, Grandmother," Cari said and kissed her cheek.

"I love you more," she responded.

They waved goodbye and went into the hotel. Cari got back into her car and pulled onto the street. Her apartment wasn't far away. She checked that her phone was connected to the Bluetooth and selected Bob's name from her favorites list.

"Hey, Cari. How was dinner?" he asked.

"It was nice. Grandmother seemed to be breathing better. Maybe it was the cold air. I guess some people have allergies this time of year," she suggested.

"Uh, maybe so. I know you've been worrying about her," Bob replied.

"I am worried about her. She hasn't seemed like herself, but she doesn't seem interested in talking about it either," Cari told him.

"Maybe she's just getting over a cold and it's nothing," Bob hypothesized. "How was the airport?"

"This missing persons case gets more intriguing by the hour. We were able to track Rebecca from her gate all the way to the E-line on the subway," Cari told him.

"Wow. I get the feeling you're going back again tomorrow?" Bob questioned.

She smiled. He knew her so well. "Yeah, we're going to try to track her through the subway and see if we can figure out where she went."

"It's been twenty-four hours now, right?" he asked.

"I guess it has been. Something isn't adding up. She hasn't called anyone to check in. Marjorie assured me she was in a safe relationship. Plus, she has kids. Something or someone convinced her to leave the airport yesterday. If I can figure out what that was, then I think we can find her," Cari said confidently.

"You and Genevieve are like two peas in a pod," Bob said with a laugh.

"What do you mean?" Cari asked.

"Well, I'm sure you're aware she doesn't think Stenoway acted alone," Bob reminded her.

"Right, but she hasn't found any proof. I kind of thought she'd let it go," Cari mused. "I looked through his accounts with her back in July and I agreed with her, but it was more of an instinct than something evidentiary."

"She definitely hasn't let it go. She took the day off today and tracked down the woman who was seducing Pierce and Follard," Bob revealed.

"What?! Where is she?" Cari asked in surprise.

"I didn't hear, but she got permission to go visit Stenoway in prison tomorrow and see if she can get him to spill who his accomplice is," Bob replied.

"Well, maybe she's making progress too. She helped us get connected with the airport police, but she didn't mention tracking down the other woman," Cari remarked. "I'll have to call her tomorrow and see if she'll give me an update."

"Always sleuthing...well, good luck," Bob replied. "I'm pretty beat. I worked a few extra hours the last few days, so it won't really look like I took two days off on my next paycheck. I'm going to get ready for bed. Talk to you tomorrow?"

"Definitely. I'll call you on my way into the city unless you're sleeping in," she offered.

"That sounds perfect. Love you, Cari. Three more days and we'll be married," Bob said sleepily.

"I can't wait. Love you too, Bob," she said with a big smile, even though he couldn't see it.

The call ended just as she reached her apartment complex. She was pretty tired too. She climbed the steps to her unit and unlocked the door. Her mind drifted back to the airport videos. Something she had seen hadn't fit with everything else. She tried to remember what was out of place, but nothing distinct came to mind. Maybe she'd remember in the morning.

Chapter 6

Cari was only ten minutes from the parking lot where she planned to catch the subway into the city. She had no desire to fight the rush hour traffic if she didn't have to. She wanted Bob to get to sleep in as much as he could, so she decided to call Genevieve first since she knew she was going to work early today.

"Hey, Cari. I'm almost to work. Did everything work out with your missing person?" Genevieve asked her.

"Uh, not yet, but we're making progress. I heard from Bob that you're interviewing Stenoway today. I hadn't realized you were still searching for his partner or accomplice," Cari told her.

"I just can't let it go. Someone else was definitely involved and I'm not comfortable letting them roam around freely," Genevieve said.

Cari bit her lip. "What does this mean for Robby?"

"Robby? Nothing. No one knows he was our informant, so he should be fine. I don't even know if his boss had any repercussions for letting Stenoway funnel money through NTS," Genevieve said flippantly.

"You at least kept him updated, right?" Cari asked.

"I don't think it's necessary. His part is finished. There's no reason to stress him out with these developments," Genevieve argued.

"I guess that makes sense. Keep me posted on what you find out. I'll need to write an addendum to my story," Cari said. "If you're getting to interview Stenoway again, does that mean Shelly told you something about the other person involved?"

"Not exactly. She just didn't know anything about Stenoway. That wasn't who she worked with, which means we're missing a link somewhere. I'm hoping the six months Stenoway has spent in prison have made him more amenable to telling us who he was working with."

"Well, I wish you luck. Talk to you soon," Cari said and ended the call.

It was well after seven now, so she figured Bob was probably awake. He confirmed her suspicions when he answered on the first ring.

"I was starting to think you were going to ghost me," he laughed.

"Ah, I would never," she assured him. "I just wanted to let you sleep in."

"Thanks. I've been awake for half an hour," he said and laughed again. "How was the drive?"

"Not terrible, but I'm still pretty far away from the city. I'm taking the subway in so I can avoid the majority of the rush hour traffic," she explained.

"Good plan. We're still on for lunch today, right?" Bob asked.

Cari cringed. She'd forgotten about it. "With your parents?"

"Yeah, I'm picking them up from the airport in about an hour," he confirmed. "My brother is flying in this afternoon with his girlfriend. Hopefully, they'll be on time for the dinner we planned. Their flight lands around four, but his girlfriend will definitely check a bag. She's super high-maintenance."

"I can't check my phone calendar right now. Remind me what time we're meeting for lunch?" she asked hoping it was closer to one.

"One o'clock at Mae's Diner," he replied.

"Got it. Thanks for the details…again," she said sheepishly.

"Of course. Hey, I was thinking about your grandma last night after we hung up," he said in a quieter tone. "How did her ankles look?"

Cari almost laughed. "Her ankles? I don't know. She was wearing pants."

"Oh, well, what about her feet? Her shoes? Were they tight?" he asked.

Cari remembered thinking her shoes did look tight when they were at the bridal shop. "Yeah, I noticed that in the morning at the dress fitting."

Bob was silent for a moment. "Um, I could be completely wrong, but it kind of sounds like she might have congestive heart failure."

Cari felt her heart sink into her stomach. "Heart failure? Like she's having a heart attack?"

"No, it's not that exactly. It's a complicated condition, but pretty common the older we get," he explained. "In many cases, it can be easily managed by medication."

Cari felt a little relief. Maybe it wasn't as serious as it sounded. "Okay. That's a lot to think about. I just reached the parking lot…I'll be in touch. Love you, Bob," she said as she parked her car.

"Love you too," he said and ended the call.

She wiped a tear from her cheek. She couldn't think about her grandmother's health right now. She pulled up her metro pass as she walked to the train platform. She scanned it and started to put her phone away when another call came in. *Officer Lochaven!*

"Officer Lochaven?" Cari asked.

"Miss Turnlyle, I went to bed thinking about Rebecca Davenport. All the video we watched yesterday pointed to a woman just leaving the airport without a care in the world, but her sister was adamant she wouldn't do that," he began. "I came in early this morning and rewatched the video right before she goes to the bathroom. That's the only other interaction she has with someone."

"Right, the other woman bumped into her and it seemed like they swapped phones," Cari agreed. Something clicked in her mind. "That's it!"

"That's what I'm trying to say—"

"Sorry to interrupt, but I was thinking about the videos too. The woman who bumps into her…she was watching everyone get off of that flight. I think she was watching for Rebecca," Cari explained.

"Well, that makes what I'm about to say even more interesting. The widescreen view didn't show us what was on the other phone screen. I went back and played it slower and zoomed in on the two women. The other woman has her phone screen facing up," he explained. "When I zoomed in, there was an image on the screen of a man with two kids. You'll never guess who the man was."

"Her husband. That's why she left. The woman was threatening her family or something," Cari surmised.

"That's what I think too," Loch agreed.

"I can't believe I didn't notice the screen," Cari remarked.

"It was zoomed out too far for any of us to notice. I saved a still of the image and I emailed it to Ms. Marino. She confirmed it was her brother-in-law just a few minutes ago," he informed Cari.

"Are we still meeting your friend at metro?" she asked.

"Yeah, but I'm going to join you. I got permission from my superior to stick with the case," he told her.

"Oh, great. That's really kind of you, Loch," she said.

"I'm up for a promotion soon. This can't hurt my chances," he admitted.

"Well, I know Rebecca's family appreciates the extra effort. I'm about to get on the subway now. I'll see you there," Cari told him.

"See you there," Loch echoed and ended the call.

* * * * *

Both Genevieve and Alex locked their service weapons into the glove box of the cruiser. It was easier than surrendering them before meeting with a prisoner. Genevieve wondered how much Salzer would let Stenoway say to them. She didn't plan to hit him with any new charges. She just wanted to know the truth.

After they walked through the metal detector, they retrieved their badges and cell phones from the little bin. Alex was brooding about something. He'd been especially quiet on the drive to the prison, but wouldn't admit to it.

"I'm sorry you are being forced to join me out here," she said to him.

His dark eyes widened. "No, you aren't."

"You're right. I'm not, but we both know this is the right thing to do," she told him.

A prison guard approached them. "For Anderson Stenoway?"

They nodded. Genevieve put out her hand. "Detective Viacorte and Detective Runimoss from Brenington PD."

"His lawyer will be here soon, but he agreed to let you come back before he arrives. I'll bring you back now," the guard said after shaking their hands.

They followed the guard through a series of hallways and doors until they reached a meeting room. Stenoway's hands were cuffed to the table and his ankles were shackled too. He wore a faded orange jumpsuit and had grown a beard since they last saw him in the summer. He had an empty paper cup in front of him.

Genevieve heard Alex mutter something under his breath. She looked at him in confusion.

"Never mind," he responded and entered the room.

They took their seats on the opposite side of the table. Genevieve thought Stenoway looked paler than he had back in July. He probably didn't get as much time outside anymore.

"I'll be outside if you need anything," the guard told them and closed the door.

"Detectives. To what do I owe the pleasure?" Stenoway asked.

"I'm not here to waste anyone's time, so let's get right to it." Genevieve pulled out a notebook and a file. "I found Shelly."

Stenoway's arrogance faded away and his eyes widened. "You're bluffing. Where is she?"

"You don't need to know. Funny thing, she has no idea who you are," Genevieve informed him. "That was a huge surprise. If you didn't 'hire' her, then who did?"

"It doesn't matter. She's useless to you. She doesn't know anything," Stenoway said quickly.

Genevieve could hear footsteps in the hallway. "The fact that she doesn't know you, tells me you did not act alone. So, who were you working with?"

Stenoway looked at the door. They heard an electronic click and it swung open. Logan Salzer walked in and took the empty seat next to his client.

"Ah, detectives. What brings you out to my favorite client today?" Salzer asked. "Were you short on cases and thought you'd waste my time by calling me out here?"

"We were just discussing some new information with Mr. Stenoway," Genevieve responded. "We thought Mr. Stenoway could help us understand it."

Alex cut in. "We aren't here to add to Mr. Stenoway's charges, so if you have somewhere else you need to be…"

"Oh, no, Detective. I'm quite happy to observe and counsel my client, as is his right," Salzer replied.

Genevieve opened her folder and pulled out a sheet of paper. "Several months ago, we were given access to another one of Mr. Stenoway's accounts. I think we're all aware he is no longer employed by the three cities, yet somehow, a monthly deposit of two thousand dollars is taking place. We exposed the blackmail scheme, so that can't be the source of the money."

"I didn't hear a question in there," Salzer said smoothly.

"Mr. Stenoway, here is the most recent statement from the account. Is this really your account?" she asked and pushed the paper toward him.

He glanced at it quickly. "Of course it is. Who else could it belong to?"

"That's what I'm asking. Who added you to this account?" Genevieve challenged him.

"Why would someone add a criminal to their account and give them two thousand dollars every month, Detective?" Salzer said in a mocking tone.

"That's what I'd like to know," she said and narrowed her eyes at Stenoway. It looked like he'd started to sweat. "Are you uncomfortable, Mr. Stenoway? We could ask the guard to bring you some water."

He barely nodded his head. "I'm fine. Thank you for the offer."

Salzer reached down and pulled a disposable bottle of water from his briefcase. "Here, Anderson. I bought a bottle from the vending machine on my way in."

Salzer untwisted the cap and passed the water to his client. Stenoway took a big drink and set the water back down.

Alex cleared his throat. "Mr. Stenoway, we feel it is in your best interest to tell us if you're covering for someone else. There's no need for you to serve life in prison for someone else's crimes."

"Why is it so hard to believe that I'm the only guilty party?" Stenoway asked.

"It's what the evidence is telling us," Genevieve replied.

"This conversation is going nowhere. GUARD!" Salzer raised his voice to get the guard's attention. "Thank you for your time. Next time, maybe we should meet in Brenington first. Then we can save everyone a trip out here, hmmm?"

Genevieve resisted the urge to roll her eyes. "If you change your mind and want to talk, you just have to tell one of the guards. They'll get in touch with us or Agent Dureski."

She and Alex stood up from the table when the guard opened the door. They nodded their goodbyes and exited the meeting room. Alex put a finger to his lips quickly before turning to follow the guard out of the prison's interior. They retraced their steps to the entrance and signed out of the visitor log.

Genevieve waited until they were outside before she spoke. "You felt it too."

"He's afraid. It really rattled him that you found Shelly. I hate to admit it, but I think you're right. We missed something back in July," he said and ran a hand through his dark hair.

"But who? How do we find this other person?" Genevieve asked. "Why wouldn't he just tell us?"

"Maybe he doesn't really know. You said Ms. Palladium didn't know who she was taking orders from. Maybe Stenoway never met the other person either," Alex proposed and unlocked the cruiser.

"They never answered the question about the account or the money. Something really feels off about all of this," Genevieve observed. "I need to look at all these accounts again. The answer is in the money. I just haven't looked in the right place yet."

* * * * *

Cari connected to the metro Wi-Fi and double-checked her phone had Wi-Fi calling enabled. She wanted to call Grandmother while she rode the train to meet Loch, Elizabeth, and the other officer. She touched the green phone icon and waited for the call to connect.

"Good morning, little bride-to-be! How are you today?" Grandmother asked in a cheerful voice.

"Uh, I'm pretty good. How are you, Grandmother?" Cari asked with a bit of trepidation.

"I'm getting really excited for Saturday. I just can't get over how beautiful you look in…that…dress," Grandmother replied. She struggled to get the last few words out.

"Thank you. Are you sure you're okay? It sounds like you're out of breath," Cari observed.

"I'm fine. I'm just old," she responded.

"I'm a little worried about you. I talked to Bob…Grandmother, have you seen your doctor recently?" Cari asked.

"I go every year because my insurance says I have to," Grandmother told her.

"Bob thought…um…based on what I told him…uh…he said you might have congestive heart failure," Cari struggled to say the words.

Her grandmother didn't respond for several seconds. "Now, Cari, let's worry about that another day. This week is *your* week. Yours and Bob's. Let's celebrate that."

Cari felt like gagging, but managed to hold it back. "Okay, Grandmother. If you need anything, you'll let me know, right?"

"Of course, sweetheart. I can hear a lot of noise around you. Where are you this morning?" she asked.

"I'm headed back into the city. We're still trying to track down this woman who went missing from the airport earlier this week," Cari explained.

"Oh, dear. It's almost been two days now, huh? That doesn't seem good," Grandmother said. "I'll let you go. Stay safe and I'll see you at dinner."

"Okay. I love you," Cari told her.

"Love you more," Grandmother said and ended the call.

Cari put her phone in her bag. Grandmother hadn't denied having congestive heart failure. Cari didn't know much about the disease, but it didn't seem good if the word failure was part of the name. Maybe Bob could tell her more about it later. The train announced her stop was next. She stood up and held onto one of the hand grips as it lumbered down the rail. She almost lost her balance when it lurched to a stop. She exited onto the platform and looked for a sign directing her to the office.

"Cari!" Elizabeth called out.

Cari turned to her right and saw Elizabeth standing with Officer Lochaven and another man. Cari realized he looked familiar; it was Keith, Rebecca's husband. Whitney was nestled into the baby wrap on Elizabeth's chest again. They waved her over.

"Perfect timing, we came from the opposite direction and just got here," Loch explained. "Officer Nitto is meeting us in the office. It's just down the walkway a bit."

"Interesting name," Cari remarked.

Loch shrugged. "I'm sure it could be worse. He's a good guy. I texted him that we were headed his way, so he'll be ready for us."

They walked about two hundred yards to the metro security office. Officer Loch waved at the people inside with his badge. A tall Black man with closely cropped hair smiled back at him. The other two just nodded and kept their eyes on the screens in front of them.

"That's Nitto who waved. He wasn't on shift today, but came in for me," Loch told them.

"Thank you for helping me, Officer Lochaven. I don't know how I'd find Rebecca without you," Elizabeth said.

"Yeah, we really appreciate it," a tired Keith mumbled.

Officer Nitto opened the door. "I didn't realize we were going to have this large of a crowd. It might be a little tight in here."

"Nitto, this is Elizabeth Marino. She's the sister of Rebecca, the missing person. This is Keith Davenport, Rebecca's husband," Loch said pointing at the members of the group. "And this is Ms. Turnlyle. She's a friend of the family."

Cari extended her hand. "Call me Cari."

Nitto shook her hand. "Cari Turnlyle? You're the journalist, right?"

Cari felt her cheeks redden. "Yes, sir. I'm an investigative journalist for the Brenington Beagle."

He raised his eyebrows and sort of grimaced. "Okay. Uh. I've never worked a case with the press before, so this will be new. Gather around this screen over here. I have it queued up for the E-line from Tuesday evening. You said she got on at the airport at 5:37 p.m., right?"

"Correct," Loch replied.

"Okay. This video feed is for the first stop after the airport. We have no way of knowing how far she rode the subway, so this could be fairly tedious," Nitto told them. "You had a good idea to keep an eye out for her suitcase, so let's do that again. By the way, I have it set at half speed so we have a better chance of seeing her if she gets off at one of the more crowded stations."

They squeezed in around the monitor as Officer Nitto clicked play. The subway train pulled up to the platform. They watched as the doors opened. A family of four pushed their way off the train and onto the platform. The doors remained open for a few more seconds and then slid closed again.

"It's pretty rare for anyone to get off at this first stop," Nitto remarked. "The next few have connections to other lines though. I'll get the video up for the next stop."

He closed the video file and opened another one. "Each stop is only a few minutes apart, so I'll start the playback a few minutes after the last one ended."

Nitto moved the cursor to the correct time and then clicked play. Soon, the train appeared on the screen and came to a stop. The doors opened and passengers piled out of the cars. Cari looked up and down the platform for a bright turquoise roller bag.

"There are so many people," Keith complained. "Wait, is that her?"

Officer Nitto paused the video. "Is that your wife, Mr. Davenport?"

Keith leaned in. "Yeah, that's Rebecca."

"Let's see where she goes," he replied.

Rebecca was still wearing sunglasses even though she was underground. She was one of about ten passengers who didn't leave the platform after getting off the E-line. She stood by herself and occasionally checked her watch.

"The F-line also stops here. It seems like she's going to switch lines," Nitto observed. "Here comes the F-line train and yep, she's getting on it."

Rebecca boarded the F-line train and the doors closed behind her. Nitto stopped the video and closed the file.

"Let me find the folder with the F-line footage," he said as he clicked through the files. "Got it. She got on the outbound train, so she wasn't headed into the city. That's good for us. Fewer people to watch."

He repeated his steps from before and clicked play on the video. Cari wondered how many stops Rebecca would ride on this line. She wasn't very familiar with the metro routes and didn't know if it crossed another line again. She leaned forward to see better as the train doors slid open again. People filed off the train and hurried out of frame.

"There! I saw turquoise," Elizabeth exclaimed.

Officer Nitto paused the video. "Let me roll it back slowly. Where did you see it?"

"Near the top of the screen. The person exited from the back car," Elizabeth told him.

He carefully adjusted the time and then started it again. Cari watched the people getting out of the last car. She saw a woman exit wearing a long turquoise coat.

"Oh, it was a coat. I'm sorry. False alarm," Elizabeth apologized.

The video continued and more people got off. No one had a turquoise roller bag. Cari could feel the disappointment in the room.

"Let's scroll on to the next stop," Officer Nitto said as he clicked through a few screens to open another file. "Here we go."

The sequence repeated as before, except only a handful of passengers exited the subway train. The doors stayed open for a few seconds and then slid closed. The train rolled out of frame.

Nitto must have sensed their defeated attitudes. He tried to encourage them. "Like I said, it could take a few stops. I'll get the next one going here."

After they'd watched people exit the next two stops without seeing Rebecca, Cari felt Elizabeth grab her hand. She squeezed it. It must be excruciating to feel helpless like this. She waited for Officer Nitto to pull up the next video.

"We know she's still on the subway at this point. It's just a matter of finding the right stop," Cari said with more confidence than she felt. She wondered what they would do if they ran out of stops.

"What do we do if we get to the end of the line and she hasn't gotten off?" Keith asked as though reading her mind.

Officer Lochaven put a hand on his shoulder. "Let's worry about that if and when we get there, okay?"

"Ready for the next video?" Nitto asked.

They nodded in confirmation and he clicked play. Cari felt Elizabeth gripping her hand tighter and tighter as people exited the subway cars. Suddenly, she released it and clapped.

"There! There she is!" Elizabeth shouted.

Baby Whitney let out a howl in response to her mother's volume.

"Oh no. I'm sorry. I woke her up. Is there a bathroom where I can change her? I brought a bottle for her this morning," Elizabeth said to the officers.

"The restroom is just down the way to your right," Officer Nitto told her.

"I'll be right back," Elizabeth said and grabbed her diaper bag from below the computer desk.

The video was still paused. Cari turned to look at the screen. Rebecca Davenport had removed the sunglasses she'd worn on her way out of the airport, but was still wearing the hat and wig. Fewer than ten people got off at the stop, which made it easier to spot her.

"Isn't that the same woman from the airport? The one who gave her the cell phone?" Cari asked.

"I think you're right. Good catch, Miss Turnlyle," Loch complimented her. "They're basically out in the suburbs now. We can follow them on the street side for a bit. Nitto, can you access those cameras for us?"

Officer Nitto looked at his watch. "I can give you a little more time."

"Thanks, Nitto," Loch said.

"Give me a minute to find the right folder," Nitto replied and closed the current video. "Let's see. She got off in Jamaica at 179th, so...here we go."

"Keep watching for her turquoise bag. That will be the quickest way to see her," Loch instructed.

Nitto set the speed to half and clicked play. They watched for Rebecca and her new acquaintance to come up the steps from the subway. After a few minutes, the two women entered the frame. Nitto paused the feed when he heard someone knock on the door to the office. He twisted the knob and Elizabeth slipped back inside with a happier Whitney. She had a bottle up to the baby's mouth and was no longer wearing the wrap. Cari moved to the side so Elizabeth could see the screen again too. Nitto clicked play again.

The other woman was on the phone. She raised her hand like she was hailing a cab as they stepped toward the curb. A dark sedan pulled up and the window rolled down. The woman slipped her phone into her coat pocket and leaned toward the car.

"Is there sound?" Keith asked.

"No, just image," Nitto replied. "We'll be able to get the license plate unless they have it covered."

The trunk of the car popped open and Rebecca put her bag inside. The woman closed the trunk and motioned for Rebecca to get inside the car.

"Rebecca! Who are these people?" Elizabeth asked the computer screen.

The two women got in the back seat and closed the car door. It slowly pulled away from the curb. Nitto paused it once the plate was in view.

"Okay, let me record the plate and I'll call over to dispatch to have them run it," Officer Nitto told them. "Loch, can I talk to you for a moment?"

Loch nodded and the two officers exited the security office. Cari watched their faces through the window. They were both nodding in agreement, but she couldn't read lips.

"What are they discussing?" Elizabeth asked with concern.

"It could be any number of things, but I think they noticed that no one forced your sister into that car. She went willingly," Cari said gently.

"But what about the image the woman showed Rebecca at the airport? She had a photo of Rebecca's family! She must have threatened her," Elizabeth argued.

"I'm sure Officer Lochaven has told his friend that, which is why they've been so helpful," Cari reminded her.

"I never saw anyone hanging around the kids and me the other day," Keith said. "Wouldn't I have noticed someone taking a photo of us?"

"Do you remember what day this happened? Was it recently?" Cari asked.

Keith thought about it for a moment. "Come to think of it. This was before Rebecca left to come here. She took the picture!"

"Maybe they just stole the photo after you or Rebecca shared it on social media," Cari suggested.

"But why Rebecca? What does she have that someone else could want?" Keith asked and swallowed. "That came out wrong, but you know what I mean. Most people don't know her from Adam. Why her?"

Nitto re-entered the office. Loch motioned to Cari to join him outside. She patted Elizabeth on the arm and went with him.

"What's up?" she asked once the door closed.

"Nitto was bothered that the woman just got in the car. No one threatened her or pushed her. She just got in like she'd known these people for ages," Loch explained. "Before you object, yes. I told him about the photo on the woman's phone. That's what has us stumped...unless..."

"Unless Rebecca had a reason to run away," Cari finished. "I asked their cousin if Rebecca was in a safe relationship. She promised me Rebecca and Keith couldn't be happier. Mrs. Marino told me the same thing."

"Nitto is going to make some other calls. If Rebecca is running because she feels unsafe, then we don't want to ruin that for her," Loch told her.

"Something just doesn't add up with that theory. Once she saw her family on the other woman's phone, she completely changed course. The woman said something to her or threatened her family in some way. That's why Rebecca is being compliant," Cari argued.

"Well, I can't disagree. I was suspicious of Mr. Davenport yesterday. He put in almost no effort to find her, but I feel like I can read people pretty well and I'm more inclined to believe that it isn't an abusive relationship like I initially thought. Something funny is going on. Mrs. Davenport is a stay-at-home parent. Her husband hasn't said anything about a ransom call, so they aren't trying to get money from the family. We need to ask more questions," Loch said.

"She has something they want or need," Cari pointed out.

"Yeah, but what? The Davenports aren't rich; they're just a regular middle-class family," Loch remarked. "I feel like we're blindfolded without a guide here."

"He's still going to trace the license plate, right?" Cari asked.

"Of course, we'll find who owns the car and see what that tells us. For now, you're going to have to let us handle it. We'll call Mr. Davenport and Mrs. Marino if we learn anything new," Loch said.

The door opened and a tearful Elizabeth exited with Keith, who looked as angry as she was sad. Cari put out a hand to Elizabeth. She grabbed it and pulled Cari toward her. Cari held her while she sobbed.

"How are we going to find my sister?" Elizabeth asked. "We can't just give up."

"We're not giving up. We're letting the police do their jobs. They'll track down this lead and keep us updated. You can call me if you think of anything else that might help them find her," Cari offered.

Her phone buzzed with an alert. It was time to go. She needed to hurry if she was going to make it to Mae's Diner in time for lunch.

Chapter 7

The laptop bounced on Genevieve's knees as Alex drove them back to Brenington. She was using her cell phone as a hotspot so she could access Stenoway's accounts again. The answer had to lie within the money trail; she just needed to sniff it out.

"Find anything new over there?" Alex asked. She knew he was smirking without even looking at him.

"Not yet. It's too bad we can't get a forensic accountant to help us with this. I know how to keep my checking account balanced and stick to a budget, but that's about it," she admitted.

"Do you know a forensic accountant?" he asked.

"No, but I know they exist," she said and clucked her tongue at him.

Her cell phone started vibrating, so she checked to see who was calling. She cringed when she saw the name. News travels fast, apparently.

"Agent Dureski?" she asked cautiously. They'd barely left Stenoway and his lawyer forty minutes ago.

"Stenoway is dead," Dureski growled into her ear. "What did you talk to him about?"

"We asked about the accounts. I have reason to believe he wasn't working alone. I was hoping he'd tell us something," Genevieve explained.

Alex looked over at her. "Put it on speaker."

Her fingers trembled as she lowered her phone and hit the speaker button.

"You need to get back out there. Did you record your interview? I need your notes. I need to know everything," Dureski ordered her.

"We're turning around now," she replied and Alex quickly took the exit. "How...what...happened?"

"We don't know yet. The warden just called me. It happened at lunch, so there's a myriad of options. I'm taking the helicopter out, so I'll beat you there," he told her.

"Sir—" she started to respond, but the call ended.

"That sounded bad," Alex said with his eyebrows raised. "I assumed Grusky approved our visit with the FBI, right?"

"He did, but now Stenoway is dead and..." she stared at her cell phone blankly.

"What?! He's *dead*?" Alex exclaimed as he steered the car through the U-turn loop.

"Yeah, I don't know any more than you do. It feels like our visit triggered this," she remarked.

"Maybe he choked or something," Alex hypothesized. "It's not necessarily a homicide."

"Push the speed so we can get there more quickly," she instructed him.

"I *am* pushing the speed, but that's not going to cut off much time. Twenty-five miles is twenty-five miles," he said. "At least the roads are clear, so we aren't fighting traffic."

"I guess. I'm going to look at these accounts some more," she said and double-checked to see if her hotspot was still active. "Okay, so we know these five-hundred-dollar weekly cash deposits are more than likely half of the blackmail money he got each week. Where did the other five go?"

"Maybe he mailed it to his mom," Alex joked. "It was cash. It's hard to follow."

"His parents are dead. He has, uh *had*, no siblings, no wife, nobody. He isn't a charitable person, so the money has to be somewhere," Genevieve argued.

"Agreed. If it still exists," Alex remarked offhandedly.

"Of course it exists. What are you talking about?" she asked.

"Maybe he spent it. Went out to eat somewhere nice every week," Alex suggested.

"By himself? And spent that much money? It doesn't fit. He was very careful about everything. Someone buying a five-hundred-dollar meal-for-one *with cash* would be noticeable," she pointed out.

"Maybe it was and we just haven't found the people who saw it happen," he countered.

"This is not helpful," she eschewed him. "This extra account...the one we didn't have access to at first..."

"What about it?" Alex asked.

"Nothing happened with it until *after* we got access," she told him. "All the payments from Pierce are there on the corresponding dates, but then the rest of the money just sat there for a month or so. Then he started getting these two-thousand-dollar payments from somewhere."

She clicked on one of the payments for the umpteenth time. It wasn't a cash deposit; it was a direct deposit from somewhere else. The transaction didn't include where it came from, only the account numbers. Genevieve tried to remember what her paycheck looked like when it deposited into her account.

"When you get paid, does it say 'City of Brenington' on your account?" she asked Alex.

"I don't know. My wife does all the money stuff. According to her, I'm 'not trustworthy,'" he replied. "Why?"

"I'm looking at the two-k deposit again. Shouldn't there be an account name associated with who is issuing the deposit? Not just a series of numbers?" she asked.

"Beats me. Maybe you were onto something with that forensic accountant idea," he said and raised his eyebrows.

"I was being serious," she said and glared at him.

"Uh, same," he said and grinned. "I'm getting pretty good at talking your language."

She rolled her eyes. "Maybe if I look at the money deposited at Robby's company from Pierce, it will make more sense."

Alex grunted, but didn't say anything.

Genevieve went to her email to get the file she'd received from Dureski. Robby had given him a pdf showing each of the deposits and withdrawals involved with the case.

"Pierce's wife's LLC sent the money to NTS and NTS sent money to the landscaping company, right?" she asked to refresh her memory.

"Yeah, but she owns the landscaping company too, or her LLC does," Alex confirmed.

"Right. Ugh. Are we in a dead zone or what? My email account is just giving me the spinning circle," she complained.

"We are kind of out in the middle of nowhere. It's weird, like they don't want to have a prison right in the middle of a major metropolitan area," he teased her.

"Hilarious. They still live in the twenty-first century and use cell phones," she grumbled.

"We're almost there. You should just save your money searches for later," he suggested.

She closed her laptop. "Fine."

She could see the prison coming into view and wondered what they would find inside. She couldn't remember the last time a prisoner had been killed at the facility, but she hadn't paid that close attention to the news either. Surely, Stenoway hadn't been killed, though. He was keeping someone else out of prison, so why would they want him dead?

Alex parked the car and they got out after storing their weapons again. He double-checked the doors were locked and then they walked inside. Just as they reached the door, Alex stopped.

"What? You aren't going to hold the door for me this time?" she asked in a mocking voice.

He shook his head. "We need to call Grusky. He's expecting us back at the precinct."

"I completely forgot," she said and put a hand to her forehead. "I'll call him."

"No, you go check in with Mr. FBI. I'll call him," Alex told her. "I'll be right behind you."

She left him outside the door and went inside. The guard at the metal detector motioned her forward.

"We heard you were coming back," he remarked. "Where's your partner?"

"He's making a quick phone call," she replied. "He'll be inside in less than a minute."

"Well, put your cell phone and stuff in the bin and come get scanned," he said. "I'm going to radio the warden that you're back."

He flicked a button on his radio and then spoke. "The two detectives are back. Should I send them your way? Okay…see you in a moment."

Genevieve passed through the detector and grabbed her badge and her cell phone. "Where should I wait?"

"The warden is coming to get you. Ah, there's your partner now," he said and pointed at the door.

"Sorry for making you wait," he said and nodded at Genevieve. "We're good."

The warden arrived as Alex was refastening his belt.

"I'm Warden Scola. I'll respond to warden or Scola," he said and extended his hand. "You must be Viacorte and Runimoss."

"Nice to meet you," Genevieve replied as she shook his hand. "Where are we headed?"

"Agent Dureski is still in the cafeteria. Two of my guys are going through the security video to see what happened. Everyone around him said he started choking, then turned purple. He fell off his stool and hit his head. Then he passed out. We had medical personnel over to him quickly, but he was already dead," the warden responded. "To answer your question, we're going to the cafeteria."

"Are there signs of a seizure or neurological response of some sort?" Genevieve asked Scola.

"I can't say. I haven't really looked at the body, yet," Scola answered. "The FBI is going to run tox screens. They'll be very thorough."

"Did Stenoway have any allergies?" she asked.

"Dureski asked me the same thing on the phone. There's nothing in his file. I'd guess he's had this meal before. He's been here long enough for us to make it through the rotation of entrees," Scola noted. "The cafeteria is just through these doors."

Scola held open one of the double doors for them. Genevieve saw Dureski in a crouch next to a body. He turned to look at them when the door clanged shut.

"Good, you're here," he said and then turned back to the others near the body. "Swab around his mouth. It looks like there's some residue."

Dureski stood up. "Warden, is there a room I can use to meet with the detectives?"

"Of course. Did you want to review the security video first?" Scola asked.

"Did anyone get in touch with his lawyer yet?" Dureski asked seemingly ignoring the warden's question.

"The number we have says it's been disconnected and is no longer in service," Scola replied. "I don't have another way to reach him."

"Viacorte, did he tell you he had a new number when you spoke with him earlier?" Dureski asked her.

"No. He didn't mention anything like that. He shut down our questions pretty quickly and that was it. We probably only saw Salzer for five minutes," she informed him.

"Let's go watch the security video," Dureski said.

The warden led the way out of the cafeteria and held the door for the three law enforcement officers. "Take a left. The security footage is near the front entrance."

Alex seemed to know where he was going and strode down the hall. Genevieve was right on the edge of jogging to keep up. When they reached the first hallway again, Alex knocked on the second door and held up his badge. An electronic lock hissed and the door opened.

"It's going to be a bit crowded, so I'll leave the three of you to it," Scola offered. "Have my guy radio me if you need anything."

"Thanks, warden. I need you to go look up his lawyer's website. Call his office if you have to," Dureski said without looking at him. "Is the video ready?"

The man in front of the screens nodded. "I've got it queued up to the start of lunch, which is eleven o'clock for his cell block. He went to lunch after he finished talking to his lawyer."

"How long did he meet with the lawyer after the detectives left?" Dureski asked.

"Just a few minutes. The lawyer signed out at 10:45 a.m. Ready to watch?"

"Let's see what we have to see," Dureski replied.

He hit the space bar and the video whirred to life. "Okay, I see him in line. He seems fine. Maybe a little sweaty."

They leaned in toward the screen. Stenoway was in line and waiting for a tray of food. He pointed at some things and shook his head at others. Once he had his tray, he went directly to a seat at the second table from the back. He opened a butter packet and used a plastic utensil to spread some on a roll. Then he took a bite followed by a drink of water. It looked like he had a bowl of soup on his tray. He picked up his plastic spoon and lowered it into the soup. Before the utensil reached his lips, he dropped it.

"Pause it and go back," Dureski ordered. "Just a few seconds. To the butter and when he spreads it. Slow it down."

The video tech rolled the feed back a few seconds and then decreased the playback speed. "I've got it on 50% now."

The tech hit play and they watched Stenoway open the butter again.

"Can you zoom in on his face?" Dureski asked.

"You got it," he replied.

"He's sweating," Genevieve observed. "Something is making him overheat."

They could see sweat stains appearing on his jumpsuit under his arms. His face was wet with sweat too. It almost looked like the roll was vibrating in his hand.

"Is he shaking already at this point?" Genevieve asked.

The tech paused the video again. "Let me put it back on regular speed for a moment."

They watched Stenoway grab the roll. Genevieve pointed at the screen. "There. Did you see it? His hand trembled. Like he was scared."

"Good catch, Viacorte," Dureski remarked. "Keep it moving. Pause it when he collapses."

The tech nodded and allowed the video to proceed. Soon, Stenoway had the spoon lifted toward his mouth again. His arm stiffened and his eyes rolled back in his head. He fell out of the seat and hit the floor almost simultaneously with the spoon.

Another inmate raised his hand to get a guard's attention right as the tech froze the image on the screen.

"Okay, half speed now," Dureski ordered.

A guard ran over. He put two fingers alongside Stenoway's neck and leaned toward his mouth. Genevieve figured he was listening for breath sounds. He shouted something into the radio clipped to his shirt. Another guard rushed over. A knot had formed on the side of Stenoway's head. His eyes looked lifeless. The second guard started CPR and was thrusting both hands at Stenoway's chest.

"Here's where the medical staff arrives," the tech said.

"Quiet," Dureski barked.

The tech pulled his hands back and closed his mouth. Genevieve watched two more people crouch by Stenoway. One took over compressions. The other tilted his head and tried to shine a light into his mouth. He swept a finger through the mouth and shook his head.

"Is this all the audio we can get?" Dureski asked.

"Yeah, there isn't really a mic to pick up voices," the tech replied.

They watched silently while the medical professionals worked to get Stenoway back. After twenty minutes, they leaned back from the body and shook their heads. The rest of the cafeteria had been evacuated.

"Go back to when he first hits the floor," Dureski ordered again.

"You got it," the tech said quickly and adjusted the video. "Here it is."

"Zoom in on his face some more," Dureski requested.

The tech zoomed in.

"I thought so. There's some foam coming out of his mouth. It must have gotten wiped away at some point during CPR even though they never did mouth to mouth. If he was poisoned, we'll find it in the tox screen. Damnit," he muttered under his breath. "Let's go talk to the warden again."

The tech hit a button to release the lock on the door. Dureski pulled it open and marched down the hallway without checking to see if Alex and Genevieve were following. Alex raised his eyebrows as they hurried after him. Genevieve shrugged. Dureski was pretty tightly wound. He knocked on the warden's office door. Scola let them inside.

"I can't find Salzer on the web. I mean, I found a Logan Salzer, attorney at law, but that guy died like a decade ago. He looks nothing like the man who's been coming here every week," Scola told the trio.

"Unbelievable," Dureski grumbled. "This is a disaster. How did this case go from closed to nowhere so fast?"

Genevieve pulled out her cell phone to look up Logan Salzer on her own. Her hands were clammy and she almost dropped her phone. Her shoulders slumped as she skimmed the results. Scola was right; Logan Salzer, attorney at law, was no longer in practice. Who was the man posing as Stenoway's lawyer?

Scola spoke up. "Let's check the security video of him leaving the prison. Maybe we can track his vehicle."

Alex opened the door and they filed out of Scola's office. The warden entered a code to get back into the room with the surveillance footage. The lock disengaged and he pulled the door open.

"Pull up the feed from the parking lot, please," Scola asked. "We need to see where the attorney went. He left about an hour ago."

They waited while the guard found the correct file. He opened the recording and adjusted the time as requested. Genevieve recognized the parking lot.

"Okay, I've got it on double time. I'll pause it once you see him get in his car," the guard explained and hit play.

They watched the quiet parking lot for several minutes before the man posing as Logan Salzer entered the frame. He got into a silver Lexus near the back of the lot. The guard paused the video just as the license plate came into view.

"Okay, somebody record that plate," Dureski ordered. "Slow it down to regular time. Let's see which way he leaves."

Genevieve wrote down the license plate. It was a New York plate and didn't look like a rental, so it seemed like they'd be able to trace it to a real person. She looked back at the monitor. Salzer had on his right blinker. He turned out of the lot and drove away.

"Wait," Genevieve said quickly. "Roll it back a few seconds. I think I saw something just before his car went out of frame."

Dureski gave her a quizzical look. The guard adjusted the time again and wisely put the playback speed at half. The Lexus' brake lights came on just before the car was out of the picture.

"There. He's slowing down for some reason. There's no intersection at that point, so why wouldn't he just accelerate and be gone?" she asked. "Maybe he threw something out the window?"

"Good catch again, Viacorte. Let's go see if he left something out there," Dureski suggested.

Scola led them out of the room and back down the hallway to the exit. They didn't bother signing out since they planned to come back in after their search. Thankfully, it was a little warmer than when they'd first arrived. The frost on the grass had melted and Genevieve could feel the wetness soaking into her shoes as they traipsed through the short grass alongside the road.

"I see a plastic bag up ahead. It could just be litter from someone else," Alex remarked. He was already pulling ahead of the rest of them.

"Put on gloves before you touch anything," Dureski hollered as he hurried to catch up with Alex. Genevieve was glad she wasn't the only one who needed to work to keep up with her tall partner.

Alex snapped on a pair of gloves from his pocket and crouched down in the ditch. Genevieve could see a white plastic bag at his feet. It had probably blended in a bit better before the frost melted. Alex removed a pencil from his coat pocket and lifted the edge of the bag.

"I thought it was just a grocery bag when I first saw it, but this is more like a ten-gallon trash bag," Alex observed.

"What's inside?" Dureski asked as he put on a pair of gloves.

"I see some kind of hair piece, a thick wrap of some sort..." Alex trailed off. "It's probably better if we take it inside and inspect it where it's dry."

"Agreed. Lead the way, Detective Runimoss," Dureski commanded.

Alex picked up the bag and they quickly returned to the prison entrance. Scola had waited for them at the door. He scanned his badge to get the door open.

"Warden, can we use your office to look through this bag?" Dureski asked.

"Of course. Let me clear off some space on my desk," he said. "We have to pass through the metal detector again. We can get a peek at the bag's contents when it goes through the scanner."

Alex set the bag on the conveyor belt and they took turns going through the metal detector. The guard turned the screen toward them so they could see what was inside the bag. Genevieve leaned in for a better look.

"What are those lumpy things at the bottom?" she asked.

"I'm not sure. It almost looks like wads of chewing gum or something," the guard remarked.

"Warden, grab a new trash bag for us to spread the contents onto it...we need to make sure we don't contaminate the evidence," Dureski instructed. "Let's just use this table rather than go back into your office. Viacorte, record this with my phone for evidence."

Genevieve took the phone from him and pulled up his camera app. She switched it to video and waited to click the start button. Scola set out two new trash bags to cover the tabletop. Once they were straightened, Alex emptied the contents of the bag onto the table.

"Okay, so he was wearing a wig. I estimated him to be in his late forties or early fifties, but that was partly because of the salt and pepper hair. We have no idea what his real hair color is," Dureski remarked.

"His arm hair was dark, so I bet his hair is dark too," Genevieve pointed out.

"This is some sort of tummy girth thing," Alex said and held up a rubber belt. "It made him appear to have a paunch, which also made me assume he was older and out of shape."

"These must be cheek embellishments," Genevieve said. "They make your face look rounder. All of these items altered his appearance."

"I'm going to gather these up and have one of our artists put together an image of what he'd look like without these on," Dureski told them.

"We should get a DNA sample from those cheek implant things," Genevieve suggested. "We can compare it to the DNA we got from Frobish's nails."

"Yes! Take those back to your CSU team. Your department is smaller and I'm guessing there isn't a line to try to bypass to get the sample run," Dureski surmised.

"Green can have his guys do it today," Alex agreed. "We have an evidence kit in our cruiser."

Scola raised his hand and spoke at the same time. "We have evidence kits. I'll grab you one. Be right back."

"I'll call in a BOLO on that car and get my guys on tracking it down. He's got a head start, but we're no longer flying blind."

Chapter 8

H er eyes were starting to cross from staring at the ledgers
for too long. Genevieve rubbed them and blinked a few
times. Alex was still down with CSU getting the cheek
inserts processed, but he'd be upstairs again any minute. Her gut
told her Salzer would come back as a match.

"Viacorte, are you still taking tomorrow off?" Grusky barked
from inside his office.

She got up from her desk and ran a hand over her face. She'd
promised Cari she would help get the church decorated and pick
up any last-minute items on Friday, but with the new
developments in the case, she was thinking of shortening it to just
a half day. She walked over to Grusky's office rather than shout
across the bay.

"I thought I might work in the morning and just take the
afternoon off. We've got a lot going on right now and I don't really
want to abandon the trail while it's hot," she explained.

"Good. Is Runimoss back up here yet?" he asked.

"I think he's still downstairs," she responded.

"Tell him to update me on his plans for tomorrow," Grusky
said. He motioned for her to leave without looking up from his
computer.

She scrolled through the list of transactions again. It seemed
like a front to her. Stenoway had refused to provide a reason for

the two-thousand-dollar deposits. The timing felt too convenient. She expanded one of the deposits and read the information again.

"I'd like to razz you one more time for looking at those accounts, but I guess that's my assignment now too," Alex said, startling her.

"Hey, Grusky wants to know your plans for tomorrow," she said as she continued to read the information on the screen.

"Tomorrow? I'll be here all day. I'm not in the wedding," Alex shrugged.

"Are you going to the wedding on Saturday?" she asked.

"Ugh. Yes. Sophia *loves* weddings. As soon as she heard about it, she went shopping and bought a new dress. She's making me wear my suit," he groaned.

"Good. You don't want to look like a bum," Genevieve laughed.

"Hey, LT!" Alex shouted. "I'll be here all day tomorrow."

"Is it so hard to walk thirty steps and not shout?" she asked and rolled her eyes.

"Yep. Work smarter not harder, remember?" he asked. "Which account are we looking at first?"

"I feel like the answer is in the two-k deposit, but I'm at a loss at how to approach it," she told him.

"You said the deposit is being issued by an unnamed account, right?" Alex asked.

"Yeah, it's just listed as a number," she concurred.

"What does an account number tell us?" he asked. "Can we run a search on it and get a name?"

"This is why I said we need a forensic accountant. They know more about this stuff," Genevieve told him.

"Let's ask Grusky if the department has one," Alex said with a shrug. He took a big breath and she grabbed his arm before he shouted. "What?"

"There's no need to shout. You could at least pick up the phone if you aren't going to walk over there," she reminded him.

"Fine," he grumbled and picked up the phone receiver. "Hey, Lieutenant. Do we have a forensic accountant who could help us with this?"

"Put him on speaker," Genevieve hissed.

Alex pressed a button and Grusky's voice came out of the desk phone.

"...contract one. I'll have to put in a request with the chief. Why?"

"We're kind of in over our heads with these accounts. We have a suspicious deposit, but no name on the account it came from," Genevieve explained.

"Chris should be able to help with that or at least point you in the right direction. If he gets stuck, then come back and we'll see about asking the chief to connect us with someone more knowledgeable."

Alex hung up the receiver. "Down to Chris? Or can we call him to come to us?"

"Let's get him up here since we have all the information pulled up," Genevieve decided. "I'll get him on the phone."

She picked up her desk phone receiver and entered the CSU extension. Chris picked up immediately.

"Hey, Viacorte. What's up?"

"We're trying to nail down an account holder's name, but don't know where to start. Could you come up here and direct us?" Genevieve asked.

"I'll be right there," Chris responded.

The line went dead and she replaced the receiver. "He's on his way up."

"Did you try running an internet search?" Alex asked.

"Like, search the account number?" Genevieve asked skeptically.

Alex merely shrugged.

"I think banks have a little more security than that," she told him.

Chris walked up to their desks. "How can I help?"

"We're trying to figure out who is making this 2-k deposit into this account every month, but it only lists the number, not a name," Genevieve said and pointed at the computer screen.

"Oh, well, you can't get a name from an account number without a warrant, but you might be able to figure out which bank the account is associated with," Chris explained.

"From the account number?" Genevieve asked in confusion.

"No, I mean, sometimes, but every bank is different, so that's not a reliable way to identify the bank," Chris responded. "The transaction should have a routing number associated with it and *that* can tell you which bank you need to talk to about the account."

Genevieve expanded the line item again. "Where is the routing number?"

"Hmmm…this system might not give you access to it," Chris said slowly. "You're going to need to get an expanded warrant for this account that specifically addresses this transaction."

"And then we'll have the account holder's name?" Alex asked.

"No, then you'll get the routing number and that will give you the name of the specific bank," Chris told him. "You'll need another warrant to get the account holder's information from that bank."

Genevieve groaned. "This could take forever."

"I don't know about forever, but it will probably take a few days. Anything else I can help with?" Chris asked.

"No, I think we're good. Thanks for your help," Genevieve responded.

"Maybe we'll get something useful from those cheek inserts and you won't have to worry about these accounts anymore,"

Chris said hopefully and stepped back from the computer screen. "I'll keep you posted if we get results today. I'll be on vacation tomorrow."

"Wedding?" Alex asked.

"Well, sort of. I didn't use all my PTO last year and they won't just pay me overtime for it. They're letting me take Fridays off this month to use four of the days from last year, but the rest are just lost to the man," Chris said and then turned to go back to the CSU.

"Well, this is annoying," Genevieve commented after he was gone.

"Maybe the FBI could get the info faster," Alex suggested.

"I don't know how helpful Dureski is feeling right now. He seemed pretty angry about our visit and Stenoway's death," she reminded him. "We're not in a very good position to ask for favors. I'll get started on the warrant application. At least now we know Stenoway had a partner."

"It feels like there's some shifting in the alliances. If they took out Stenoway, they might take out Pierce and Follard too," Alex proposed.

"I guess that's possible. It's probably too much to hope that the fake lawyer will just run away and try not to get caught," Genevieve mused. "While I draft the warrant, you go talk to Grusky about having someone keep an eye on Follard. Pierce is in prison, so he should be fine."

"I mean, people never get killed in prison..." Alex said sarcastically. "I'll see if Grusky can alert the prison to the risks too."

"I don't think anyone else knows where Shelly is. I already asked the Microtel to delete her address from their system. I wouldn't have found her without their help," Genevieve remarked.

"That's good because we're already stretched thin. Grusky is probably going to balk at the idea of sitting someone on Follard as it is," Alex said.

Genevieve just nodded. She wondered if Robby needed to be warned about suspicious activity. At least he spent the majority of his waking hours at the same place as Follard.

* * * * *

Bob drummed his fingers on his thighs. Cari was not known for being on time, but she usually called if she was running late.

"She's only a couple of minutes late, Bobby," Jack said, using Bob's legal name.

He flinched at the name. "Dad…"

"Sorry, old habit," Jack apologized. "Look, I just saw her pull in like her car was on fire."

Bob grinned. "She sure loves to cut it close."

They watched Cari rush into the diner. Her winter coat was unzipped and flapping in the wind. Her brown curls were tied back in a ponytail or Bob knew they would have been completely askew around her face. Her face registered surprise when she saw them waiting in the alcove for her.

"Sorry I'm late. I swear, I stopped at every traffic light between the metro lot and here," she said. "Wow, it is cold outside."

Bob pulled her into a hug and kissed the top of her head. "Your cheeks are bright red. Any luck with the metro search?"

Cari started to answer when Margie, Bob's mom, put up her hand. "Let's get a table first, then we can talk about the latest sleuthing adventure."

"Good idea, Margie," Cari agreed.

They stepped up to the hostess stand. "Party of four for Hursley."

"You're all here now?" the hostess asked.

Bob wanted to make a sarcastic comment about counting to four, but he just nodded instead.

"Right this way," she replied.

She seated them at a booth near the window. Bob could feel the draft and scooted into the seat closest to the window to block some of the cold from Cari. His dad followed suit on the opposite side.

"What a fun little diner!" Margie exclaimed after glancing at the menu. "Do you have any favorites?"

"I like to get either chicken salad or egg salad during the summer. It's so cold out today, I might go for a little more comfort food and get something with potatoes and gravy," Cari told her.

"Chicken fried steak for me," Bob said and rubbed his stomach. "Mae is a great cook. You'll love whatever you order."

"What's the cuisine tonight?" Jack asked.

"It's *much* fancier," Cari said. "Fancy cuts of meat, specialty sides...dessert...we're going to eat well today."

"Maybe I should just get a sandwich now to save room for later," Margie laughed.

"What can I get everyone to drink?"

Bob looked up and smiled. "Justin, great to see you again. Mom, Dad, this is Mae's grandson, Justin. He's a college student."

"Nice to meet you, Justin. I'll just have water," Margie told him.

"Same for me," Cari replied.

"Unsweet iced tea for me," Jack answered next.

"Make it three waters, please," Bob requested.

"Are you ready to order or do you need a few more minutes?" Justin asked with his pen ready.

"I'll get your chicken fried steak with potatoes and gravy. Lunch-size, please," Jack said.

"Uh, make it two of those, please," Bob added.

"And for the ladies?" Justin asked.

"Chicken and dumplings, please," Cari said after staring at the menu for a few more seconds.

"Umm...I'll get the chicken noodle soup," Margie responded. "It all looks so good. It was hard to decide."

Justin gathered their menus. "I'll have those drinks out in just a moment."

"Okay, Cari. Bob told us you're helping someone from a previous investigation. Is that right?" Margie asked.

Cari nodded. "The girlfriend of a victim from almost two years ago called me the other day. Her cousin is missing."

"Tell us all about it," Margie said and leaned forward.

Bob smirked as Cari began to rattle off the details surrounding Rebecca Davenport. He was glad his parents got along so well with Cari.

* * * * *

"Pick up, pick up, pick up," Cari said frantically into her cell phone.

"Hey, Cari. I thought you had a big family dinner tonight," Genevieve said when she answered.

"I do, but I can't find my shoes. I promised everyone I wouldn't be late for once, but if I don't find my shoes soon, I'm going to be late again," she said urgently.

"Um, right. Why do you think I know where your shoes are?" Genevieve asked.

"You helped me pack some of these boxes last weekend, remember? We did my closet. Everything that I didn't need for the wedding this week," she reminded her friend.

"We labeled all the boxes, so if they got packed by accident, they'll be in one of the boxes with 'closet' written on top of it," Genevieve told her.

"Right. Right. Right. I didn't label any of the boxes I packed on my own, so I just need to find one of the ones you labeled for me," Cari said as she navigated around the stacks of boxes in her apartment.

"Which shoes are you looking for? I really thought we left everything out. You made a list for me, remember?" Genevieve said patiently.

"They're black flats. I wear them to work all the time, but I can't find them anywhere," Cari said and moved another box off of the top of a pile. "Ugh, none of these say 'closet' on them."

"Just curious, but did you go to work today?" Gen asked.

"Well, sort of. I went into the city to help with this missing person case I told you about. Thanks again for getting us connected with Officer Lochaven. He's really been helpful. He and a metro guy hooked us up with surveillance video for the subway—"

Genevieve interrupted. "Right, um, I'm just asking what you did because I thought if you worked today, you might have worn the shoes."

"Oh my gosh, Gen! You're brilliant. You should really put those detective skills to work more often. I did wear the shoes today. They're in my bathroom. Sorry for the panic call," Cari apologized.

Gen laughed. "No problem. By the way, I hate to do this to you, but I need to work tomorrow morning. We've had some new developments with the Stenoway thing…wait. Off the record?"

It was Cari's turn to laugh. "Yes, off the record. I'm not working for the Beagle at all this week."

"Well, Stenoway might have been poisoned today. He's dead," Gen spilled.

"What? What does that mean? Did you tell Robby?" Cari asked. The hair on the back of her neck rose and she felt suddenly chilled.

"We're still investigating. He might have just had an allergic reaction or something. The FBI is involved again. I need to track a few things down in the morning. I'll get over to the church to help decorate as soon as I can," her friend promised.

"No problem. Keep me posted about this. My gut just went on high alert with that piece of news," Cari confessed and looked at her watch. "Eek! I've got to go. Thanks for your help!"

She ended the call and slipped her shoes on. She could still be on time if she made all the traffic lights. They were eating at The Yellow Duckling, which had grown to be one of her and Bob's favorites. Cari had a special connection to one of the owner's longtime friends. She'd helped solve his daughter's murder. He'd arranged for them to get a private room for their family dinner. She jumped in her car and hurried out of the parking lot.

It was a short drive to the restaurant, but she still thought she had time to give Marjorie a call. Something about Rebecca's disappearance didn't sit right with her. She hoped Marjorie could fill in the gaps.

"Hey, Cari. I haven't heard from Elizabeth tonight. Any news?" Marjorie asked.

"I think we're on the right trail. We were able to track her movements from the subway to Jamaica today. The police are working on determining the owners of the car she got into," Cari explained. "What's confusing is that she seemed completely at ease with getting in this stranger's car."

"That is odd. Elizabeth sent me the photo of the woman. I don't recognize her either," Marjorie said. "Do you know who she is?"

"We haven't figured that out yet," Cari replied. "What else can you tell me about Rebecca? Does she have any special skill that someone might want to exploit? Some hidden talent?"

"Wow, I don't know. She's a mom, but I can't imagine she'd get abducted to be a nanny or something," Marjorie said. "I don't know her super well; she's several years older than me."

"Why is there such a huge gap between her and Elizabeth?" Cari asked. "I mean, my sister is eight years older than me, so I know it happens."

"Oh, she was adopted. My aunt and uncle had fertility problems. They decided to adopt a baby after years of not getting pregnant. Then Elizabeth came along as a surprise later," Marjorie said. "My mom talks about Rebecca's adoption all the time. Like it was a big deal for the family."

"I'm sure it was a really momentous occasion," Cari acknowledged. "Was it a closed adoption? Rebecca never tried to connect with her biological parents?"

"Yeah, it was a closed adoption. As far as I know, she's never tried to locate her birth parents. She was adopted as an infant, so this is the only family she's ever known," Marjorie explained.

"That makes sense," Cari agreed. "Thanks for the information. I've got to run...big family dinner tonight."

"Enjoy! And congrats again on your wedding. That's really exciting," Marjorie replied and ended the call.

Cari parked her car and looked at the clock on the dashboard. She made it with a minute to spare! She climbed out of the driver's seat and closed the door. Bob and his parents were walking down the sidewalk toward her along with a man she recognized as Bob's brother Jordan and a young woman with blonde hair. She waved.

"Right on time, Cari," Bob said with a knowing smile.

"I'm guessing my family is probably already inside," Cari told them. "Wait. I thought your grandparents were joining us. Didn't they ride with you?"

The group shared a laugh. "My grandparents decided to book a rideshare to the restaurant. They explained to me how it was the latest and most convenient form of travel," Bob said with an amused grin.

"How very modern of them," Cari laughed.

"They might have beaten us here, for all I know," Margie told her.

"Cari, you remember my brother Jordan. This is his girlfriend, Rachel."

"Nice to meet you, Rachel," Cari said and shook her hand.

"Likewise," Rachel responded with a hint of a southern accent.

Jack pulled open the heavy wooden door and the six of them stepped inside the restaurant.

"Oh, here they are!" Cari heard her mom exclaim.

Her family was gathered around the hostess stand with two older couples she assumed were Bob's grandparents.

"See, Patricia, I told you they'd all be on time," Cari's grandmother said proudly.

Her mom looked a little hurt. "Did you ride here together?"

"No, I pulled up at the same time they did," Cari explained.

"Is everyone here?" the hostess asked.

"Yes, ma'am," Darren, Cari's dad answered.

"Right this way. We reserved our private dining room for you. Mr. Kastener sends his congratulations to the happy couple," she said and smiled at the group.

"Thank you," Cari and Bob said in unison as their group of seventeen followed the hostess past other diners.

"Cari, you should send this Mr. Kastener a thank-you note for getting a private room for our party. That was a really nice gesture on his part. Who is he, anyway?" Patricia asked.

"Patricia, remember? He's the father of the young woman who was killed. Cari helped solve her murder a year or two ago," Darren reminded her.

"Maybe we could not talk about murder at dinner," Patricia retorted.

Darren muttered something under his breath.

Cari grabbed Bob's hand and squeezed it. He leaned over and kissed the top of her head. The hostess held the door open and they filed into the room. The large table was covered in a Navy-blue tablecloth and set with cream-colored napkins.

"Should we sit wherever we want or do you have a seating chart in mind?" one of Bob's grandmas asked. She was petite with dark greyish hair that almost had a purple tint to it.

"Sit wherever you'd like, Grandma Doreen," Bob said.

"The food here looks delicious," Jack commented after pulling out a chair for his mother. "I looked at the menu before we left. It is fancy, just like Cari told us at lunch."

Hilary and Joel raced to grab a seat next to Darren. "I want to sit by Grandpa!" Joel pouted when Hilary beat him to the chair.

"You can sit on the other side, dude. Grandma won't mind, will you?" Darren said and pulled out the chair on his left for Joel.

"Not at all. Now you get to sit by both your grandparents," Patricia said and smiled.

"Ha!" Joel said triumphantly to Hilary. She rolled her eyes.

"Ann Margaret, where are you sitting?" Bob's other grandma asked Grandmother.

Grandmother looked left and right. "It looks like I'm sitting next to you, Treva."

Bob's grandpa unwrapped his silverware and took out his spoon. He had thick white hair and bushy eyebrows. He clinked it against his water glass. Everyone stopped talking and sat in their seats.

"I think we should figure out what we want to eat and drink before we hold up the waitress and the restaurant. Once we've made our orders, we can go around the table and introduce ourselves," he said and nodded.

Everyone picked up their menus. Cari looked at Bob. She already knew what she wanted to drink.

"Is that Grandpa Dave or Grandpa Bill?" she whispered.

"Oh, that's Grandpa Bill. You'll hear a lot from him this weekend," Bob said and chuckled. "He is not afraid to direct traffic."

Two waitresses entered their dining room. Cari wasn't surprised since they had such a large party.

"Good evening, everyone. We'll be working together to take care of you tonight. I'll get the drink orders for the left side of the table and she'll take the right side," she said and pulled a notepad with a pen out of her apron.

"Mom, can I get a soda?" Joel asked before it was his turn.

"Yes, baby," Bea said quickly.

"Is everyone ready with their entrees too?" Bill asked in a loud voice.

"Bill, you can't order everyone around here. You promised Jack you'd sit and listen," Doreen told him.

"Well, if we're ready, we might as well order entrees. No need to prolong the inevitable," Bill grumbled.

"I'll be getting the check once the meal is over," Bob's other grandpa, Dave said with a finger raised. He was mostly bald with bright blue eyes that reminded Cari of Bob's.

The first waitress smiled. "Oh, um, the meal has been spoken for by someone else already, sir. Thank you."

Dave's eyes shot daggers toward Bill. "Was that you? Margie told me I could pay tonight if I wanted to."

"Uh, another patron of our restaurant is covering the tab," the waitress explained. "Feel free to order whatever you'd like."

Dave glared at Bill one more time. Cari wondered if they always got along so well at family functions. She'd have to ask Bob about it later. The two waitresses made their way around the table quickly despite the outbursts.

"We'll be right back with your drinks and then we can take the rest of your order."

The waitresses left the room and Bill rose to his feet. "Now, does everyone know what they're ordering?"

No one said anything for several seconds. "Well, if we're all ready, then let's go around and introduce ourselves. I'm Bill. I'm the paternal grandfather of the groom and this is my wife of fifty-five years, Doreen."

Doreen smiled at everyone. Dave waited for Bill to sit down before standing up. "I'm Dave and I'm Bob's maternal grandpa. We're happy to meet all of the Turnlyles today."

"And I'm Dave's wife, the final grandparent on Bob's side. Grandma Treva. Congratulations, you two," she said and smiled at Cari and Bob.

The waitresses returned with their drinks, which put a pause on the introductions. Cari knew everyone else in the room. She had been surprised to hear the meal was being paid for by someone else. She wondered if Mr. Kastener had arranged that too. She felt like the evening was going well, but couldn't help but let her mind wander back to Rebecca. Had Nitto found the owners of the car yet? It had been forty-eight hours since Rebecca left the airport. She knew they needed to find her soon.

Chapter 9

The phone on Genevieve's desk was ringing when she got to the station on Friday. She hurried over and picked up the receiver.

"Detective Viacorte," she answered.

"I thought you might get here early today," Lieutenant Grusky said. "The judge approved the warrant for the lawyer's cell phone records. The number is disconnected, so we can't try tracing it, but at least we can look through the calls he made over the last six months."

"I'll get started on it right after I pour myself some coffee," Genevieve assured him.

"I've got Judith with CSU looking through the data of which towers his phone pinged off of while it was still on. We can get a feel for where he's been and probably where he was living too," Grusky informed her.

"What about the DNA results? Did those come back yet?" she asked anxiously.

"Green hasn't said anything. I'll give him a call while you get started on the phone records."

"Perfect. I'll keep you posted," Genevieve said.

She draped her messenger bag over her desk chair and picked up her coffee mug. She didn't know what she expected to find on the call records, but hopefully, it would get them a lead into finding Salzer or whatever his name really was.

After fixing her coffee, she sat down at her desk and logged into her computer. Grusky had forwarded her two attachments. One was labeled phone bills and the other was a transcribed copy of all the texts Salzer had sent over the last six months. She opened the pdf file with the bills first and started scanning the numbers for something familiar. The records started with incoming and outgoing calls. The last few pages were incoming and outgoing texts. She scrolled back up to the top. They'd requested phone records for the lawyer's number, but didn't include his name in the warrant since they didn't know it.

"You weren't that clever, were you, Mr. Brensteiner?" she said as she read the name on the bill.

She looked up when she heard the door to the detective's bay open. Alex gave her a nod and joined her at their desks.

"Phone records?" he asked as he looked at her computer screen.

"Yeah. Turns out Logan Salzer was really Gregory Brensteiner," she said and pointed at the screen.

Her cell phone rang and she fished it out of her bag.

"Hello, Agent Dureski. Is it okay if I put the call on speaker? I'm at the station with Alex," she told him.

"Fine. We found the car the lawyer was driving. He parked it at the bus station. We're looking through footage to see which bus he got on, but haven't seen him yet," Dureski updated them.

Genevieve held the phone between her and Alex. "We got his cell records. His real name is Gregory Brensteiner," she told him. "We just started reviewing them."

"Text me that name. Did you get the DNA results back yesterday?" Dureski asked.

"My lieutenant is checking on those right now. Hopefully, we'll find out something soon," she said as she picked up the phone to send the text.

119

"My gut says it must be him. He knew we'd recognize him, but they couldn't call in a real lawyer or they'd risk someone else knowing their secrets," Dureski mused. "Call me as soon as you have the DNA results."

The line went dead before she could say goodbye. She looked at Alex and shrugged.

"How about we split up the phone records? Since you don't like texting at all, you take the old school records and I'll start reading through his texts for a clue," Genevieve suggested.

"Deal," Alex agreed. "You're making a face. What is it?"

"I was just thinking. Now that we know Salzer's real name, or at least, I think we do, maybe we should look to see how he and Stenoway met. He's obviously not really Stenoway's lawyer, so how did their paths first cross?" Genevieve asked.

"Ask Chris to run a search. He can find it faster than we can," Alex said and she gave him a look. "Okay, faster than I can."

"Chris isn't working today, remember? He's probably got a New York driver's license. Let me look him up. Then we can dig up his background," Genevieve told him.

She typed the name into the search bar of the Department of Motor Vehicles. They estimated him to be in his forties and they knew he was white with brown hair and brown eyes. She clicked the search button and waited for results to appear.

"Luckily, Brensteiner is not the most popular name in the state," Alex observed as the search results pulled up three names. "Expand those names. Let's see who we found."

Genevieve clicked on the first Gregory Brensteiner and the database loaded his information onto the screen. "This isn't him. The hair is too light. It also lists him as only five and a half feet tall. The man we met is much taller than five-foot-six." Alex remarked.

"Agreed," Genevieve said and expanded the next Brensteiner on the list. "Now this could be our guy. What do you think?"

She watched Alex stare at the screen. He rubbed his jaw and tilted his head.

"Where are the driver's license photos we found from before? I know they don't really look like the fake lawyer, but I want to compare them to this," he told her.

She minimized the window and opened her file explorer. "They're in the case folder still. Let me find it...okay. Here we go."

She opened both driver's license photos and resized the windows so they could fit on the screen at the same time. Then she enlarged the DMV window to add the third image to the screen. The two driver's license photos were very similar, but the third one with Gregory Brensteiner on it had some differences. The man's face was fuller and his hair was greyer. She flicked her eyes from image to image. She finally saw it.

"It's him. Look above his left eye. There's a small scar," she pointed at the screen. "See it?"

"You're right. I hadn't noticed it in person. Maybe he conceals it with makeup?" Alex suggested.

"Or it just looks like another wrinkle. I wasn't scrutinizing Salzer or whatever his name is, so I didn't see it either," she responded. "Let's give Grusky an update. I need to call Dureski with this too."

"I'll get Grusky on the phone," Alex offered. "You call the feds."

Genevieve found Dureski in her contacts and hit talk. He answered immediately.

"What's the update, Viacorte?" he asked in rapid-fire speech.

"We found Gregory Brensteiner's driver's license photo and compared it to the two fake IDs that were used to rent vehicles in the Frobish and Aguirre murders," she explained. "We confirmed it by looking him up in the Department of Motor Vehicles."

"Great. We got the same name on the car," Dureski remarked. "What about the DNA?"

"No word yet on that," she reported. "Hopefully, soon. Did you figure out which bus he got on yet?"

"No, several buses left at the same time, so we haven't caught up with him yet. We were just getting ready to pull his driver's license too," Dureski told her. "Our ME confirmed Stenoway was poisoned. Strychnine."

Genevieve replayed their interview of Stenoway in her mind. "The bottle of water."

"Good catch, Detective. We retrieved the paper cup and the bottle of water. The cup tested negative for Strychnine, but the concentration in the water was well over the level necessary to kill someone," Dureski informed her.

"He said he bought it at the vending machine," Genevieve pointed out.

"He did buy a bottle of water from the vending machine. He had a second bottle in his jacket pocket. It wasn't picked up by the metal detector, of course. He stopped by the restroom before meeting with you. He must have switched the bottles then," Dureski hypothesized.

Alex snapped his fingers to get her attention. "DNA is a match. Brensteiner is our killer."

"We just got the DNA match; it's Brensteiner," Genevieve told Dureski.

"Have them send me those results for my file," Dureski said and ended the call.

Genevieve looked at Alex. "What did Grusky say?"

"I called Green first," Alex replied. "I wanted to see if the FBI had any other orders for us before I talked to Grusky. I guess they were working together, but Brensteiner was the leader. Maybe he's tired of paying Stenoway two-k a month?"

Genevieve nodded slowly as she considered the possibilities. "We need to dig into their backgrounds more. Figure out when they met. Stenoway didn't have a next of kin, but maybe Brensteiner does. Dureski said the silver Lexus was registered to a Gregory Brensteiner too, so I think we have his name now."

Grusky burst out of his office before Alex could respond. "I heard the DNA was a match. Fantastic! What else?"

"His name is Gregory Brensteiner. We found him from his cell phone records, which match the car registration *and* a New York driver's license," Genevieve told him. She motioned him to look at her computer screen. "This is him. We're developing a theory of how he and Stenoway were working together."

Grusky nodded. "Let's hear it."

Alex motioned for her to speak. "Well, it seems like Brensteiner was the alpha in the relationship. We need to figure out how they met. We don't know much about the man posing as his lawyer, so we're going to try to get in touch with family members and so forth."

Grusky looked at his watch. "Are you still working a half day, Viacorte?"

She checked her watch in response. It was only nine o'clock. "Yes, sir. I need to be there for Cari. The FBI is gathering intel on this guy too, so we'll be covered."

"Keep up the good work. I'll put together a warrant to search his residence. Send me his address and I'll get it submitted," Grusky said and turned back to his office.

"Well, this is a first," Alex remarked.

She frowned in confusion. "What?"

"I'm going to work more hours today than you are," he said smugly.

"I'll be sure to bring you a medal to recognize your achievement," she said with a laugh. "I'm going to look at these phone records and see if anything stands out."

"What do we know about Brensteiner?" Alex asked.

"Basically nothing, why?"

"While you look through those phone records, I'm going to see what else I can find on the guy. Family members, education, and so on," Alex told her.

She gave him a thumbs-up while she scrolled through the man's call history. One number showed up every Thursday evening. She opened their database and typed it into the search bar.

"He's got a sister who is local. He calls her every Thursday night," Genevieve said.

"I was just looking at her. She's a teacher," Alex said. "Maybe she knows where he is."

"Nicole Hamilton. I'll call the school and let them know we're coming by," Genevieve said.

* * * * *

Cari had started her day with a four-mile run. She needed to clear her head. The big family dinner had gone fairly well the night before, but she was less than thirty-six hours from getting married. The thought overwhelmed her. She loved Bob and was excited for their future, but also nervous she'd disappoint him as a wife. She wasn't domestic by any definition of the word. She was messy, non-maternal, and career-driven. Bob was kind, patient, and supportive in every way. He was organized and logical and very, very neat.

"And he loves me," she reminded herself aloud as she stepped from the shower.

She put on a pair of old jeans and a sweater. Her coffeemaker beeped to announce its readiness from the kitchen. She poured herself a cup and then went back to her bedroom to finish getting ready. Her cell phone buzzed with an incoming call, so she hurried to get it from the charger.

"Elizabeth, do you have an update?" Cari asked her.

"Yes, Officer Lochaven just called me. They were able to get the name of the car owner," Elizabeth responded.

"Great! Have they gone to their home to see if your sister is there?" Cari asked with anticipation.

"Not yet. They're putting a warrant together in case they need to demand access to the house," Elizabeth explained.

"Did they give you the name?" Cari asked.

"Yeah, but not the address. I think they were worried Keith and I would go over ourselves," Elizabeth said with a sigh. "The car owner is Noah Ridgeway. Can you find his address?"

Cari hesitated. "Uh, I probably could, but…"

"I get it. I know I shouldn't be marching over there demanding to see my sister," Elizabeth lamented. "It feels like we're so close. I just want to know she's okay."

"I know. This is hard for me and I've never met her," Cari commiserated. "I'll call Officer Loch and see if he has an update, but first, I have a question for you or maybe Keith. Is he with you?"

"I can go knock on his door. We're still at the hotel," Elizabeth told her. "I'm just getting ready to put Whitney down for a nap."

Cari heard a door squeak and then slam closed. She listened while Elizabeth knocked on the door to Keith's room. The background noise increased and Cari wondered if Elizabeth had switched the call to speaker.

"Hey, do you have an update?" Keith asked.

"This is Cari. She wanted to ask us a question," Elizabeth replied. "Can we come in?"

"Sure. What's up?" Keith asked.

"I spoke to Marjorie last night. She mentioned Rebecca was adopted as an infant," Cari told them.

"Yeah, so?" Keith asked. "That was years ago, decades ago even. Why is it relevant?"

"I'm not sure. Has Rebecca ever gotten in touch with her biological parents?" Cari asked.

"No," Keith and Elizabeth said simultaneously.

"And they haven't reached out to her at any point? I'm not sure if that's legal. I'm not very familiar with the adoption process," Cari admitted.

"No contact at all," Keith confirmed.

An idea flashed in Cari's mind. "What about those DNA tests? The ones you send off for analysis to see what your heritage is? Italian? German?" she asked.

"No, I don't think so," Keith said, but Elizabeth didn't respond.

"Elizabeth? Did she mention something?" Cari pressed.

"Well, I…I didn't really think about it. We both did one while I was still pregnant. Just for fun. We wanted to see how similar we were even though we aren't blood relatives technically," Elizabeth said quietly. "Is this my fault?"

"Did you get the results back?" Cari asked, goosebumps rising on her arms.

"I just got mine this week. Maybe Rebecca got hers too? I didn't think to ask her. New mom brain," she said with a nervous laugh.

"I saw an envelope on her dresser this week," Keith admitted. "I didn't look in it, but maybe it was her results," Keith hypothesized. "I can call my mom and ask her to find them."

"My results were emailed to me. Surely, hers were too?"

"Oh, well, we can try to look in her email app on her phone. I need to charge it first," Keith replied. "Will her parents' names be on there?"

"Well, only if they've used a company that submits results to the same database *and* Rebecca marked hers as shareable. You can just get your own results and not look for connections, I think," Cari told him.

"As soon as her phone gets a little charge in it, we'll see if we can find her results in her email," Keith said.

"Great. This could be nothing; I don't want to get your hopes up," Cari said gently. Her watch buzzed. An incoming call from Bea. "I'm getting another call. I need to take it. I'll be in touch." Cari switched calls. "Hey, Bea. What's up?"

"Mom is wanting your opinion on these decorations. She's getting irritated that you aren't here yet. Aspen got here before everyone. She's been delegating jobs. I think it's fine, but…well, you know how Mom is," Bea told her.

Cari checked her watch. It was after 9:30. "I'm so sorry I'm late! I was getting an update about the missing woman. I'll be there in less than ten minutes."

"Okay, love you, Care-bear," Bea said and ended the call.

Cari twisted her curls into a messy bun and tugged on her coat. She picked up her messenger bag and double-checked it for her keys and wallet. She locked her apartment and hurried out to her car. The wind blew her coat open and she struggled to keep it closed as she climbed into her car. She scrolled through her contacts list and found Officer Lochaven's name.

"Ms. Turnlyle?" Loch asked in a hurried voice. "We're waiting for the warrant to come through so we can search the car owners' home. Do you need something or can it wait?"

"I just have a quick update. It might not be relevant," Cari told him.

"Okay…" he said and sounded impatient.

"Mrs. Davenport's cousin told me Rebecca was adopted as an infant. It feels like it might be relevant to her abduction," Cari explained.

"She's thirty-five years old. Has she been looking for her biological parents?" he asked.

"Not that her family knows of. I suppose we could check the call history on her phone," Cari suggested.

"I don't know. I'll keep it in mind, but I don't think it's important," Loch replied.

"Does the person who owns the car resemble the woman from the airport?" Cari asked.

"No, but Nitto and I thought it could have been their daughter or other younger relative in the video. We didn't see the driver in the video, so that could have been anyone," he reminded her.

"True. Well, I hope you get some answers when you talk to them," Cari said encouragingly.

"I'll keep you posted," Loch said and ended the call.

* * * * *

Genevieve checked her watch again as she waited for Alex to park the cruiser. The morning was getting away from her quickly. She regretted getting out of her car before he did. The wind was howling and the temperature felt like it was still below freezing. She hoped Brensteiner's sister would cooperate with them. Nicole Hamilton was a middle school science teacher. The school said she had a planning period in the morning and that would be the best time to speak with her. The two detectives had driven separately so Genevieve could get to the church and help with the decorations like she promised.

They entered the school and pressed the button to be admitted into the main office. Alex held up his detective's shield when the secretary looked their way. They heard a click and pulled the door open.

"You must be the detectives from Brenington," the secretary commented. "Mrs. Hamilton's planning period just started. Let me give her a call."

She picked up the receiver and ran her finger down a sheet of paper. She pressed five numbers on the keypad and waited for Mrs. Hamilton to pick up.

"While we're waiting, if you could get your IDs out, I'll get them scanned," she said with the receiver away from her mouth.

Genevieve and Alex slid their IDs across the counter to the woman. She picked one up and inserted it into a small scanner device on her desk. Another device printed a sticker with Alex's face and name on it. She put Genevieve's in next.

"Mrs. Hamilton?" she paused. "Yes, the detectives are here...I'll let them know."

She handed the two stickers to them. "Please put these on your shirts. Return them to me so I can check you out once you're ready to leave. Mrs. Hamilton's room is 112A. Take a right out of the office, then follow the hallway on your left to almost the very end. Her room is the last one on the right. She said she'd stand in the hallway to watch for you."

"Thanks," Genevieve said. She was still cold from being outside, so she stuck the sticker to her coat instead.

The secretary hit another button to release the lock out of the office. Alex held the door for her and they turned to the right. A sign on the wall indicated the science hallway was to their left. They entered the next hallway which was lined with paper posters made by students. They were decorated with colorful bar graphs from what looked to be a recent science project.

"Man, I do not miss this stuff," Alex remarked. "Group projects and coloring. No sir."

Genevieve laughed. "I'm not sure anyone remembers middle school with fondness, though, it probably wasn't the coloring aspect they hated the most."

A tall woman with straight brown hair stood near the end of the hallway. She raised her hand in a kind of half-wave. Genevieve waved back.

"Take the lead with the questions," Alex said quickly. "I think she'll respond better to you."

She nodded in agreement as they reached the woman.

"Mrs. Hamilton?" Genevieve asked when they reached her classroom. The woman nodded. "I'm Detective Viacorte and this is my partner, Detective Runimoss. Thanks for giving us a few minutes of your free time."

The woman looked uneasy, but welcomed them into her classroom. Alex closed the door behind them.

"I only have stools for seats in here, sorry. It's part classroom and part lab," Mrs. Hamilton explained.

"No problem," Genevieve replied and pulled out a stool to sit on. "We're here to talk about your brother, Gregory Brensteiner."

The woman lifted her hand to tuck a strand of hair behind her ear. Genevieve noticed her hand was trembling slightly. "Greg? Did something happen?"

"No, Mr. Brensteiner is fine as far as we know. He visited an inmate yesterday and then had his cell phone turned off. Have you heard from him in the last twenty-four hours?" Genevieve asked.

Mrs. Hamilton clasped her hands together and put them in her lap. "Uh, I don't...let me think...I don't hear from Greg very often. It might have been a month or more since we last spoke. Why would he visit someone in prison?"

"He was posing as the man's lawyer," Genevieve explained.

Hamilton flinched. "But...Greg doesn't...huh..."

"Greg doesn't what?" Alex asked. His voice startled Hamilton and she flinched again.

"He doesn't practice criminal law. Why would he have a client in prison?" she asked in confusion.

"What kind of law does your brother practice?" Genevieve asked.

"I think he does wills and estates mostly. I don't know if he's ever been in a courtroom. Who did he visit?" Hamilton asked.

"Anderson Stenoway," Genevieve responded. She watched the woman's face for a sign of recognition.

Hamilton chewed on the inside of her cheek before responding. "I didn't realize they were still friends."

Genevieve wasn't sure she believed her. "When did your brother meet Mr. Stenoway?"

"In college. They were roommates their freshmen year, but I never got the sense they were friends. It was just who they were assigned to live with in the dorms," she explained.

Genevieve flipped back a page in her notebook. Brensteiner had attended Brooklyn College and then CUNY-Queens for law school. "Was this at Brooklyn College?"

Hamilton nodded. "Is Greg in trouble for something? You said he was posing as Anderson's lawyer. What does that mean?"

"He told us his name was Logan Salzer, who was a criminal attorney until a decade ago. Unfortunately, Mr. Stenoway died shortly after being with your brother. Now, we can't find Mr. Brensteiner, which doesn't paint him in a favorable light," Genevieve told her. "Are you sure you haven't heard from him?"

Hamilton blinked and then shook her head. "I don't think so."

"Mrs. Hamilton, we have his phone records," Genevieve explained. "We know you talk to him every week."

Her face blanched. "I don't know where he is. If you have the records, then you know we usually talk on Thursdays. He didn't call last night. I've been really worried that something was wrong."

"Yet, you didn't call him to see if everything was okay?" Genevieve asked.

"I did try! Like you said, the number was no longer in service," Hamilton said sadly. "When you showed up, I thought you were going to tell me he'd died."

"Please let us know if you hear from him, Mrs. Hamilton," Genevieve requested. "We don't want anyone else to get hurt."

The woman nodded. Genevieve wasn't sure if she was agreeing to contact them or agreeing that she didn't want anyone else to get hurt.

Alex stood up from his stool. Genevieve couldn't think of anything else to ask her. "I think we've taken up enough of your time for today. Here's my card. It has my cell on it. If you think of anything else or your brother contacts you, please let us know."

Hamilton took the card from Genevieve. "Sure. Nice to meet you. You can leave the door open. My next class starts in twenty minutes."

Alex opened the door to her classroom and waited for Genevieve to exit first. They retraced their steps to the main office and returned their temporary ID stickers to the secretary.

"She's lying," Genevieve said once they were outside. "She's talked to her brother. Or maybe she got a text. But she's definitely heard from him."

"I agree. Dureski can probably get a warrant faster than we can for her phone records. Why don't you call him and see what he says?" Alex suggested. "I'll drive back to the station, unless we hear from Grusky that he got the warrant to search Brensteiner's residence."

Genevieve waited until she was in the car to pull out her phone. The wind chill was below freezing and she had forgotten her gloves in her car. She buckled her seatbelt and then hit the phone icon next to Dureski's name.

"More good news?" Dureski asked.

"We spoke with Brensteiner's sister. She told us Stenoway was Brensteiner's freshman roommate at Brooklyn College," Genevieve told him.

"Interesting. See if you can find a mutual friend from their college years who can tell us more about their relationship," Dureski suggested. "By the way, we still haven't found him. He isn't at his house."

"You've searched his house already?" Genevieve asked.

"I'm here now with two other agents. Your DNA match helped us get a warrant fast. No sign of him here. What else do you know?" he asked impatiently.

"Like I said, we visited his sister. She claimed she hasn't heard from him in a month. We knew that was a lie and called her out on it. I think she has talked to him and thought you could get a warrant to monitor her phone," Genevieve explained.

"Send me the number and I'll make it happen," Dureski said and ended the call.

She called Alex to update him.

"What did he say?" Alex asked.

"He said he'd do it. I'm texting him the number now," she told him. "Dureski also said they're searching Brensteiner's home right now."

"And?" Alex asked.

"Nothing so far. He had a good suggestion. Let's call Brooklyn College and see if they can give us some contact information for some of Brensteiner's classmates. Maybe they have a yearbook or an alumni directory?" she suggested.

"Dial away," Alex said sarcastically.

"I've got to get over to the church to help decorate like I promised," Genevieve said reluctantly. "You're going to have to call the school on your own."

"Look up the number for me?" he begged.

She rolled her eyes. "Once a dinosaur, always a dinosaur."

Chapter 10

Officers Lochaven and Nitto knocked on the door of 231 Park Road. Loch saw the curtains move and a woman's face peek out. He tried to smile and look unalarming. Nitto was a bigger man: close to six-foot-four with broad shoulders and muscles to spare. He dwarfed Loch's six-foot lean frame, but Loch thought he could still outrun his academy classmate.

"Police, ma'am. We just have a few questions," Loch said through the closed door.

He heard a chain slide along the door, but couldn't tell if it was going on or coming off. The door opened a few inches.

"Are you sure you have the right house? What is this in regards to?" the woman asked.

"Is Mr. Ridgeway home?" Nitto asked. His deep voice was intimidating too.

"Why?" she asked.

"Ma'am, could you let us inside so we can have a proper conversation?" Loch asked.

"Let me see some identification," she demanded.

They both got out their shields and held them up so she could see them. After a few seconds the door closed and then re-opened the whole way. Now that he could see her, he wasn't sure they were at the right house. She was at least a decade older than the woman in the video, maybe even two decades. Her hair was short and grey and her skin was wrinkled with age. She wore thick bifocals and house slippers. She stepped back. "You can come in."

"Thanks. Is anyone else home?" Nitto asked.

"No, just me," she said quickly.

"Noah is...?" Loch asked.

"He's at...work. What's the problem?" Mrs. Ridgeway asked with a tremble in her voice.

"Do you own a dark blue Mazda-3?" Nitto asked her.

"That's my husband's work car. Why?" Mrs. Ridgeway asked quietly. Her eyes darted around the room.

"Ma'am, are you sure no one else is here?" Loch repeated his friend's question.

"Yes, just me. Noah keeps saying he'll retire soon, but I think he likes working too much to ever quit."

"Do you mind if we take a look around?" Nitto asked.

"Don't you need a warrant for that?" Mrs. Ridgeway asked and pursed her lips.

Loch reached inside his jacket pocket. "We have a warrant. Feel free to sit down and read it while we walk through the house."

"I told you no one is here!" she exclaimed.

"Please, just let us do our jobs," Nitto said firmly. "It's not a big house. It won't take us long."

She frowned, but moved further out of the way. The house was only one story and he could see the kitchen from the living room. The hallway to the right must lead to the bedrooms.

"Check the kitchen while I look in the bedrooms," Loch told his friend.

Nitto crossed the room to the kitchen while Loch entered the hallway. The hallway split in two directions. To his left was what he guessed was the master bedroom. To his right was a bathroom and another bedroom. He went right first. The guest bedroom was empty. He looked under the bed and in the closet, but the room was spotless.

"Guest room is empty!" he called out to Nitto.

"Kitchen and pantry are empty too," his friend responded. "So is the garage. No car in there either."

Nitto entered the hallway and followed Loch into the guest bathroom. They checked the linen closet and pushed the shower curtain back, but the room was vacant too. They returned to the hallway and made their way to the master bedroom.

"Is this really necessary?" Mrs. Ridgeway hollered from the living room.

"Almost finished, ma'am," Nitto replied.

The master bedroom had a pale-yellow bedspread and pale-yellow curtains. Loch picked up the framed photos one by one and examined the faces. None of the people resembled the woman from the airport. Nitto was already in the master bathroom.

"Clear," he said and shrugged. "Let's go see what she says about the car."

The older woman was sitting on the cream-colored sofa. Her cell phone was up to her ear.

"Okay, I just thought you should know," she said and pulled the phone away from her face. "I called my husband to tell him you were here."

"Tell us about the Mazda," Nitto said and sat down in an empty chair.

"My husband has it at work right now," she said simply.

"Did he drive to the airport on Tuesday night?" Loch asked.

She swallowed. "No, he was here with me. All night."

"Did you drive it to the airport?" Nitto asked.

"I just told you I was here all night. Are you deaf or just a bad listener?" she grumbled at him.

Nitto grimaced. "Ma'am, a missing person was spotted entering your vehicle at the airport on Tuesday evening. Who else has access to your car?"

She shrugged and settled deeper into the sofa. "No one else has keys to our car."

Loch frowned. "That's not what Officer Nitto asked. Who has access to your car?"

They heard a noise coming from the garage. Loch realized it was the garage door and stepped to the window to look outside. The dark sedan he'd seen on the surveillance video was pulling into the driveway.

"Did you ask your husband to come home?" Loch asked.

She shook her head, but didn't say anything. Loch looked at Nitto who shrugged. Thirty seconds later the door to the garage burst open and a pudgy man with tufts of grey hair above his ears stomped inside.

"Let me see this so-called warrant," the man demanded.

"It's right over here, Noah," Mrs. Ridgeway said and waved the warrant at him.

He marched over to the sofa and took it from her. "What are you looking for?"

"The better question is who," Loch explained. "Who are we looking for?"

"They said some woman went missing and they saw her get into your car. I told them we were here the whole time," she said proudly.

"Mr. Ridgeway, did you let someone borrow your vehicle on Tuesday evening?" Nitto asked.

The man licked his lips. "Is that a crime? To share your car?"

"Noah!" his wife hissed, but he shushed her.

"No, it's not a crime, though your insurance probably won't like it," Loch told him. "Are you saying you did allow someone else to use your car?"

137

"Noah, you can't. We promised," his wife begged. "It hasn't been seventy-two hours yet."

"I never said I'd go to jail for them. We have to be honest," Mr. Ridgeway said. He'd calmed significantly in the last minute. "Our neighbors asked if they could use it."

"Why did they need to use your car?" Loch asked.

The older couple exchanged a glance before Mr. Ridgeway spoke again. "They needed to pick someone up."

"Who?" Nitto asked and leaned forward.

"Someone who could save their daughter," Mrs. Ridgeway said and burst into tears.

Loch looked at Nitto; it was clear he hadn't been expecting that answer either.

* * * * *

It took the five women almost three hours to go through all the tables and chairs the custodian had left in the reception hall and arrange them in an orderly fashion. It wasn't that they needed every table; Patricia wanted them to look the same and be level. They selected the ten best tables and then put the others away. Each table needed a white tablecloth, which Cari's mom had to re-center to perfection every time. They'd ordered pizza for lunch before noon, which was a welcome break for everyone. Cari was relieved when her mom suggested the two of them take care of the decorations for the sanctuary once Genevieve arrived. She was tired of moving furniture.

The sanctuary looked peaceful with the afternoon sunlight streaming in through the stained-glass windows. Cari hadn't been at the church except for morning services and loved the way the light danced off the bows she and her mom had placed on each of the pews.

"What do you think?" her mom called out from near the altar.

Cari beamed. "It's beautiful, Mom. I love it."

"Let's see…we got all the bows on the pews, so we can check that off the list," her mom read from a sheet of paper. "I printed out the to-do list Aspen made for us."

Cari nodded and walked up to the front of the sanctuary. "What's next?"

"I put the two white candles on the altar and the wedding candle in the center as requested," her mom replied. "We need to set the wedding announcements on the two stands in the back. Aspen said it was rare for anyone to just show up at the church, but this way, no one will just walk in during the middle of the ceremony. The posters are in the first pew."

Cari returned to the first pew and picked up the two posters. "They go on the easels, right? Should I put one in each of the hallways leading into the sanctuary?"

"That makes sense," her mom agreed. "I'll be right there. I'm just centering these candles."

The easels were set up in the back of the sanctuary. Cari set the posters down and then moved the easels to the two hallways. The posters listed the date and read "Turnlyle and Hursley wedding today" in scripted font. Simple and to the point. She set one on each easel and waited for her mom to inspect her work.

"Looks good, Cari. Let's go see how your sister and Genevieve are faring in the reception hall," her mom said when she reached her. "Bea will need to leave soon to get her kids from the bus stop. Your dad is spending the day with his mother until the nail party later."

"Oh, right. School gets out in about an hour for Joel," Cari remembered as they walked down the hallway.

The doors to the reception hall were open. Cari's jaw dropped when she saw the decorations. Each table had a light green candle in the middle with a white satin bow tied around it. Bea was straightening one of the tablecloths while Aspen was adjusting the ivy on the trellis behind the cake table. The screen above the stage was playing a slideshow of photos of her and Bob over the last two years as well as some of them from their childhoods. She stood and watched the photos.

"I didn't know you were coming in here right now! This was supposed to be a surprise," Bea said.

"I love it and I was surprised," Cari said and squeezed her hand. "Bob is going to love this too! I can't believe you got all these photos of both of us. Sneaky!"

"Your in-laws-to-be are so much fun. I really enjoyed setting up tables with Margie this morning. She told me so many family stories," Bea said with a smile.

"She is very nice," Cari agreed. "Did I miss Genevieve leaving?"

"She got a phone call and took off a few minutes ago. She is efficient, though," Bea assured her. "She tied all the bows on these candles in record time."

"She's a great friend," Cari smiled. "Wow. I can't believe this is really happening. Did you ever think I'd be getting married?"

"I was starting to wonder," her mom said from across the room.

"No doubt in my mind," Bea said and hugged her. "Aspen, what else is on our to-do list?"

"Let me check. We might be finished for now," the wedding planner said and picked up her tablet from the cake table. "Tables are finished; trellis is finished...the QR codes are out...you're happy with the sanctuary?"

"It looks incredible," Cari said. "The bows are perfect. Thanks for making them, Bea and Mom."

"I think we finished early today...until the actual rehearsal. We're starting at six o'clock sharp. Don't be late!" she glanced at Cari.

"I promise not to be late for my own rehearsal," Cari said with her hand over her heart.

"Good. Tomorrow, I'll get here at one o'clock to put the flowers in the sanctuary. The bridesmaids' corsages will be in the reception refrigerator and the groomsmen's flowers will be in the main kitchen refrigerator. The mothers' and grandmothers' corsages will be with the bridesmaids' flowers too," Aspen told them. "The only other thing is the programs, which you have, right?"

"Oh, yeah. They're in my car. I can go grab them," Bea said.

"I'd just leave them in there for now. Someone on staff might move them where we can't find them if we bring them in now," Aspen explained.

"Okay, that makes sense," Bea replied. "Thanks for all your help. This has gone so smoothly."

"She's fantastic, right?" Cari said. "I'll definitely be recommending you any chance I get."

Aspen blushed. "Thank you both. I appreciate it. Let's turn the lights off and I'll check out with the office."

"Is someone's phone vibrating?" Patricia asked.

Cari looked at her watch and saw she was getting an incoming call from Elizabeth. "Oh, it's me."

She fished her phone out of her messenger bag and answered it. "Elizabeth? Is everything okay?" she asked and stepped out of the reception hall.

"I'm getting so anxious just sitting around waiting. I haven't heard anything from either officer since this morning," Elizabeth said, her voice catching on the last word.

"I'm sure they're still looking for Rebecca. You said they had to get a warrant. That can take some time," Cari tried to encourage her.

"I know your wedding is tomorrow, but do you have time to help us figure out the DNA test information? We got Rebecca's phone charged and got into her email app," Elizabeth explained. "We were able to login to her account with the DNA thing, but

141

none of the names are familiar and none of them have photos, so we're sort of at a loss. We tried looking on social media, but we couldn't find anyone."

"We finished decorating early, so why not?" Cari asked. "Should I meet you at your hotel?"

"Sure. I'll text you the address. Whitney is about to go down for a nap, so as long as we're quiet, we won't have to multitask with entertaining the baby and scouring the internet for an abductor," Elizabeth said.

"I got your text. It says it will take me thirty minutes to get there," Cari told her. "Luckily, you picked a hotel between me and the airport, or it would be over an hour before I got there."

"See you soon. Thanks, Cari," Elizabeth said and ended the call.

Cari started to walk out to her car and then remembered everyone else had been with her in the reception hall. She shouldn't just leave without saying something. She turned back to the hall, but it was dark. *Everyone must be waiting for me outside.* She did a one-eighty and walked out to the parking lot. At first, she didn't see anyone, then she realized they were in their cars. No one wanted to stand outside in the wind today. After waving goodbye to Aspen, she walked over to Bea's car. Her mom was in the front seat.

"Hey, sorry to just walk out. That was the young woman I've been helping this week," Cari told them.

"I'm going to drop Mom at the hotel and then go meet the kids off their buses. We'll see you at the nail salon at 3:30," Bea said.

"Okay, give Grandmother a hug from me, okay, Mom?" Cari said and waved goodbye.

She hoped Grandmother was okay. She'd been so busy all day she hadn't had a chance to call and check in with her. Her coughing fits seemed to be a little less frequent at dinner the night before, so maybe Cari was just obsessing over nothing. She walked over to her car and unlocked it. She'd need to leave the hotel by 2:45 to get to the nail appointment on time.

She pulled out of the church parking lot and called Bob from her Bluetooth. She didn't know what grooms had to do the day before the wedding, but hopefully, he had a minute to chat.

"Hey there, almost-Mrs.-Hursley," Bob said when he answered the phone.

"Hey there, yourself," she responded. "What are you up to?"

"My mom and I just beat my brother and dad at bridge, so I'm sitting here gloating a little bit," Bob replied.

Cari heard voices in the background. "Did I hear Lydia's voice?"

"Yeah, we're all in the lobby of my parents' hotel...well, the whole family is staying here," Bob said. "You're driving. Where are you off to?"

"I'm still trying to help find Marjorie's cousin. They found the car owners, but that was the last update. It turns out one of Marjorie's cousins is adopted!" Cari exclaimed.

"The older one who's missing?" Bob asked her.

"Yeah, she was adopted as an infant. The younger one, Elizabeth, asked if I'd help them go through the DNA results her sister got recently. It's electronic, but they don't know how to find any of the people on the list. One of those ancestry things, you know?" Cari asked him.

"Do you think her biological family abducted her?" Bob asked in a confused voice.

"I don't know, but her adoption seems relevant to her abduction. The police are hopefully talking to the owners of the car she got into, but maybe we can help by coming at it from a different direction," Cari suggested.

"It could work. Or it could be unrelated," Bob said.

"I'm choosing to be optimistic," Cari told him.

"Well, I wish you luck," Bob responded. "I need to hang out with my family some more before my mom leaves for the big nail party."

"I'm so glad she wants to come. Have fun with your family. Tell everyone I said hi. Love you, Bob," Cari said.

"Love you forever, Cari. One more day and we'll be married! I almost can't believe it. See you soon," he said and ended the call.

* * * * *

"Alex, I think the department might need to sign you up for technology for dummies or dinosaurs class," Genevieve told him. "What's the problem again? I couldn't hear much over the wind, but I'm in my vehicle now. My take away was that you need help using a website."

"Very funny. I was going to apologize for bothering you on your afternoon off, but now I'm not," he grumbled. "I called the registrar's office at Brooklyn College. I thought maybe they could direct me to someone who knew both Brensteiner and Stenoway."

"Oh, like their residence advisor or something?" Genevieve asked.

"Yeah. Unfortunately, they wouldn't give me that information without a warrant. However, she was willing to look up some information on the alumni and told me they were in the same fraternity," Alex informed her.

"So, they're fraternity brothers. That makes me think the sister *is* lying to us," Genevieve commented.

"Agreed. She gave me their website, but I can't find a phone number on it anywhere. Do you have a few minutes to look at this with me over the phone? I know you're trying to be a dutiful bridesmaid, but this is pretty important too," Alex reminded her.

"You're lucky I like you. You could have just called Chris, you know..." she teased him. "If it makes you feel better, we're finished decorating. I have about an hour until I need to be back at the church for the rehearsal. Should I join you at the precinct? I'm only a few minutes away."

She smiled to herself as she parked her car in the precinct lot. She was just a little bit closer than she'd told him.

"Chris is on vacation, remember? And Bob isn't here. I'd rather not have everyone think I'm completely incompetent with computers, plus I know you hate taking time off. You even work on the weekends for free," Alex told her. "I'll see you when you get here."

The call ended and she got out of her Expedition. She grabbed her badge and clipped it back onto her belt. She was apparently really terrible at taking time off. This was the second time this week she'd chosen to come in after requesting time off. She opened the door to the detectives' bay and Alex's head snapped up.

"Were you just mocking me from the parking lot?" he asked her.

"Do you want my help or not?" she said with a smirk.

He rolled his eyes, but rolled back from his desk to give her space to look at the screen.

"Here's their main website, but the only form of contact they have is this form," he said and pointed at the screen. "I'd rather talk to someone than wait for them to realize we aren't newbies wanting to rush or something."

Genevieve grabbed the mouse and clicked on the three lines for the menu options. "Let's see what they have under history."

"I don't really need a history lesson of their fraternity," Alex told her grumpily.

"It might have past officers. We can find their contact information," she explained. "Look, we know they were in college in the early 2000s. Here's a list of the past fraternity presidents for the Brooklyn College chapter. We just need to scroll down to the turn of the century, back when the dinosaurs roamed the earth—"

"Not funny. I was already in the academy at that point," he said and crossed his arms.

"Here we go. Elliott Peterson was the president the year they graduated. Let's look him up," Genevieve said and walked over to her desk to get her chair.

"I can search the database," Alex said with his chin raised. He rolled his chair back up to the computer. "Ell-i-ott Pe-ter-son...he's probably in his forties and hopefully, still a resident of New York...and enter."

Genevieve pushed his chair a bit so she could see the screen better. "It's a pretty common name, but with the age restriction, we might get lucky."

The database gave them twelve names. Genevieve reached to grab the mouse, but Alex swatted her hand away.

"Hey, I got this," Alex said proudly.

"Go back to the frat page. See if it has any sort of bio for past presidents," she suggested.

Alex clicked over to the fraternity website. "Where do I find that?"

"Hover the mouse over his name," Genevieve told him.

"Ah, I can click on his name," he said and did so. "Peterson lives in Beacon...so if we look on our list...bingo! Numero five."

"Cool. Now you have a phone number," Genevieve said and patted him on the back.

"Do you want to call...?" he asked and raised his eyebrows.

She rolled her eyes. "Really?"

"I know you like working for free. I'm just trying to be accommodating," Alex said with a shrug. "I'll call him."

He picked up the receiver from his desk phone and punched in the phone number. "I'll put it on speaker so you can hear."

The line rang three times and then clicked. Genevieve expected to hear a voicemail message.

"Hello? Hello? Did I catch you?" a man's voice asked.

"You got us," Alex said. "Is this a landline?"

"Yeah, I just hate the idea of giving it up...uh, who is this?" the man asked.

"Detectives Runimoss and Viacorte with Brenington PD. We're looking for Elliott Peterson," Alex told him.

"Detectives?" the man asked in a higher voice. "Is everything okay?"

"Yes. Please, is this Mr. Peterson?" Alex asked impatiently.

"Uh, yes. I'm Elliott Peterson," he replied.

"We found your name on your fraternity's website as a past president of the Brooklyn College charter. Is that you?" Alex asked.

"Uh, yeah, I was president in the early 2000s," Peterson said.

"Perfect. Did you know Anderson Stenoway and Gregory Brensteiner?" Genevieve asked him.

"I did. Why do you ask?" Peterson questioned them.

"The two men have stayed in touch and we're trying to get a better sense of their relationship as part of an investigation," Alex responded ambiguously.

"Well, Greg was only sort of friends with Anderson. I mean, they had been roommates, if I remember correctly, but I got the impression Greg allowed him to tag along," Peterson explained. "Greg was better friends with another member...I can't think of his name off the top of my head."

Genevieve's shoulders slumped. "Any chance you have a directory or old photos that might jog your memory?"

"Oh! Good thought. We have a photo book of sorts from that year. The only problem is the photos aren't labeled or anything. They're just printed photos in a book the guys gave me for graduation. I can look through that and get back to you at some point," Peterson offered. "There's a chance seeing his face will jog my memory."

"Sooner would be a lot better than later, Mr. Peterson," Genevieve told him.

"Hey, is this about Anderson getting arrested last summer? For *murdering* people?" Peterson asked. "I'd kind of forgotten about that, but now that we're talking about him…I guess it floated back to the surface."

Genevieve and Alex looked at each other. "Sir, do you think you can look through your photos for us this afternoon?"

"Uh, sure. It's on my bookshelf. I'll go start flipping through it now," Peterson offered.

Genevieve started to thank him and then had another thought. "Do you have a cell phone, Mr. Peterson?"

"Of course. Doesn't everyone?" he asked with a laugh.

"When you find the photos of Stenoway and Brensteiner, can you text us a photo of them?" she asked and then looked at Alex. "Or send it as an email?"

"I can a text a photo. No problem," he responded.

"Great. Here's my number," she said and recited her cell to him. "Send me a text so I know we're connected."

"Okay. Just a sec while I type a message out," he said. "Done."

Genevieve's phone buzzed. "Got it. Thanks, Mr. Peterson. We appreciate your assistance."

"I'll be in touch before the end of the day," he replied.

She ended the call. "I'm not sure how available I'll be the rest of the afternoon. We're getting our nails done in a bit, so I won't be able to check my phone while that's happening. I'll let you know if I get anything from Peterson as soon as I can."

"I'll keep looking through Brensteiner's text and call history. Maybe something will turn up," Alex told her. "Enjoy your mani-pedi."

"I will sign you up for one if you tease me about it again," she told him as she got up from the desks. "And it's just a manicure."

Chapter 11

The older couple was seated on their sofa. Loch thought Mrs. Ridgeway might cry again. Her face was still red and splotchy from her last outburst. Her husband had a protective arm around her shoulder. Loch sat down in an overstuffed chair next to where Nitto was standing. They'd been talking to the couple for over an hour and it felt like they were being intentionally obtuse. Loch had taken a bathroom break to clear his head. He nodded at Nitto.

"Mr. and Mrs. Ridgeway, let's start from the beginning again," Nitto said calmly. "Your neighbors needed to borrow your car…"

Mr. Ridgeway nodded. "Yes, their young daughter is sick. She needs a bone marrow transplant."

Loch looked from one to the other. "And how does your car help them with that?"

The couple exchanged a glance before Ridgeway continued. "They've been begging people to get screened to see if they were a match for Sarah, but they hadn't found anyone. Everyone knows a sibling would be the best match, but Sarah was an only child."

Mrs. Ridgeway sniffled. "We *thought* Sarah was an only child. When they started asking people to join the donor registry, I suggested they do one of those DNA test thingies. You know, where you swab your mouth and then send it off to see what your ancestry is? I thought maybe they'd find a distant relative or something. I guess they sort of did..."

When she didn't continue, Nitto leaned forward. "What do you mean?"

"Well, when they first got the results back, there wasn't anyone whose name they didn't recognize," she told him. "Then, about a week or so ago, they got an email. A new relative had been entered into the database or whatever. A full sibling of Sarah's.

"When they told us they'd found a sibling, we were obviously confused. As far as we knew, this was a second marriage for both of them. We knew they'd been friends in high school, but never realized it had been more than that. They told us they'd gone their separate ways after graduation. One to college and medical school, the other to nursing school. They married other people, but never had children. Then, by some chance, they ended up at the same hospital here in New York. They fell in love, again, and got married. Then Sarah was born five years ago," Mrs. Ridgeway said and smiled.

Loch started to speak, but Mr. Ridgeway put up his hand. "You have to understand, officers. Sarah is like a granddaughter to us. We even babysit sometimes. She was diagnosed with leukemia about a year ago and it's been so hard on all of them. That's why we agreed to loan them our car. Matthew and Jennifer had another child...over thirty years ago. That's who turned up on the DNA registry. A full sibling to Sarah: Rebecca Davenport. She's a match to Sarah. She can save her life."

Nitto looked at Loch. "They just called this woman up and asked her to come to New York and donate her bone marrow?"

The couple exchanged another glance. "Uh, not exactly."

Loch narrowed his gaze. "I didn't think so. They coerced her into leaving the airport. Why wouldn't they ask first?"

"Think about it. They have lived with this guilt of *abandoning* their first child for more than half their lives. They gave their baby up for adoption all those years ago. It was a closed adoption, so they only knew she was female at birth. They've never met the young woman and suddenly, they're going to show up in her life and say, 'Oh, hi, we're your biological parents. Also, can we have your bone marrow?'" Ridgeway asked.

"Instead, they threaten her with an image of her family while she's traveling alone? And then what? Mrs. Davenport is a missing person. She should have been flagged at a hospital," Nitto retorted.

"Yes, she probably would have been, if she'd been at a regular hospital," Mrs. Ridgeway agreed. "Remember how I told you that Sarah's parents are medical workers? Matthew is a surgeon and Jennifer is a surgical nurse. They bought a brand-new RV and sterilized it. Then, they borrowed some equipment from their hospital and set it up in the RV. A bone marrow extraction isn't that complicated. It's painful, but it's usually an outpatient procedure. They performed the two procedures in the RV on Wednesday morning."

Loch's jaw dropped. "That has to be malpractice. They should both lose their licenses."

"It was worth the risk to them if it could save Sarah," Mr. Ridgeway argued.

"Where are they now?" Nitto asked as he stood up. "You said something about seventy-two hours? Why?"

"They asked us to keep all of this quiet for three days to give them time to get away. They're going somewhere west of here. They aren't coming back," Mrs. Ridgeway said.

"What about their older daughter? The missing woman? Where is she?" Loch asked.

"Well, she had a bit of a complication following the procedure. It might not have been related, but they asked me to drive her to the hospital this morning, right before lunch. I just came from there. She had a slight fever and they were worried she might have an infection," Mr. Ridgeway explained. "But, she's actually fine. She has to stay overnight for observation."

"Why didn't the hospital call the police when she showed up there this morning?" Nitto asked. "We should have been notified!"

"I'm sure someone will call soon. Mrs. Davenport didn't want to press charges; she went with them willingly on Tuesday," Mr. Ridgeway told them. "I'm guessing you've watched surveillance video if you made it all the way to us."

"I have so many questions and I'm sure her family does too," Loch remarked and unclipped his radio. "We're going to have to bring you both in."

"What? Why? We didn't do anything wrong. We helped save a little girl's life!" Mrs. Ridgeway exclaimed. "We told you Rebecca isn't going to press charges. She even promised to wait until the afternoon to call her family and let them know she was okay. She wanted to give them more time to get away."

"You assisted in the abduction of another person. This all could have been handled in a much more civilized manner," Nitto told her. "Loch, I'll let my precinct know we're bringing these two in. You get someone to start tracking down that RV."

Nitto pulled out his cell phone and stepped outside to make the phone call.

"How long ago did the Hendricksons leave? How much of a head start do they have?" Loch asked the couple.

Mr. Ridgeway glanced at his wife before he responded. "We're cooperating, so if I tell you, will you reconsider charging us in this whole thing?"

"*How long, Mr. Ridgeway?!*" Loch raised his voice.

The man's shoulders slumped as he looked at his watch. "It's been about two hours give or take. I left with Mrs. Davenport before they took off in the RV," he said quietly.

"Two hours?!" Loch exclaimed. "That's forever. You have been purposefully stalling this interview to give them more time."

"No. Please, we're trying to do the right thing." Mrs. Ridgeway's lip quivered. "It hasn't been that long, actually. They weren't planning on needing to leave so soon, so they weren't quite ready to go. They knew once Mrs. Davenport got to the hospital, it wouldn't be long before the story came out. They tried to hurry, but they barely left before you knocked on our door earlier."

"What does the RV look like? Does it have a name or color scheme? Who is it registered under?" Nitto asked.

"It's a big one, um, it doesn't have a name on it. They just bought it. I'm sure it's registered to them," Mr. Ridgeway said plainly.

Loch nodded. "We know they're headed west. We can start driving that way while dispatch finds the registration information. It probably doesn't have a license plate yet. Just a temporary one," he paused and looked at the older couple. "What else can you tell us? You said you wanted to cooperate. Now is the time."

Tears ran down Mrs. Ridgeway's face again. She shook her head and grabbed her husband's hand. He finally nodded, as though in surrender. "They're traveling on I-78. They turned their phones off, so you won't be able to track them. Please, be careful with Sarah. Her health is very fragile right now."

The door opened and Nitto stepped back inside.

"The other officers will be here in about five minutes to bring these two in. Then we can be on our way," Nitto told Loch.

"I'll call Mrs. Marino and let her know where her sister is once we get the Ridgeways squared away," Loch replied. "What a bizarre turn of events."

* * * * *

The hotel parking lot was pretty full when Cari pulled into it. She found a space in the back near the dumpster. After she locked

154

her car, she called Elizabeth to find out which room she was staying in.

"Hey, I just parked. Which room?" Cari asked her as she entered the hotel.

"1247," Elizabeth said. "Thanks again for coming out here."

"I hope I can help," Cari said. "I'm getting on the elevator. See you in a moment."

She rode the elevator to the twelfth floor. The signs on the wall directed her to go right in the hallway for rooms 1230-1250. She was almost to room 1247 when the door opened and Elizabeth poked her head out.

"We're in here. Whitney woke up, so I'm trying to bounce her and keep her entertained while we look at the list," Elizabeth said. Baby Whitney had tear-rimmed eyes and looked at Cari with unease.

"Hi, sweetheart. It's just me. Remember me?" Cari asked and smiled.

Whitney's lip pouted out and more tears fell onto her cheeks.

"Guess not," Cari said and cringed. "Where's the list?"

"Right here," Keith said from his spot on the sofa. "I have it pulled up on my laptop."

Cari sat down next to him and looked at the computer screen. "Okay, so it lists a mother and father…who are married."

She turned to Elizabeth who was trying to get Whitney to eat some baby food. "What do you know about your sister's adoption?"

Elizabeth sucked in a breath. "Hmm…my mom said they were told the parents were like fifteen and sixteen years old. They weren't ready to be a mom and dad."

"It seems like they must have stayed together or something. They have the same last name," Cari remarked. "Jennifer and Matthew Hendrickson. Jennifer is fifty and Matthew is fifty-one. That fits with what you told me. Rebecca is thirty-five, right?"

"Yeah, that's correct. We entered their names onto social media sites, but didn't find anyone who looked like the woman at the airport," Keith said. "Are there other places you could look?"

"Uh, I have access to LexisNexis for work, but I'm off this week…normally, I'm all about stretching the limits for an investigation, but this isn't for the newspaper and it's having budget issues…" Cari trailed off. Keith and Elizabeth looked crestfallen. "I might be able to call and—"

"Oh, my phone is ringing!" Elizabeth exclaimed and ran over to the kitchenette counter. "Hello? Hello? Is anyone…Rebecca?! Is it really you?"

Cari felt goosebumps on her arms. She watched tears spill down Elizabeth's cheeks.

"Where are you? A hospital? Are you kidding me?! We're on our way. Keith is here with me and Whitney. Oh my gosh, Rebecca. I've been so worried. You're sure you're okay? We're coming right now…uh, which hospital?" Elizabeth spoke so fast Cari almost didn't register what she was saying.

Keith rushed over from the sofa. "Can I say hi?"

"Here it's on speaker," Elizabeth said and set the phone on the counter. Whitney smiled up at her mama.

"Keith? I tried your phone first, but it went to voicemail," Rebecca told him.

"Shoot. I forgot to pack a charger and we were talking to Mom earlier…I guess it's dead," Keith apologized. "Why are you in the hospital?"

"It's a really long story, but I saved a little girl's life. I'll tell you all about it when you get here," Rebecca said. "I'm kind of tired, so I'm going to rest until you arrive."

The call ended. Elizabeth started rapidly throwing baby toys into a diaper bag. She pulled a bottle out of the refrigerator. "Whitney, do you want to try the bottle again while we ride in the car? Uncle Keith can drive us to see Auntie Rebecca."

"I'll let you go reunite with Rebecca," Cari told them. "I'm so glad she's okay. Let me know if you need anything else."

Elizabeth picked up the diaper bag. She walked over to the hotel room door with Cari. "You've been such a huge help. I can't thank you enough."

"I'm not sure I did anything. Rebecca seems to have turned up on her own," Cari said and smiled.

"But all the help from the police. Oh, the police! I should call them," Elizabeth said with her hands full. "Where did I put my phone?"

"It's on the counter here, but it just flashed a 1% warning...and it's dead," Keith told her. I'll grab your charger if you tell me where it is."

"It's in the bathroom. Maybe we can charge it in the rental if it has the right type of connection," Elizabeth suggested.

"So, we have two dead phones," Keith said with a frown. "Hopefully, we can charge one of them in the car."

"I can give Officer Lochaven a call and let him know Rebecca contacted you," Cari offered. "He might want to talk to you and her. Which hospital?"

"Memorial Hospital in Greenway," Elizabeth said. "Is there only one hospital in Greenway?"

Cari nodded. "That sounds right. I'll let him know. It was nice to meet you both."

"Congrats on your wedding!" Elizabeth said joyfully as Cari exited the hotel room.

Cari turned back and smiled. "Thanks."

She pulled out her cell phone and found Officer Lochaven's number while she waited for the elevator to arrive. She was relieved to see it was just after 2:40, so she was mostly still on schedule and would hopefully be on time for the nail appointments. She rode the elevator to the ground floor and then hit the call button for Loch.

"Ms. Turnlyle, we were just trying to call Mrs. Marino. Are you with her?" Loch asked.

"I just left her hotel room. Her cell phone died, so she asked me to call you," Cari explained as she walked out to her car. "Her sister just called her. She's in the hospital, but it sounded like she was okay. Keith and Elizabeth are headed over there now with the baby."

"We just learned of Mrs. Davenport's location as well. There's a BOLO out for the parents and their RV. We found the owners of the sedan and got the story out of them," Loch told her. "It's pretty convoluted."

Cari listened as the officer recounted Rebecca's abduction from the airport three days ago. "They were so afraid she'd say no that they threatened to harm her family?"

"Well, I'm not totally sure on that part. They did have recent images of her family. It sounds like they insinuated that if she loved them, she would leave the airport with that woman without making a scene. Once she learned why they needed her to come with them, she agreed to the procedure," Loch said.

"But why didn't they let her contact her family? Everyone has been so worried about her," Cari argued. She crossed the parking lot to her car and turned it on.

"They were afraid someone would put a stop to the transplant and their daughter would die without it. They didn't have time to go through legal proceedings if they got caught before the transplant took place," Loch said. "Like I said, it's convoluted. I mean, it's their daughter and they were trying to save her life, but at what expense?"

"What happens with their little girl now? Won't they both have to go to prison?" Cari asked as she exited the hotel parking lot.

"We have to find them first," Loch told her. "I'm sure we'll catch up with them before too long. It's hard to hide in a big RV. After that, I don't know. It's up to the courts."

* * * * *

The nail salon reeked of chemical smells. Genevieve wondered if they had proper ventilation or if all the employees left with a headache each day. She walked up to the front desk to check in.

"I'm here with the Cari Turnlyle bridal party," she told the woman behind the desk.

"Oh, you're the first one here," the woman told her. "Name?"

"Genevieve Viacorte," Genevieve told her.

"Okay, go ahead and have a seat. We'll call you back as a group after everyone has arrived," she explained.

A bell sounded to indicate the door had opened again. Genevieve turned to look and saw Bea entering with her daughter Hilary. She smiled.

"Cari is on her way, I'm sure," Bea told them. "She's always certain she can get one more thing done before she needs to leave. My mom and Grandmother are just getting parked. Bob's mother is coming, right?"

"I guess so? I was just told to be here by 3:30 this afternoon," Genevieve answered.

Bea walked up to the counter. "Hilary and Beatrice Rialto with the bridal party."

"Got you checked in," the clerk responded.

The bell rang again and Cari's grandmother and mother stepped inside. Genevieve hadn't seen Cari's mom in years, but recognized her from when they were in high school.

"Hi, Mrs. Turnlyle. Good to see you again," Genevieve said to her.

"Genevieve! Wow! It's been a long time. It's so great that you and Cari have reconnected. Please, call me Patricia," her mom said.

"I'll get you checked in, if you give me your names," the clerk called out from the desk. "I heard a Patricia in there. Who else is here?"

"Ann Margaret," Cari's grandmother said and raised her hand. "Margie Hursley," said another voice.

Genevieve looked up and would have recognized Bob's mother without hearing her name. They had the same friendly smile.

"You must have slipped in right behind us, Margie," Cari's grandmother remarked.

"I was running to get out of that wind," she said and smoothed out her hair. "Is Cari here?"

Patricia gave a half-smile, half-smirk. "She's late as usual."

The bell above the door rang again and Cari rushed inside. "I made it! Just a minute or so late. I didn't expect the traffic to be so heavy."

"Is everybody here now?" the clerk asked.

Cari looked around the room. "Yes, ma'am. All present and accounted for."

"We have your seats ready in the back. Just follow me," the clerk told the group.

She led them through a doorway and past the regular manicure tables and pedicure chairs. They went down a hallway and she motioned for them to enter a room on the right.

"Your nail specialists will be back shortly. All wedding party members are getting the same color, correct?" she asked for clarification.

"Yes, we're all getting coral with a light green accent nail," Bea responded.

Genevieve didn't know what an accent nail was. Alex was going to tease her endlessly for this. She followed the rest of the women into the private room. There were four reclining chairs on both sides of the room and two tables in the middle. A light knock sounded at the door and two women in green scrubs entered.

"Your manicurists are ready for you," the clerk said with a smile. "Sit wherever you'd like."

"Who wants to go first?" one of the manicurists asked.

Hilary timidly raised her hand. "Can my mom and I go first?"

"Of course, sweetheart. Are you going to be the flower girl tomorrow?" the manicurist asked her.

Hilary nodded and sat down in front of the woman. "My brother is the ring bearer."

"Who wants a mimosa? Or just orange juice?" the clerk asked. "And don't worry, it's all included in your party package."

Genevieve didn't want a mimosa; she wanted a mask, but she raised her water bottle instead. "Nothing for me. Thanks."

"I'm going to stick with water this afternoon too," Cari replied.

"Well, I'll have a mimosa. How about you, Patricia?" Margie asked.

"Count me in," Cari's mom responded.

"So, two mimosas?" the clerk asked.

"Um, make it three and an orange juice," Bea said at the last second.

"I'll have someone bring those back shortly."

Cari sat down next to Genevieve. "The missing woman turned up today. She's in a hospital."

Genevieve turned to look at her. "Was she in an accident?"

"No, it's sort of unbelievable. She was basically coerced into donating her bone marrow," Cari said.

"That sounds completely against the law," Genevieve said pointedly.

"I'm not sure what's going to happen with it. The investigating officer said he'd keep me updated. The people who abducted her or whatever you want to call it? They are trying to escape in an RV," Cari said with her eyebrows raised.

"That should be easy to spot," Genevieve commented.

"They have their daughter inside and she's recovering from the transplant procedure. It sounds pretty risky to me," Cari remarked.

"It sounds like they must have been desperate," Cari's grandma interjected. "Parents are willing to risk a lot for their children."

"That's true," Genevieve agreed. "Still, I'm not sure the end justified the means in this case. You can't just abduct people and demand they become a donor for your sick child."

A voice interrupted their discussion. "Who ordered mimosas and a plain orange juice back here?"

"That's the mothers of the bride and groom and the two ladies getting their nails painted," Margie answered from the opposite side of the room.

The young woman passed out the three mimosas and one orange juice in a paper cup. "Enjoy."

"Who's next?" one of the manicurists asked. Patricia took a sip of her mimosa and then got out of her chair.

Bea stood up and took a chair next to her grandma who was seated on the other side of Cari. "You know these are massage chairs, right?" she asked them.

"What?" Cari asked.

Genevieve looked at the panel of buttons on the arm rest. It had three settings for heat and three for vibration level. She put the heat on low and the massage level on medium. It felt pretty good.

"I could get used to this," she commented.

"Agreed," Cari said and laughed.

Hilary stood up and looked at the four of them. Genevieve could see she was reluctant to sit by Bob's mom. She turned the massage chair off and waved Hilary over.

"Come have a seat next to your aunt, Hilary. I'll go next," she volunteered.

Hilary smiled with relief. "Thanks."

"Be careful not to touch anything for fifteen minutes. You don't want to smudge it," the manicurist reminded Hilary.

Genevieve put her hands palm down on the table. The manicurist grabbed one and immediately started picking and pushing at her cuticles. She resisted the urge to pull her hand away. She didn't understand why anyone would choose to do this regularly. After a few minutes, the manicurist finally put down the cuticle torture device and picked up a nail file. Genevieve's nails were short and fairly even. The woman buffed a few of the edges with the file and then set it down.

"Bridesmaid?" she asked.

"Uh, yeah. Bridesmaid," Genevieve responded.

The woman grabbed the bottle of coral-colored nail polish and painted it onto her thumbnail and three of her fingernails. She skipped her ring finger. Genevieve remembered Bea mentioning an accent nail and finally understood what it referred to. The woman brushed light green polish onto the nail of her ring finger. She set her right hand aside and picked up the left. This time she started with the ring finger before switching back to the coral polish.

Genevieve heard a cell phone buzzing and realized it was coming from her messenger bag. She cringed. Both of her hands had wet polish on them, so she couldn't look at her phone. The buzzing ended, but was followed by a quick vibration she recognized as a text message. It couldn't be Alex; he doesn't text. She wondered if Peterson had sent her a photo and wished she could look at it. The buzzing sound resumed.

"Oh, that's me," Bea said and awkwardly pressed her watch face. "Hey, Robby. I'm on the watch. The whole room can hear you."

"Bad news. My car battery is dead. Can you come pick me up?" Robby asked.

Genevieve tried to act like she couldn't hear the conversation and stared at her nails. The woman was using a clear polish now.

That meant she was almost finished. She heard her cell phone vibrate with another text message again.

"Put your fingers in the bowl. Five minutes," the manicurist instructed.

Genevieve nodded and slid her fingers into the warm solution on the table. She had to admit it felt nice.

Robby's voice filled the room again. "I know we all need to get ready for the rehearsal. Your dad is with Joel right now, right?"

"Yeah, Hilary and I were planning on leaving here in about a half hour," Bea told him.

"Why don't I take Hilary to your house? We can bring your dress to the rehearsal. It's not like you'll have a ton of instructions, right?" Patricia interjected from Genevieve's right.

"That could work, right?" Robby asked. "I'm sorry. I didn't realize the battery was on its last legs. It started fine this morning. I thought I was making great time by getting out of the office early, but now my car won't start."

"I need a few more minutes for my nails to dry. Then I'll be on my way. It might be five o'clock before I get there. I don't know what the traffic will be like today."

"I have my coat and gloves, but it's pretty chilly, so the sooner the better," Robby begged.

"I'll do my best. Love you," Bea said and ended the call.

"I'd offer to go get him, but I hate driving in the city," Patricia said. "I'm just not used to that kind of traffic."

"Totally fine, Mom," Bea replied. "Thanks for helping with the kids."

Bea blew on her nails and shook her hands in the air. "Do you think I'm good to use my fingers again?"

The manicurist looked at the clock on the wall. It was 4:15. "You should be fine."

Bea smiled. "Thanks...Hilary, Grandma is going to take you home from here, okay?"

"Okay, Mom," Hilary answered. "We'll see you at the rehearsal though, right?"

"Definitely. I'll get there as soon as I can," Bea replied and then turned to Cari. "I'm sorry if this throws a wrench in the rehearsal. I'll do my best not to be late."

"It will be fine either way. Be safe. Love you," Cari told her.

"Next!" Genevieve's manicurist called out and then looked her in the eye. "Fifteen minutes."

"Got it," Genevieve said obediently. She was itching to look at her phone.

Cari took her seat at the table. Margie was taking her turn at the other table. Genevieve sat down next to Hilary and turned the massage chair back on. At least she could get pampered a bit while she waited for her nails to dry.

Chapter 12

Loch rode in the passenger seat while his friend Nitto drove along the interstate. He was enjoying the change of pace from the last few days. Though, their current speed was a little faster than he'd like. They needed to catch up to the RV, so Nitto was driving well over eighty miles per hour. The Hendricksons wouldn't want to draw attention to themselves, so they were probably staying around the required speed limit for RVs, or fifty-five miles per hour. They'd been driving for almost two hours. He hoped they would catch up to the RV soon.

"At least there's no traffic clear out here," Loch remarked.

"Yeah, we'd never catch up if we were stuck in city traffic," Nitto agreed.

"I could get used to this," he said to Nitto.

"To what?" Nitto asked.

"I've been an airport cop for a few years, but tracking down this woman and the RV...it's been way more exciting than most of my airport days," Loch explained.

"Have you applied to be a detective?" Nitto asked him.

"I've been putting it off. Being a detective with the NYPD sounds like more action than I'm looking for," Loch told him.

"Looking for that Goldilocks position, huh?" Nitto laughed.

"I guess so. Something where people aren't shooting at me, but where I'm doing more than calming down unruly travelers," Loch responded.

"Maybe you need to switch to a suburb instead of working in the city," Nitto suggested.

"Maybe. I wonder what it would take to be a PI," he mused.

"Go private? Really?" Nitto frowned at him.

"I know…it's kind of discouraged, but I could choose my hours and my cases," Loch argued.

"And lose your benefits and…some respect?" Nitto added.

"Yeah, I kind of liked working with the reporter, though. I was really skeptical about it when my detective friend called, but Turnlyle was great to work with. She had some good ideas and she didn't try to go around me or over my head," Loch told him.

"Wow, now you're really talking about the dark side. A reporter?" Nitto asked.

"I guess technically she's a journalist," Loch said with a shrug. "She was right on the money with this too. Once she learned the woman was adopted, she told me it was relevant. She was right."

The radio squawked. "Nitto?"

"This is Officer Nitto," he responded. "I'm with Officer Lochaven."

"We spotted your RV on I-78. We can attempt to pull them over or wait for you to catch up. We're approaching exit 57 for Lehigh St…uh, that's in Pennsylvania."

Loch looked out the window. "We're not far from Pennsylvania now. I see a sign for St. Andrew's Lutheran Church."

"I know where that is. You're only five minutes from here," the man on the radio said.

Nitto looked at Loch and nodded. "Light 'em up. We'll be there shortly."

Nitto turned on the cruiser's lights as well. Loch could feel them accelerating down the interstate. The cars ahead of them pulled over as they raced along the road. Loch resisted the urge to grab the handle above the window for support. After a few minutes, he saw blue and red flashing lights ahead on the shoulder. He grabbed the binoculars and looked.

"That's them," he confirmed to Nitto.

Nitto eased off the gas and pulled up behind the other cruiser. "I'm going to call in our location. We're in New Jersey now."

"Dispatch, it's Lochaven and Nitto. We've got the RV headed west on I-78 approaching exit 57. Requesting assistance," Loch said into the radio.

"Your captain is on the line with the local PD. They have one cruiser out there already and are sending more units. Your captain wants you to wait for a negotiator before engaging with the suspects."

Nitto shook his head. "No way. These people aren't dangerous. They're medical workers. They're trying to keep their daughter alive. They aren't going to put her at risk of gunfire."

"Be advised—"

Nitto flipped the radio off. Loch raised his eyebrows but didn't say anything.

"If you have something to say, now's the time," Nitto told him.

"If you're good, I'm good," Loch replied.

Loch heard more sirens and saw two cruisers get on the interstate just behind them. Nitto pulled past the RV and blocked it in. He turned the cruiser off and got out. Loch joined him at the back of the car and Nitto removed a bullhorn from the trunk. Loch's radio chirped.

"Is this Officer Lochaven?"

"Speaking," Loch responded.

"How do you want to handle this? We were instructed to wait for a negotiator to arrive, but to be honest with you, that could be over an hour or more."

Nitto leaned toward Loch and spoke up. "I've got the bullhorn out. I'm going to ask them to exit the vehicle. If you can have the other two cruisers position themselves to the left of the RV, that will keep them from trying to escape."

"Got it."

Loch watched the two cruisers slowly pull alongside the RV and give them a thumbs up.

Nitto put the bullhorn up to his mouth and pressed the trigger. "This is the police. Turn off the vehicle. We need everyone to exit with their hands in the air."

The driver's door opened and a man with wild hair and scrubs climbed out. He had his hands up, but Loch could see fear in his eyes. The man kept looking back and forth between them and the RV.

"Please," he shouted. "My wife and child are inside. They can't get out. My child is recovering from surgery and my wife is with her."

"Dr. Hendrickson?" Nitto asked.

The man nodded.

"Is the RV off?" Loch asked. He couldn't hear with the wind howling in his ears.

"It's off. We're done running. We just…we just wanted to save her," he said with tears in his eyes.

"You're going to need to come with us," Nitto said. "Your wife too."

"What about my daughter? It's critical that she not be exposed to any sort of infection right now," the doctor told them. He was shivering in the cold air.

"I'll call for a bus," Loch assured him.

He stepped to the shoulder and pulled his radio from his shirt. "Officer Lochaven requesting an ambulance to our location. We're on the shoulder of I-78 west—"

"It needs to be extra sterile. They'll be transporting an immunocompromised patient who just underwent a bone marrow transplant," the doctor shouted.

"Dispatch, the victim is recovering from a bone marrow transplant. Be advised," Loch added.

"We need your wife to get out of the RV too, Dr. Hendrickson," Nitto told him.

"She has to stay with our daughter," he begged. "She's only five years old."

"We understand, sir. Officer Loch is going to take her place," Nitto said and jerked his head at Loch.

"No, he could have some sort of infection. He can't enter the RV. It's a sterile environment," Hendrickson said, his eyes frantic.

"Sir, we cannot allow your wife to remain in the vehicle," Nitto told him.

Loch went back to the cruiser and grabbed some hand sanitizer. "Look, I'm putting this on my hands, okay? I'll put on a mask and gloves. I won't touch anything. Your daughter will be safe. I'll keep my distance."

The man's shoulders slumped. He motioned for Loch to proceed. Nitto approached the man and pulled out his handcuffs.

"You have the right to remain silent..." Nitto began as Loch walked to the other side of the RV.

He pulled on a pair of gloves and a mask he'd taken from the first aid kit. Then he tried the door handle. It was locked.

"This is Officer Lochaven, ma'am. I need you to unlock the door. I have on gloves and a mask," he informed her.

He leaned toward the door to listen. He heard a child whimpering and a woman speaking quietly. He heard the locks disengage and pulled on the handle again. The door opened.

"Don't leave me, Mommy. I'm scared," the child begged.

Loch gulped. The little girl's head was void of hair and her skin was very pale. He felt guilty for making the mother leave.

"I have to, baby. I'm sorry. I love you so much. Forever. I love you, Sarah," the woman said as Loch climbed the steps into the RV.

"I'm Officer Lochaven. Mrs. Hendrickson, please step away from the child and raise your hands. I'm going to stay in the front seat after you exit. I won't engage with your daughter, but you have to get out now," he told her.

The woman's face was wet with tears. She wore a surgical mask and kissed her daughter through it on her scalp before rising to her feet. The child was strapped to a bed and had an IV in her right arm. The IV pole had two bags hanging from it. It was secured to the wall of the RV with cables.

"Goodbye, Sarah. I love you," the woman said one last time as she went down the steps and out the side door.

The child raised her arms and sobbed. "Mommy! No!"

Loch felt his own eyes tear up. He wanted to go to the child and comfort her, but he'd promised to stay back.

"I heard your name is Sarah. Is it okay if I call you Sarah?" he asked in a quiet voice.

Her big brown eyes flicked to his face. "Why did you make my mommy leave?"

"I'm sorry, Sarah. Your mommy and daddy...they made a mistake...um...they have to talk to some people," Loch struggled to find the words.

"What kind of mistake? They're helping me get better! They said the other lady was my sister and she wanted to help me," Sarah cried.

Loch nodded. "That's what I heard too. I don't know what's going to happen, but we're going to keep you safe, okay? You can trust me, Sarah."

"I want my mommy!" she wailed.

A knock sounded at the side door. "EMS here. We're going to open the door now,"

A woman in a mask and gloves stood on the shoulder outside the RV.

"Hi, Sarah. My name is Sarah too. I'm going to help get you to the hospital," the EMT said calmly.

"My daddy said I needed to stay in the RV. It's clean," Sarah told her and sniffled.

"I talked to your daddy, Sarah," the EMT told her. "He gave me the keys to your RV. My partner and I are going to drive you to the hospital and get you into a safer place. It will be warm and stationary."

"And my mommy and daddy will be there?" Sarah asked.

The EMT bit her lip. "We'll see what happens."

"We'll see always means no," Sarah said sadly.

"It was nice to meet you, Sarah," Loch said as he opened the front door again. "I'm going to let the EMTs take over now, okay? You're safe, Sarah."

Sarah continued to cry and refused to look at Loch. He wiped a tear from his left eye and climbed out of the RV. A male EMT was waiting on the grass.

"Tough case," the EMT said. "It feels like there are only wrong answers here."

Loch only nodded and walked back to the cruiser. Nitto was just getting into the driver's seat. Another officer was helping Mrs. Hendrickson into his cruiser.

"This was not how I saw this ending when you called me about a missing person," Nitto said once they were both in the car.

"Me neither. Where'd you put the doctor?" Loch asked him.

"Another team arrived and took him away already," Nitto said. "It's out of our hands now."

* * * * *

Elizabeth unbuckled Whitney from the car seat. "Okay, let's go see Auntie Rebecca!"

Whitney cooed at her. Keith locked the rental car and adjusted the strap of the diaper bag on his shoulder.

"I didn't think I'd be carrying one of these again for a long time...maybe ever," he joked.

"Thanks for helping. I probably should have left Whitney home, but I didn't know how long I'd be gone and she's so little," Elizabeth remarked.

"I get it. Rebecca was with our kids all the time when they were that small too," Keith acknowledged. "Do you think they'll let all three of us see her at the same time?"

"I don't know. I hope so," Elizabeth said as they entered the hospital.

She walked up to the check-in desk. "Hi, I'm Elizabeth Marino. We're here to see Rebecca Davenport."

The woman typed on her keyboard. "Second floor. Room 206. Visiting hours end at seven."

"Thank you," Elizabeth responded.

She looked to her right and saw the elevator bay. "This way, Keith."

Keith pressed the up button and the doors immediately opened. He stepped inside and put his hand on the edge of the door to keep it open.

"Thanks. I'm always terrified the doors are going to close on me," Elizabeth admitted. "I know they're supposed to go back if they encounter resistance, but I don't want to test the mechanism."

"Probably wise," he agreed and pressed the button with a two on it.

The elevator doors closed and quickly rose up one floor. A sign on the wall outside the elevator indicated rooms 200-220 were to their left. Elizabeth adjusted Whitney and followed Keith down the hallway. They found room 206, four doors down on the left-hand side. Keith knocked on the open door as he stepped inside.

"Rebecca! You're okay. I've been so worried," Keith said and rushed to her bedside.

She had an IV inserted into her right arm and a blood pressure cuff on her left arm. Elizabeth's eyes filled with tears when she saw her sister.

"Hey, no need to cry," Rebecca said with tears in her eyes too. "You know how I am!"

"Sorry," Elizabeth said and swiped her tears away. She pulled up a chair on the other side of the bed. "I didn't know if we were going to find you. I'm still really confused about what happened."

"I was on the phone with you at the airport, right?" Rebecca reminded her. Elizabeth nodded and let her continue. "This woman bumped into me and I dropped my phone. When I bent down to pick it up, she was showing me a photo of Keith…and the kids! She said, 'Do you love them?' and what else could I say? Of course. I'd do anything for my family, for my babies. She told me to end the call and not say anything and they'd stay safe. She gave me her phone and took mine. Taped to the back of her phone was a set of instructions. I was to go to the bathroom and I'd find a bag with a wig and a hat and sunglasses.

"I went to the women's restroom and found the bag with the items in it and put them on in one of the stalls. The cell phone rang and a man told me to exit the gate area. He gave me directions on how to meet up with the woman again."

"We saw you on the surveillance video," Elizabeth said. "So, we know how you left the airport."

"Oh, okay. Uh, let's see. The woman…her name is Jennifer, by the way, got on the second train with me. When we got outside after riding the metro, a man picked us up in a car. Once I was inside, the woman told me about her daughter, Sarah. She was dying of leukemia and was in desperate need of a bone marrow transplant. They didn't know how much longer she could make it," Rebecca told them.

"That's heartbreaking. Was it the Hendricksons? We found them on your DNA results," Elizabeth explained.

"So, you know then. They're my birth parents. I…was really blindsided by that. It felt…violating and like I was being used, but Sarah," Rebecca paused. "How could I say no to a child who was dying?"

"The police are looking for them, Rebecca," Keith said and stroked her hair. Elizabeth saw his hand trembling. "They're in an RV. Who knows? They may have found them already."

"I don't want to press charges," Rebecca said indignantly. "I don't want to break up their family. I'm fine. I didn't even really have a fever. They sent me here out of the utmost concern for my well-being."

"They abducted you. From an airport," Keith raised his voice a bit. Elizabeth flinched.

"Keith, surely you understand. What would you do if one of our kids was sick and you weren't a match, so you couldn't help them?" Rebecca asked.

"I wouldn't kidnap people and coerce them into helping my child. That's not okay, Becky," Keith argued. "They could have let you call me. They could have told us you were safe and okay. They could have just asked permission."

"They didn't know what I'd say. It wasn't worth the risk to them," Rebecca said gently. "I probably saved her life. They were running tests on her and said things were looking good so far."

"I hope she's going to be okay, Rebecca. Truly, I do," Keith told her. "I'm not okay with how they did this."

Elizabeth wasn't sure what to say. It felt awkward in a hundred ways. "When will you get discharged?"

"I'm waiting for the results of some sort of test…white blood cell count or something. If it isn't elevated, then I think they'll let me leave in the morning," Rebecca said.

Whitney reached out and grabbed Rebecca's index finger. She cooed. Rebecca smiled back at her.

"Let me raise the bed. Can I hold her? I've been looking forward to meeting her for so long. Look how sweet she is," Rebecca said to Elizabeth.

"Sure," Elizabeth said and waited for the bed to lift her sister into a seated position.

She passed Whitney to Rebecca. Whitney touched Rebecca's hair and tugged on it. She cooed some more and then leaned toward her face and sucked on her nose. Rebecca laughed.

"Nice to meet you, Whitney. That's quite the greeting," she said as she loosened her hair from the baby's fingers. "She's beautiful, Elizabeth."

"Thanks," Elizabeth said. "She's had an adventure this week. This was not how I expected your introduction to go, but I'm glad we're together now."

Keith cleared his throat. "The police are at the door."

Elizabeth swung her head to the doorway. She saw two police officers standing outside the room.

"We're sorry to interrupt the reunion. We need to speak with Mrs. Davenport for a few minutes," one of them said. "Mr. Davenport, you're welcome to stay."

Elizabeth lifted Whitney from Rebecca's arms and got up from the chair. The officers stepped back to let her out of the room. They closed the door behind her once they were inside. She wasn't sure if Rebecca would really have a say in pressing charges against the Hendricksons. It felt like a mess. She wished the older couple had just asked Rebecca for help instead of being manipulative. Elizabeth paced the hallway outside the room and wondered what the police were telling Rebecca and Keith.

* * * * *

The second hand seemed to tick slower and slower as it made its way around the wall clock. Genevieve felt guilty for not giving Cari more attention, but she really wanted to get a look at her cell phone. She hoped it was a photo from Peterson or maybe that he'd remembered another name.

"Are you trying to use the force to change time, Genevieve?" Patricia asked.

Genevieve felt herself redden. "I guess I'm not very good at sitting still and not using my hands."

"Right?" Cari agreed. "I love these colors together. As soon as we can get our phones out, we have to take a picture of all our hands. Too bad Bea won't be in it. Maybe we should do it at dinner tonight instead."

Genevieve smiled at her. "That could work. I forgot to ask you: did you and Bob decide on a honeymoon location?"

"Sort of. It's not that exciting. I mean, we've been on a trip together already, so that could count…" Cari babbled.

"But…?" Genevieve tried to get her back on track.

"We're unpacking my boxes at his apartment for two days," Cari said and laughed. "Is that lame? We just really need to get it finished and I have to be out of my apartment by next Sunday."

"It's very practical," Grandmother assured her from the nail station. "Take a trip this summer when you're settled."

Genevieve heard Patricia cough and wondered if there was some tension about the 'honeymoon' plans. She looked at the clock. Finally, her fifteen-minute imprisonment was over. She pulled out her cell phone and unlocked it. She had a missed call from Peterson, a voicemail, and a text. She opened the text first.

"Get anything good?" Cari asked and raised her eyebrows.

Genevieve frowned. The image was completely blurry. It looked like he'd moved the phone or the photograph as he was taking the picture. "Not really. I hate to leave early too, but I need to call this person and get them to resend the photo."

Cari blinked and then smiled. "Of course. Is everything okay?"

"It's a mess," Genevieve told her quietly. She wasn't sure if Hilary could hear her or not. "I think we found the accomplice."

Cari leaned in. "Did you make an arrest?"

"Not yet. The guy has been one step ahead of us this whole time. And now Stenoway was murdered in prison. His lawyer was a fake and we don't know where he is. Like I said, it's a mess," Genevieve whispered. "I don't really want to get into it here. Maybe we can chat next week after your...box date is over?"

Cari laughed. "I'm in. Drive safe out there. It's really windy."

"Will do," Genevieve replied. "See you at the church."

She zipped her coat and wrapped her scarf around her neck. She had a beanie in her pocket and pulled that onto her head. Her car was right out front, which was good since she didn't have her gloves. She used her key fob to unlock the Expedition and then hurried outside.

The temperature felt even colder than when she'd arrived an hour before. She instantly regretted not putting on her gloves. The steering wheel felt like ice. She steered the vehicle to the parking lot exit and then accessed her Bluetooth to call Peterson.

"Detective Viacorte?" Peterson asked.

"Hi, Mr. Peterson. I got the photo you sent. I'm not sure if you noticed, but it's very blurry and out of focus. I can't make out anything in the image," Genevieve told him.

"Oh shoot. I didn't even look at it. I just snapped it really quick and went on with my afternoon. I'm out running an errand right now, but I'll be back home in half an hour or so. Would that work? I could email it to you instead if you think that's better," he offered.

"Either way is fine," she recited her email address for him. "I'm on my way home right now, but I'll be able to check my email remotely. I take it you didn't remember the other man's name?"

"It's in my head somewhere. I just can't quite pull it out yet," Peterson lamented. "Sucks to get old sometimes. I'll send the photo again. Let me know if you can't open it or whatever."

"I appreciate the help," Genevieve said. "Have a good evening."

She ended the call as she pulled into her parking space. She quickly pulled on her gloves before turning her vehicle off. Her fingers were chilled to the bone after just a few minutes of touching the steering wheel. She put her phone back in her messenger bag and then hurried inside her apartment building.

Her laptop was sitting on her kitchen table. She unlocked it and pulled up her departmental email account remotely so she'd hear a ding when Peterson's message came through. She checked her watch and saw it was almost 4:45. She had some time before she needed to start getting ready for the rehearsal, so she decided to look at Robby's file again. They hadn't gotten a response back on their warrant for the account number making deposits into Stenoway's account yet, but maybe something in one of the transactions would help her tease out the information.

Genevieve ran a search in her email for the ledger file they'd received from Robby back in July. It wasn't the same as live access, but they hadn't requested that since Follard was only guilty of thinking with his little brain and not fraud like Pierce. She opened the file and scrolled through the information.

"Oh my gosh. I can't..." she whispered and opened another browser window.

She quickly accessed Stenoway's account with the mysterious two-k deposits to confirm what her memory was telling her. This didn't make any sense. She picked up her cell phone and dialed Robby's number.

"Genevieve? I wasn't expecting to hear from you. Bea just got here and we're getting ready to jump my car," Robby told her.

"I'll be quick. I was just looking at all these deposits and transfers from the Stenoway case again. Do you know your company's account numbers by heart?" she asked him.

"Uh, I can probably look it up remotely if I don't recognize it. Why?" he asked.

"I'm looking at the statement you sent me from the NTS account. Let me read you the account number," she said and read the numbers off the screen.

"Right, that's our main account," Robby confirmed.

"Okay, so I've got another account number that starts with the same first...eight digits and then has six different ones," she explained and read those to him. "Is that an NTS account too?"

"Let me get back in the car and out of the wind," Robby said. The background noise lessened. "Okay, I'm just logging in remotely. Yeah, that's our Expansion and Recruitment account."

"That account is transferring two thousand dollars to Stenoway's account every month and has been since last summer," she told him.

"Wait. You're saying NTS is still paying Stenoway?" Robby asked.

"It sure looks that way. Who is in charge of Expansion and Recruitment at NTS?" she asked.

"Someone in marketing? I'm not sure," Robby replied. "E and R is basically our advertising and marketing division."

"I can't come up with a reason your company would pay Stenoway for advertising. Something isn't adding up here," Genevieve told him. "Is Follard still your acting CEO?"

"Yes, though I've heard some of the other department heads holding secret meetings to discuss if they should ask him to resign," Robby told her. "The blackmail thing didn't really sit well with them, but they also understood he was in a tough position."

Genevieve rolled her eyes. "He put himself in that position, so he should expect consequences. Whatever. That's not really my problem, I guess. The money transfer from your Expansion and Recruitment account...is that a transfer you would initiate?"

"We have a whole house of finance guys, so in some cases, other people can authorize transfers. I seem to remember some paperwork about a new ad series we're running that was going to be a recurring charge of two-k. I don't know why it would go to Stenoway though."

"Yeah, something is off with it. I'll try to tease it out from my end. Thanks, Robby," Genevieve said gratefully.

"Any other questions? We really need to get this car jumped," he reminded her.

"I think that's it. I guess I'll be seeing you at the rehearsal in a bit," she replied.

"Hopefully, we won't be late," Robby said and ended the call.

It was almost five o'clock, so Genevieve decided to call Alex and get his thoughts on her recent discovery. She hit talk and waited for him to pick up.

"Gen! You just can't quit working even when you take time off," Alex rebuked her.

"I figured out who owns that account," she told him, ignoring his derision.

"The account making the deposits to Stenoway?" he asked.

"Yes. It's an NTS account," she informed him.

"That doesn't make sense. Why would Follard still be paying Stenoway?" Alex argued.

"Maybe it isn't Follard. Maybe it's someone else at NTS. Peterson is supposed to be sending me that photo. He was not meant to be a photographer. The first image he sent me was terrible. Everything was blurry and pixelated. He said he'd try again when he got home. Hopefully, he'll do it soon. I need to start getting ready for the rehearsal too," Genevieve remarked.

"It's Friday and it's officially after five o'clock, so I'm going to call it a day. Don't call me unless it's an emergency. I have plans tomorrow," he told her.

"Yeah, you're going to a wedding," she reminded him.

"That's like an hour, maybe two if Sophia wants to stay for the whole reception," he argued. "I'm going to watch some football playoffs and sit on my couch. You should try it."

"I'm not really a football person," she retorted.

"Don't call me," he said again and ended the call.

Genevieve turned the volume up on her laptop and went to her bedroom to change into leggings and a long sweater. It was way too cold to wear a dress. She already had to suffer through that tomorrow and one day of wearing a dress was enough. She tugged on the clothes and put on some heels even though they weren't very practical or comfortable. Then she went to the bathroom to brush out her hair. Her dark tresses had a nice wave to them after being bound up in the bun all day. She heard the wind howling and decided the bun was still a better choice than letting her hair fly into her face all evening. She was only a bridesmaid. No one was looking at her anyway. A ding sounded from her computer. She dropped her hairbrush on the counter and ran out to her laptop. She quickly navigated back to her email and saw an unread message from Peterson.

She clicked on the email and opened the attachment. A chill went up her spine. She looked around the laptop for her cell phone. It was sitting on the table behind the laptop. She grabbed it and quickly opened her phone app. Robby's name was the second on the list. She touched it and hit redial. The call connected and rang three times.

Hello, you've reach Robby Rialto. Please leave me a message.

"Robby, call me as soon as you get this!" she practically shouted into the phone.

She ended the call and tried Bea's number instead. Maybe they were already driving to the rehearsal and only took one car. Bea's voicemail picked up after the third ring too.

"Ugh!" she groaned. "Alex, you said only if it was an emergency. You'd better freaking pick up the phone."

She hit redial by Alex's name and waited for it to connect. He answered on the second ring.

"Gen, Gen, Ge—" he started to say.

"Alex! It *is* an emergency. I got the photo from Peterson. The other friend is Follard," she told him frantically. "I talked to Robby, like twenty minutes ago and had him access their accounts. Now he isn't answering his phone and neither is Bea. We need to warn them."

"You think he has an alert set up to see if someone looks at that account? C'mon, that's a stretch. It's Friday night," Alex argued. "What are Robby and Bea going to do if you warn them? Skip the rehearsal and dinner? Brensteiner left the prison over twenty-four hours ago. If they knew about Robby, they'd have already gotten to him."

"I guess that's true. I just have a bad feeling about it," Gen admitted. "Regardless, we know Follard is involved in a completely different way than we thought. We need to bring Follard in for an interview. Brensteiner is still in the wind. They could be planning to run off with their money together. Call Grusky and make it happen."

"Okay, okay," Alex relented. "Do you have time to call Shelly? Did she talk about Follard the other day?"

"No, good idea. I never asked her about Follard. She was so ashamed; I didn't want to rub salt in the wound. I'm replaying the conversation in my mind. She never mentioned Follard's name. It all makes sense now. He wasn't being blackmailed. He just told Dureski the same story as Pierce and we all fell for it," Genevieve realized.

"Hook, line, and sinker," Alex agreed. "You call Shelly and make sure she didn't seduce Follard too. At least we already have someone watching Follard. I'll check in with them and see if he's still at work. Maybe he'll lead us to Brensteiner."

"Deal. Thanks, Alex," she said and ended the call.

Genevieve called Shelly next, but it went to voicemail too. Apparently, no one except Alex answered their phone on a Friday evening.

"Hi, Shelly. It's Detective Viacorte. I have one more question for you, if you have a minute to talk. Call me any time."

She ended the call and looked at her watch. She needed to call Dureski and update him too. She had time to make another call before she left for the rehearsal.

"I was just about to call you, Viacorte," Dureski said when he answered the phone. "The sister got a call from Brensteiner. He told her he left the keys to his car in the usual place and he was taking her car to run some errands."

"Do you have someone watching her car now?" Genevieve asked hopefully.

"We think the car might have LoJack. We're just getting access to it now. What's your update?" he asked.

"Brensteiner and Stenoway were in the same fraternity in college. We got in touch with the president from their senior year. He told us Stenoway was a tag along with Brensteiner and one other guy. They, uh, tolerated Stenoway, but the other two were better friends," Genevieve explained. "He couldn't remember this other guy's name, so he sent me a photo. It's Follard."

"What?! But...Follard told me about the blackmail. Same story as Pierce," Dureski argued.

"I know, but it was just that: a story. He knew what was happening because he was telling people what to do. He and Brensteiner were calling the shots," Genevieve told him.

184

Dureski cursed under his breath. "I need to get someone on Follard too. Or did you guys already track him down?"

"We thought he might be in danger after Stenoway was poisoned, so we've been having someone keep an eye on him. My partner is calling for an update now," she added.

"I'll get a trace on his phone and put out a BOLO for his car too," Dureski said and then paused. "Hell. Where is the accountant...Rialto? Where is he?"

Genevieve felt like her stomach flipped over. "Robby? Uh, he should be on his way to my friend's wedding rehearsal. I tried to call him, but he didn't answer."

"I wasn't worried about his safety when I thought his boss was a victim too, but this news changes things," Dureski remarked. "Rialto's name was kept out of everything, but this news about Follard makes me nervous."

"I'll keep trying him," Genevieve promised. "Hopefully, he's just driving and can't take the call."

"Keep me posted," Dureski said. "Anything else?"

"Can you share access to the LoJack with us? We can help track Brensteiner down," she offered.

"I'll add your email to it and your partner's too," Dureski said. "Keep me posted on Rialto."

The call ended. Genevieve tugged on her winter gear again, minus the beanie. She slipped her hood over her hair and hoped her hair would be mostly presentable by the time she arrived at the rehearsal. She kept her phone in her hand and would keep redialing Robby until he answered.

Chapter 13

The door to Rebecca's hospital room opened and the officers motioned Elizabeth back inside. She looked at Rebecca and saw she had been crying again. Keith still looked angry.

"What's wrong?" she asked.

Rebecca glanced at Keith and then the two officers.

"It's fine, Mrs. Davenport. You're free to share with your sister. We'll be back with a statement for you to sign in a bit," one of the officers told Rebecca.

Elizabeth waited for them to leave before she repeated her question. "Everyone seems upset. What's going on?"

Rebecca's eyes flicked toward Keith again, but he wouldn't meet her gaze. "I told the officers I didn't want to press charges. Keith disagrees."

"But...they coerced you! They made you think they were going to hurt your family," Elizabeth argued.

Keith raised his hands in an agreeable gesture but remained silent. Rebecca tried to reach for one of his hands, but he pulled it away.

"They were desperate. Their child was going to die. If I hadn't sent off my DNA for that thing when I did, it probably would have been too late," Rebecca said with tears in her eyes.

"But how did they know you were going to be in New York? Did they stalk you on social media or something?" Elizabeth asked.

Keith nodded and grimaced.

"I mean, they looked me up, yes. It was my choice to post about traveling through JFK, but so fortuitous for their little girl, for Sarah," Rebecca explained. "The best match for a bone marrow transplant is usually a sibling. Does it suck that they never tried to meet me before they needed something from me? Probably, but I don't care. Helping that little girl, who also happens to be my sister, was the right thing to do. I would have done it if they'd asked me."

"But they didn't really ask! They just whisked you out of the airport and kept you secluded from your *real* family," Elizabeth argued. "They shouldn't be able to do that."

"The officer said at the very least, they would be put on probation, but they might lose their licenses too," Rebecca told her. "What choice did they have?"

"They could have been decent human beings and just asked you," Keith said angrily. "They don't get to demand help for their child. Her life is not more important than yours. They deserve to go to jail."

"She's a child, Keith. Wouldn't you do anything to save one of our kids?" Rebecca asked him. "You think they deserve to go to jail for trying to save their daughter's life?"

Keith sighed. "I don't know, Rebecca. The whole thing is a mess. They acted out of a place of entitlement. At the very least, it's unethical."

"I'm glad you're okay, Bec," Elizabeth said after a few moments. "I was really worried and scared."

"Are they at least going to pay your hospital bills?" Keith asked in exasperation.

Elizabeth cringed. She was tired of arguing.

"I'm not sure. I didn't fill out any paperwork when they admitted me. I think the Hendricksons work here and sent instructions electronically, but I don't know," Rebecca said. "They asked me if I had any allergies or other medical concerns before they had me taken here."

"They didn't even drive you here themselves?" Keith growled.

"Their neighbor drove me. He made sure I was okay before he left," Rebecca explained.

Keith's face was red and his eyes were angry. Elizabeth felt terrible for Rebecca. This couple just kept abandoning their oldest daughter, like she didn't really matter to them.

"I know what you're thinking," Rebecca said. "You think they just abandoned me all over again. I don't feel abandoned. They're just people to me. I grew up with a loving family and a loving set of parents. I have no attachment to the Hendricksons. They found themselves in an unimaginable position. I had the power to make it better. Why wouldn't I offer that to them?"

* * * * *

Cari was proud of herself for being ready on time for the rehearsal. It helped that Bob wanted to pick her up half an hour early. His apartment was in between her complex and the church, but he wanted to drive there together. She had to admit, she was really excited about their wedding. Maybe that helped her get outside before Bob arrived, though she was regretting not waiting inside as the wind whipped her dark curls into her face. She waved when she saw Bob's car enter the parking lot. He pulled into the guest parking space and his jaw dropped. She hurried into the passenger seat and closed the door.

"This has to be a first. I'm impressed," he teased her.

"Thank you. I like being impressive," she responded and leaned over to kiss him. "What's the surprise you wanted to show me?"

"It's at my apartment," he said vaguely as he backed out of the parking spot. "You'll have to wait and see."

She smiled at him and patted him on the leg. "I'm so curious!"

He winked at her, but didn't offer any other hints. Her cell phone rang before she could beg for more information.

"Oh, it's Marjorie. I'll try to make it quick," she promised. "Hello, Marjorie?"

"Cari! I'm so relieved that Rebecca is back and found. I've been really worried," Marjorie said quickly.

"I haven't heard from Elizabeth since she and Keith went to the hospital to see her. Is everything okay?" Cari asked.

"Yes! I mean, that's not really why I called. I just wanted to thank you again for helping us find her. Without you, Elizabeth and Keith might still be begging the police to look at the surveillance footage," Marjorie replied.

"Well, Rebecca actually contacted Elizabeth. We didn't find her," Cari reminded Marjorie. "But I'm glad I could help. I know it was scary not to know where she was. She called from the hospital. Is she sick?"

"No, they thought she might have an infection, but she's okay. Sort of okay, I guess. She's safe and she's not injured or sick or anything like that, but..." Marjorie paused. "She is refusing to press charges against the couple who abducted her!"

"They turned out to be her biological parents, right?" Cari asked.

"Yeah, and once they had her in the car, they explained how they found her—public social media posts about her trips—and told her they were her bio-parents," Marjorie explained.

"That must have been a shock," Cari remarked.

"Right?" Marjorie agreed. "But there was more. Apparently, they dated in high school. That's when Jennifer got pregnant. They were only, like, fifteen and sixteen years old, so their parents made them give the baby up for adoption. By the time they graduated, they were no longer together. Jennifer went to one college and then nursing school and Matthew chose a different school and did pre-med, then medical school and a residency, and so on. He's a doctor now. Fast forward something like twenty-five or thirty years," Marjorie said and took a breath. "They both got positions at the same hospital in New York. In the *quarter of a century* since they'd last been together, they'd both gotten married and subsequently divorced."

"Oh, that's too bad," Cari interjected.

"Yeah, it's sad. But they felt like fate was offering them a second chance and they started dating again and eventually married. And Jennifer got pregnant again," Marjorie informed Cari. "It's a sweet story until you get to the part where they coerced the offspring they never knew into being a bone marrow donor."

Cari's eyes widened as Marjorie continued with the story. She mouthed an apology to Bob. They'd reached his apartment complex and he'd parked in a spot further away from his unit than usual. She wondered what he would think of Marjorie's tale.

"…it's so far-fetched, I can hardly believe it. This couple is so sus," Marjorie declared. "And Rebecca is refusing to press charges even though clearly these people broke the law."

"It does seem unethical, if not illegal, but I suppose it is Rebecca's choice. She can choose not to press charges," Cari said gently.

"The district attorney met with her this evening. She told Rebecca they won't bring the case to trial without her support. They don't think a jury will convict these people if the victim won't speak on her own behalf," Marjorie said grumpily. "She said the most she can do is get their licenses revoked, but more than likely, they'll just be suspended."

"I'm sorry. I know that's frustrating, but it is Rebecca's decision, right?" Cari asked.

"I guess. It sounds like a mess. Keith isn't happy about it either," Marjorie told her. "Rebecca keeps saying as a mom, she knows how much she would do for one of her kids. She thinks the Hendricksons deserve forgiveness. Do you think you can get Stockholm syndrome after just two or three days?"

Cari raised her eyebrows. "I have no idea. Why?"

"I don't know. It's just really frustrating. I guess I don't know the right answer…" Marjorie trailed off.

"I'm sorry, Marjorie…and I really need to go. It's almost time for the wedding rehearsal," Cari reminded her.

"Oh, right. My bad. I'll let you go," Marjorie said sheepishly.

"Thanks for calling me with an update. Be patient with Rebecca. This has been traumatic for her. If she doesn't want to press charges, that can be okay, right?" Cari asked.

"Yeah, I guess," Marjorie agreed. "Congrats again. I know you'll make a beautiful bride."

Cari ended the call and looked at Bob. "Sorry. She had a lot to say."

"I gathered. We still have time to see the surprise. Ready?" he asked.

"Let's do it!"

He led her to the steps, but went to the right instead of the left.

"Where are you going?" Cari asked in confusion.

"This is part of the surprise," Bob explained. "Follow me."

He led her to the end of the walkway and unlocked the last door. "I put in for an upgrade back in September. This is our new home. It's a two-bedroom, one and a half bath apartment."

"What?! That's incredible. Can we afford it?" she asked hesitantly.

"They were having a special for long-time residents. Upgrade your unit and get half off on your new rental payment. It costs basically the same as what I was paying for the one-bedroom. We'll be fine," he assured her.

"This is amazing!" she said as she looked around the empty space. "Thank you, Bob! Let's go rehearse for the best day of our lives."

"One more thing," he said and drew her into his arms for a kiss. "I can't wait to start our life together, Cari."

"I love you, Bob Hursley," she said and kissed him.

* * * * *

Alex smirked when he saw Gen's name show up in the little screen on his flip phone. "Such a workaholic, Gen."

"I don't have time for jokes right now, Alex," she said crisply. "The Beagle posted a congratulatory wedding announcement for Cari and Bob."

"Woo-hoo," he said half-heartedly.

"Listen already," she snapped at him. "They listed the wedding party's names. It says 'Beatrice *Rialto*, matron of honor. They're going to connect Cari's name to Robby's."

"I mean, it feels like a long shot for Follard and Brensteiner to see that *and* connect the dots that our favorite crime-solving journalist is related to NTS' CFO…and take it a step further to realize he's the one who turned over the financials to us," Alex challenged.

"Follard commented on it five minutes ago," Gen hissed at him.

"Crap," Alex said. "Let me call the guy who's watching him again. He said he left work early when I called earlier. We need to bring Follard in now," Alex agreed. "Our guy said he'd stick with him in case Brensteiner showed up."

"You should have gotten an email with access to the LoJack on Brensteiner's sister's car," Genevieve told him. "Did you see it?"

"Uh, yeah. I haven't tried to pull it up," Alex confessed.

"Your dino-phone won't let you. Get Grusky or Green to sign out one of the department's tablets to you. You can track him with that," Genevieve instructed.

"I'll do that right after I call the guy on Follard," Alex assured her. "Thanks to your previous call, I'm back at the precinct."

He found the sticky note with the officer's contact information and dialed him from the desk phone.

"Hey, it's Runimoss again. Is Follard still on the move?" he asked.

"No, he pulled over on the highway headed into Brenington...you know, the one on the north side?" the officer said. "Should I stay with him? I saw him pull onto the shoulder, so I went past him and pulled into the gas station on the opposite side of the highway."

"Stay on him. Call me if he moves. I'll be in touch," Alex said and grabbed his coat.

He patted his pocket to check for his keys and then zipped up the coat.

"LT!" he shouted as he walked toward the stairs. "I'm headed out to help find Brensteiner and maybe Follard too. I need to check out a tablet from Green first."

"Hold up," the lieutenant said and stepped out of his office. "What's going on?"

Alex stopped and let him catch up. He told him about the connection between Brensteiner and Follard and the post from the Beagle. "I just checked in with the uni that's been watching Follard. He said he left work early today and he isn't driving toward his house like he usually does. Viacorte is trying to get in touch with Rialto, but he isn't answering his phone."

"You're worried he's going after Rialto?" Grusky asked. "It makes sense."

"We can't be sure, but better safe than sorry. Maybe he's meeting Brensteiner somewhere and they're leaving town for good," Alex proposed and started inching toward the stairs again.

"Viacorte is off with the rehearsal thing?" Grusky asked.

"Yeah, she got Dureski to give me access to the LoJack on Brensteiner's sister's SUV. That's why I need the tablet," Alex said and hoped Grusky would let him leave already.

"Okay. Keep me posted," Grusky said and turned to go back to his office.

Alex took the stairs two at a time. He knocked on Dr. Green's office door and turned the knob at the same time.

"Detective Runimoss?' Dr. Green asked when he looked up.

"I need to take a tablet. I need to track a vehicle and my phone isn't capable," Alex explained.

Green grabbed his keys off his desk and stood up. "They're in the CSU office. Follow me."

Alex stepped out of Green's office and followed the older man to the crime scene unit. He opened one of the double doors and nodded to a woman seated at a desk.

"We're checking out a tablet," Green informed her.

She shrugged with indifference.

Green took a tablet from the charging cart and then scanned the code on the device. "I just need to enter your name into our spreadsheet. You break it, you buy it. Got it?"

Alex frowned. "I'll be careful with it."

Green handed him the tablet. "Happy hunting."

"Thanks, I'll bring it back on Monday," Alex assured him.

He hurried outside to his truck. It had four-wheel drive and he felt safer in it than in one of the old departmental cruisers. He climbed inside and tugged on his seatbelt. The tablet let him log in the same way he did for his desktop computer, which was a relief. He hated coming up with new passwords. He found the email from Dureski with the LoJack instructions. It took him a minute to get the tracking pulled up, but he finally saw the SUV's location on a map. It looked like it was headed toward Follard and Brenington. He put his phone up to his ear. For once he regretted not having a smart phone. He really needed two hands to steer in the wind.

"Gen! It's Alex. I'm heading out to find Brensteiner," he said and gave her a quick update. "Can you get Dureski to call me so we can work together on this?"

"Of course. I'm just about to park at the church. I'll get him your number and ask him to call," Gen replied.

"Did you get in touch with Robby?" he asked.

"No, but I have an idea about how to find him. I'll keep you posted," she promised and ended the call.

He set his phone in his lap next to the tablet and steered the truck toward the highway the patrolman had directed him to. It wasn't too far away, and since he'd be driving toward the city instead of away from it, he would avoid the rush hour traffic. His phone rang with an incoming call. He put the call on speaker.

"This is Runimoss," he said quickly.

"Detective. It's Agent Dureski. We're on our way to intercept Brensteiner, but I think you might be closer," Dureski informed him.

"Headed toward Brenington?" Alex asked.

"Yeah. I'm on my way out there now. We have no idea if he's armed and need to proceed with caution. Viacorte said you wanted to coordinate?" Dureski asked.

"Yeah, we have a guy on Follard, but now that we know he's not a victim, we need to bring him in. I'm worried he's going after Rialto," Alex added.

"I'm not sure he's going to connect the dots and realize Rialto is the whistleblower—" Dureski began.

"Rialto's sister-in-law is getting married tomorrow. They listed his wife's name in a social media post about the wedding. Follard commented on it. I think he knows," Alex explained.

"Shoot," Dureski said. "Okay, I'll call you back when I'm on Brensteiner."

"Can we just stay on the line?" Alex requested. "I feel like this could go sideways fast."

"Fine, but I don't want to hear any chitchat. Only talk to me if you have something relevant to say," Dureski demanded.

"Just how I like it," Alex said and set his phone in the passenger seat.

He was almost to the highway on the north side of Brenington. Hopefully, he'd come across the SUV soon.

* * * * *

The rehearsal was off to a rough start. Bob's friend Chad had irritated Aspen and possibly Cari's mom by going straight to the church kitchen to eat some of the refreshments for the wedding. Luckily, Bob had found him before he finished off more than one frozen fruit custard. Patricia had slaved away over those yesterday and was going to be mad that they were one short. Chad's comment of "my compliments to the chef" didn't win her over. Bob promised to keep Chad out of the kitchen.

On top of that, Jordan's girlfriend was wearing a very short white dress with at least four-inch stiletto heels. She tripped walking down the aisle and caught herself by grabbing one of the satin bows on the end of the pews. Aspen retied it, but not to Patricia's satisfaction, who felt it was necessary to make a big display of tying it herself. Several people were talking on their cell phones with the calls on speaker while they waited in the pews, which was sort of comical, but clearly irritating to Aspen. Cari's watch alerted her to an incoming call. She could feel Aspen's eyes on her as she answered her cell phone. The rehearsal was supposed to start soon, but neither Bea nor Genevieve were there yet. She showed the screen to Bob and he encouraged her to take the call.

"Hey, Gen. Are you close?" Cari asked. She didn't nag her friend about being late. It felt way too hypocritical.

"Uh, I'm in the hallway, but I need your help with something," Gen said vaguely.

Cari could hear an edge to her friend's voice. "Of course, I'm walking your way. What's going on?"

"I'll tell you when you get out here," Gen responded.

She kept her eyes down as she walked past Aspen. She wondered if she was the most frustrating bride the wedding planner had ever managed. Cari pushed open the sanctuary door and stepped into the hallway.

"Okay, I'm here," Cari said when she reached Gen.

"I need you to stay calm. Everything is under control and I'm only asking you this out of an abundance of caution," Gen began.

"Well, that's all basically freaking me out," Cari acknowledged.

Gen put her hands up. "Bear with me. There have been some updates in the last hour or so in the case Robby helped us with last summer. I'm concerned that people might have realized his role in taking down Stenoway and…whatever," she crossed her arms like she was wiping the slate clean. "I need to know where he is. Right now."

"You told me Robby wasn't in danger. You flat-out told me he was safe," Cari said feeling her heart rate quicken.

"I know and I'm sorry, but I can't help him if I can't find him," Gen replied.

"I mean, you know as much as me. Bea went to help him get his car started…" Cari reminded her.

"No, like his location. Didn't you mention their family has one of those locator-tracking things?" Gen asked.

197

"Yeah, Hilary has it on her phone. We can get her to give you access," Cari realized.

"I don't want to scare an eleven-year-old girl," Gen cautioned.

The door to the sanctuary opened and Hilary appeared. "Aunt Cari? I can't get my mom on the phone. Miss Aspen asked me to call her."

Cari jumped at the opportunity. "Let's see where your mom is...can you open the app you guys use for that?"

Hilary's face brightened. "Of course! I'd forgotten all about that."

She pressed her index finger against the phone's screen and swiped across it twice. "Here it is."

Genevieve reached across Cari to take the phone. "Oh, I see where she is. Your dad is there too. Looks like they're just a handful of miles away."

"I'll go let Miss Aspen know!" Hilary declared after retrieving her phone from Genevieve.

Cari turned to walk back toward the sanctuary, but Gen stopped her.

"I'm sorry, Cari. I know I'm supposed to be at this rehearsal and I'm a terrible friend for choosing work over your wedding rehearsal, but I need to go make sure they're okay," Genevieve said earnestly.

"Please, don't apologize. Just bring them here safely," Cari told her friend.

Genevieve rushed down the hallway toward the exit as Cari hurried back to the sanctuary. She paused before she opened the door. Part of her wanted to chase after Genevieve and help find Robby and Bea, but she owed it to Bob to stay at the rehearsal. She opened the door and saw everyone's heads turn her way when she walked in.

"Uh, hi. Slight change of plans. We might need to start a little late," Cari said. "And I know we're already starting late. At least it isn't my fault this time."

Chapter 14

Genevieve tried Robby's phone again. It went straight to voicemail. She knew the area they were in had spotty cell phone reception. She pulled onto the highway and watched for Bea's car in the oncoming traffic. She couldn't remember what Robby drove, but figured one vehicle would be right in front of the other one.

She used her Bluetooth to try to connect with Alex instead. The call rang through to his voicemail. He didn't like to talk on the phone and drive.

"Who am I kidding?" she asked herself out loud. "He doesn't like to talk on the phone period."

As a last-ditch effort, she dialed Dureski's phone.

"Viacorte, I've got your partner on the line too. He didn't know how to add a caller, so I told him to just not answer your call," Dureksi told her. "We're just about to catch up with Brensteiner. I thought you had a wedding thing this evening."

She grimaced. "I do, but I begged off…I mean, I'm going in a bit. I just needed to make sure Rialto and his wife are okay."

"Did you hear from them?" Alex asked her.

"No, but I got their location. They're on the highway north of Brenington. They were just about to reach the big curve that's cut into the hillside," she told him.

"I see Brensteiner," Dureksi remarked. "He's weaving in and out of traffic. How close are you, Runimoss?"

"I'm almost to the curve. I gotta go. My guy on Follard is calling. I'll let you handle Brensteiner," Alex said.

"How close are you to this curve, Viacorte?" Dureski asked.

"I think I'm a mile or two out still," she estimated.

Dureski swore into the phone. "Do the Rialtos drive a small sedan? A Honda maybe? Grey?"

"Uh, his wife has a car like that," Genevieve said. She pressed the gas pedal to pick up speed.

"Put your siren and lights on, Viacorte. This is about to go down. I'll call you back," Dureski said and ended the call.

"What?!" she asked to the dead connection.

Thankfully, she had her button light in the glove compartment. She pulled it out and put her window down so she could affix it to the roof of the Expedition. It had started to snow and several flakes blew into her car. The siren rang loud in her ears and she quickly put her window back up. She didn't know what Dureski had seen, but she hoped she got to Robby and Bea in time.

* * * * *

Bea gripped the steering wheel tighter. She wished she'd taken Robby up on his offer to drive her car to the rehearsal. They hadn't been able to get his car to start with the jumper cables, so they'd left it at the park and ride and would deal with it later. She hoped they wouldn't be too late for the rehearsal.

"So, is Cari a bridezilla?" Robby asked her.

"What?!" Bea glanced at him in surprise. "She's not at all. Really? You see Cari as a bridezilla?"

He laughed. "No, not really, but some people get a little crazy when it's their wedding day."

"She's been really chill. My mom is more of a diva about things than she is," she said. "It is really windy. The snow from last weekend is blowing across the road now."

"I think that's new snow. You could pull over and let me drive if you're uncomfortable," Robby offered.

"You're from the south. What do you know about driving in blowing snow?" she scoffed.

"I've lived here over a year now. I'm a fast learner," he reminded her.

"The SUV behind me is really close too. I'm not going that much under the speed limit," she complained. "I don't feel comfortable driving any faster than this. I wish they'd just go around me. There has been a passing lane from time to time. They just aren't using it."

Robby looked over his shoulder. "They do seem really close."

"*And* they have their brights on," Bea told him and squinted in the glare.

"Super annoying. Maybe they're from the south too," Robby said and gave a nervous laugh.

"Can't trust those Southerners," she teased him.

She could see the bend in the road up ahead. The lanes were a bit narrow as the road had been cut into the rocky hillside. Bea didn't like driving around it in the summer in broad daylight. It seemed especially hazardous now that it was dark and the wind was so strong. She looked in her rearview mirror. The other car seemed like it was even closer, but now she couldn't pull over. This part of the road didn't have a shoulder for about three miles. The guardrail was the only thing between them and the edge of a steep drop.

"Did you hear from the kids?" Robby asked. She knew he was trying to keep her mind off of the other driver.

"My dad texted that they were dressed and ready to go," she said. "My mom is bringing my dress to the church for me to put on before dinner."

"Right," he said and looked over his shoulder again. "What is this guy's problem? He's practically touching our bumper at this point."

Suddenly, her car lurched and she felt her body jerk forward. "Did he just bump my car?"

"What the hell?!" Robby said, unable to keep the fear out of his voice.

"We're catching up to the car in front of us now," Bea told him. "They're going really slow."

"I think they're trying to box us in," Robby told her.

"What do I do?" Bea asked in a panic.

"Stay calm. I'm going to call 911," he said and pulled out his phone. "Ugh. I only have one bar and it keeps disappearing. Service is always spotty between the park and ride and Brenington."

He lifted his phone and moved it around to get a better signal. "C'mon…okay, I think it's going to—"

"Ahh!"

Bea screamed as the other driver rammed them again. Robby dropped his phone into the foot well. He leaned down to pick it up. She wished she'd taken her car in to get the Bluetooth feature fixed. Her phone was in her purse in the back seat. They were almost through the big curve. Once the lanes widened again, she could move over to the shoulder and get out of the man's way. Robby was still trying to get his phone from under his seat.

"Just leave it. He's going to hit us again. You don't want to hit the dashboard," Bea told him.

"We have to call for help!" Robby exclaimed.

"Reach for my purse in the backseat instead. You can try my phone," she suggested.

The driver behind them pulled into the opposite lane. At first, Bea was relieved and started to slow down so he could pass them. Then he started to slow down too. He was going to try to force them over the edge.

"Got it!" Robby shouted.

"He's moved over to the left now. I think he's going to try to force us off the road," Bea told him.

"Maybe we can make him miss," Robby suggested.

"How?" Bea looked at him, her eyes wild with fear.

"Right as he swerves toward us, hit your brake. He'll miss and go over the edge himself," Robby explained.

"What if I spin out?" Bea asked.

"We have to hope for the best," Robby told her.

"Another car is coming from the other way now," she said and looked to see if she could move to the right any more.

"The SUV moved back behind us again. Maybe it's just an aggressive driver," Robby proposed.

The vehicle traveling in the opposite direction laid on his horn as he passed their car and the SUV.

"That's going to dissuade him," Bea said sarcastically. "Should I still try to brake if he gets back in the other lane?"

"Yes. Trust me. Here he comes. Brake!" Robby shouted at her.

She slammed her foot on the brake and their car started to fishtail. She gripped the steering wheel and watched in horror as the other car shot across their lane and toward the guard rail. The SUV clipped their front bumper and they started spinning. The airbag punched her in the face and her head whipped back into the headrest. Her shoulder ached too. She felt the car lurch again and figured they must have hit the vehicle in front of them. It reversed their spin back toward the edge of the road. A sickening crunch sounded in her ears and she realized the SUV had collided with the guardrail. She only caught a glimpse of the SUV rolling over the edge as their car spun closer and closer to the broken section of the railing. She tried to remember her driving lessons as a teenager and pumped the brake pedal instead of holding her foot onto it. The airbag slowly deflated and she swatted at it to try to keep control of the car. She wasn't sure which direction they were facing at first. The car was at an angle and she could see the drop off to her left instead of her right, which meant they were facing oncoming traffic. She looked over at Robby. His head bobbed like he was trying to shake himself out of a daze. They needed to get out of the car before it shifted and rolled down the steep hillside too.

"Robby? Are you okay? Did you hit your head?" she asked frantically. "Robby?!"

* * * * *

Genevieve twisted her steering wheel hard to the left. The Expedition wasn't great at making a U-turn, but she just needed to get to the edge of the road to shield the vehicles from oncoming traffic. She saw Bea's car teetering on the edge of the soft shoulder. The guardrail had been torn apart, leaving a ten-foot opening. She slammed her vehicle into park and jumped out. Up ahead, she could see Dureski with his phone up to his ear as he ran toward Bea's car. She raced down the road to catch up to him. She felt the post snap on one of her heels. She reached down and tore it off. She should have worn flats.

"Where's Robby?" she shouted as she got closer to him.

"He's in the car. He has a head injury. I don't know how bad it is. I'm calling for an ambulance," Dureski shouted back.

They reached the grey Honda and Genevieve saw Bea's panicked face through the cracked windshield. Robby was slumped against the passenger window. She could see a cut on his head and blood running down the window as well as his face.

Dureski opened the back passenger side door. Papers fluttered out into the wind.

"Ma'am, we're going to get you out of the car just as soon as the paramedics get here to assess your husband," Dureski assured her. "Did you see him hit his head? Do you think he might have a neck injury?"

"I don't know. The car rocks any time he moves at all. He was conscious just a moment ago, but now he's out again. He's breathing. I can see his chest moving," she told them. "I think I might have dislocated my shoulder. It's happened to me before."

"Bea, you said he was awake and moved?" Genevieve asked. She felt like that was a good sign.

"Yeah, he turned toward me and the car rocked toward the embankment over here. I screamed and leaned toward him to try to shift the weight back. He grabbed my hand for a second and then mumbled something and tilted against the window," she said over the howling wind. More papers flew out of the car. "Oh no! The wedding programs!"

"Cari will forgive you," Genevieve assured her. She heard approaching sirens. "I think the ambulance is arriving. They'll be able to stabilize Robby's neck and get him out of the car."

"But, if they take him out of the car, won't that throw off the balance?" Bea asked fearfully.

Dureski nodded. "She's right. Do you have any cables in your Expo? Or rope? Anything we can tie to the axles and use to keep this car on the road?"

Bea called out from the front seat. "I have jumper cables. Would those work?"

Dureski considered it. "It's worth a try. Viacorte. Pull your vehicle up closer and be sure to pull your parking brake. I have a rope in the Suburban we can use for the back axle. We'll tie the jumper cables to the front one."

"The jumper cables are on the back seat," Bea said and pointed.

Dureski grabbed them and handed them to Genevieve.

"Wait, where is Alex?" she asked realizing he'd been part of the tracking team too.

"He's chasing down Follard. The Rialto's car clipped his on its way toward the edge of the road, but he managed to keep from spinning and took off back north, away from Brenington. That happened right as Runimoss arrived on scene, so he just stayed on him," Dureski explained.

"I'll call him after we tie off this vehicle," Genevieve said.

"I requested a blockade, but it's possible Follard will get off the highway before he reaches it," Dureski told her. "I've also asked them to get a chopper out to track him."

Two ambulances and a firetruck pulled up just as Genevieve reached her vehicle. The firetruck blocked the traffic coming from Brenington. One ambulance pulled around her and positioned itself next to Bea's car. The other pulled alongside the guardrail right behind her. She put her vehicle in drive and closed the gap between her vehicle and Bea's Honda. She climbed out of the driver's seat and slammed the door.

"We're going to check out the vehicle below," the paramedics behind her shouted as they got out of the ambulance.

"Car below?" she asked in confusion.

"Yeah, the one that broke the guardrail," one of the paramedics responded.

Dureski was on his back under the Suburban. He inched himself back out and held up the opposite end of the rope.

"There's another vehicle?" Genevieve asked him.

"Brensteiner. There's no way he survived the crash. He slammed into the guardrail and went through the windshield," Dureski told her. "No seatbelt."

"You saw it happen?" she asked in surprise.

"Yeah, he tried to ram the Rialtos from the side and they hit the brakes just in the nick of time. He shot past them, right into the guardrail," Dureski said and pantomimed a car sailing over the edge.

"Did anyone look?" Genevieve asked with trepidation.

"I saw his head go through the windshield, Viacorte. He's dead," Dureski assured her.

She heard a radio crackle and looked toward the firemen standing nearby.

We've got one dead body down here. Lacerations to neck, face, and chest. Vehicle is probably totaled.

"Copy that."

"Told you," Dureski said and shrugged. "Hey, you're small. Want to tie this other end to their rear axle for me?"

She cringed inwardly. Her nice clothes were going to get ruined along with her shoes. She handed him the jumper cables and took the end of the rope from him. "The Expo is further off the ground. You can work on it while I tie this off."

He grinned. "Good bargaining skills."

She got on the ground and looped the rope over the axle. After tying a square knot, she tugged on the rope to be sure it was secure. The ground was cold and her fingers ached through her gloves as she pushed herself back upright.

"Done!" she called out.

"We've got the patient's neck secure. We'll pull him from the vehicle once you give us the go ahead," a paramedic told her.

Genevieve got out her cell phone and unlocked it. She only had a bar or two of signal. Time to get an update from Alex. Before she could touch the phone symbol next to his name, a call came in from Shelly.

"Shelly! Thanks for returning my call," Genevieve said. "I'm sorry to bother you on a Friday evening, but I need to know about the other man you were seducing."

"Other man...?" Shelly asked in a confused tone. "I only seduced Pierce. That was it."

"You don't know anyone named Follard?" Genevieve asked.

"I have no idea who that is," Shelly told her. "If it helps, I can show you the envelope of photos. They're only of me with Pierce. You can ask the guy from that terrible motel. I was only with Pierce."

"It's okay, I believe you. I regret not asking about Follard before. We maybe could have prevented some things, but hindsight is twenty-twenty, right?"

"If you say so," Shelly responded. "Anything else?"

"No, that's all I needed," Genevieve said and ended the call.

* * * * *

Alex scowled at the man in the driver's seat. "Do you realize how much trouble you're in?"

Follard smirked at him with a bloody smile. "Prove it. I'm a victim, remember?"

"Nice try. We've been enlightened. You fooled us and the FBI last summer, but now we know the whole story. Step out of the car with your hands up," Alex instructed him.

"I need medical assistance. I could have a neck injury!" Follard whined. "I hit my mouth on the steering wheel when that idiot clipped me back there."

"Might have chipped a tooth too," Alex observed. "And you should know better than to leave the scene of an accident. Especially one you were involved in."

"I was scared. The other drivers were all over the road. I didn't know if it was safe," Follard claimed.

"Keep your hands where I can see them. The paramedics should be here any second," Alex informed him and read him his rights. "I'm going to cuff you to your steering wheel for now."

He got out his handcuffs and secured Follard to the steering wheel. He heard another siren approaching and looked back to see an ambulance.

"See? What did I tell you? Medical assistance has arrived," Alex told Follard.

The paramedics walked over to where Alex was standing. "Are the handcuffs necessary?"

"I haven't been able to check for a weapon. This man is accused of killing five, maybe even six people," Alex told them. "He claims he might have a neck injury."

"We'll get him in a C-collar and then we'll need you to uncuff him so we can put him on a stretcher. You can cuff him to that," the paramedic said.

"Cool. My cell phone is ringing. I'll be right over here if you need me," he said and pointed to the hood of the car. "Follard. I've got my eyes on you. Don't try anything."

Follard rolled his eyes.

Alex answered the incoming call from Gen. "Hey, Gen. Got an update for me?"

"Brensteiner is dead. He went through the windshield," Gen said crisply.

He cringed. "Yuck. That sounds like a mess. What else?"

He listened as she relayed her conversation with Shelly to him. "And the Rialtos?"

"They're getting Robby out of the car now. We tied off their vehicle to keep it from rolling over the edge. Once Robby is out, they can help Bea climb over the middle and onto solid ground," Gen explained. "Their car is totaled. What's the story with Follard? It doesn't sound like you're still driving, but I can tell you're outside. The wind is loud."

"The roadblock caught him. The paramedics are checking him out now. He requested medical assistance for a neck injury," Alex said. "I think he's making it up."

"Dureski wants to be part of the interview," Gen said. "I'd love to be there too, but I need to go to the rehearsal and give Cari an update."

"You said the paramedics had to help Robby out of the car. What's his status?" Alex asked with concern.

"He's been in and out of consciousness. I'm not sure if it's a bad concussion or something more," Gen said quietly.

"So, what's his wife going to do? Rehearsal or hospital?" Alex asked.

"She needs to go to the hospital. The airbag slammed into her. She might have whiplash from it and I think I heard her say something about a dislocated shoulder. I told her I'd get back to the church and explain everything to the family," Genevieve said.

"What happens with the wedding now?" Alex asked.

"I have no idea. Cari's packed and ready to move into Bob's apartment. Her lease is up any day now," Genevieve explained. "But I can't imagine her getting married without her sister there. I need to let you go. Bea just got out of the car. I'll be in touch."

Alex closed his flip phone and stuffed it into his pocket. Follard had on the C-collar and the paramedics were waving him over. He took out his keys.

"I'll unlock these as soon as you have the stretcher over here," he told the paramedics. "Where are you going to take him?"

"Probably Brenington West. It's the closest. I think that's where the other ambulance is headed too," the paramedic said.

"Good to know," Alex responded.

They brought the stretcher over to Follard's vehicle. Alex leaned into the front seat and unlocked one handcuff. He kept his hand on Follard's wrist as he removed the chain from the steering wheel. Then he clamped the handcuff back down on Follard's wrist.

"Hey, they said you could cuff me to the stretcher," Follard complained.

"Newsflash, idiot. No one trusts you," Alex remarked.

They helped him out of the vehicle and onto the stretcher. Alex repeated the process and secured one side of the handcuffs to the stretcher. He got out a zip tie and tightened Follard's other wrist to the opposite side.

"He's good to go. I'll meet you at the hospital," Alex told them.

Chapter 15

Genevieve slowly got out of her car and let out a long breath. She wasn't looking forward to talking to the family inside the church. They'd been waiting for her to return for almost an hour. She hoped they'd gone ahead and started the rehearsal without her and Bea. She looked down at her coat and cringed. It was covered in streaks of dirt and gravel from her time on the asphalt. She brushed it off as best she could and kept walking in her broken heels.

She made her way inside the church and heard music coming from the sanctuary. That seemed like a good sign. Maybe people weren't fearfully wondering what was happening with Bea and Robby. She wondered if Hilary was suspicious by this point. The girl was quiet, but very observant.

Genevieve pulled open the door to the sanctuary. The singing stopped as one by one, they all turned to look her way. She gave a slight smile and walked down the aisle. She hadn't met Bob's groomsmen yet, but knew the best man was his brother. The other young man wore a Hawaiian shirt and looked like he should be holding a surfboard on the beach instead of standing near the altar of a church. She remembered Cari had mentioned Bob's college roommate lived in California and was a bit of a trip. She tried to smile at everyone, but felt certain it looked like more of a grimace.

"I'm sorry for keeping you waiting. Uh, I'm glad you went ahead and started without me," she said when she reached the front few pews. "I have an update."

Bob looked from her to Hilary and Joel. He raised his eyebrows. She gave him a quick nod. Bob squeezed Cari's hand and tugged her to sit down next to the two children. Hilary's eyes filled with tears.

"Oh no! What happened? Where are my parents?" she sobbed.

Joel looked from Bob to Genevieve. "They aren't with you. Where are they?"

Genevieve put her hands up. "Let me say first, that your parents are fine. They are okay."

She heard several people exhale. She crouched down in front of the two children.

"They were in a car accident on their way to the rehearsal and your dad hit his head, but I spoke with him before I left to come back here. He was a little shaken up, but the paramedics both assured me that his vitals look good and he's going to be fine," she said and put a hand on Joel's knee. "They took both your parents to get checked out at the hospital in Brenington and that's where they are right now."

"You're sure they're okay?" Hilary asked in a small voice.

"Yes, sweet girl. I wouldn't lie to you, right?" Genevieve said and looked into her eyes.

Hilary nodded and wiped away another tear.

Bob looked at Cari. "What do you want to do?"

Cari tried to carefully wipe her tears away without smudging her makeup. "I don't know. I…I…I should go be with Bea, but I need to be here too."

"Go be with your sister," Bob said confidently. "We know how to get married, right?"

Cari pulled him into a hug and he kissed the top of her head. Genevieve heard someone stand up and looked over her shoulder. The wedding planner was on her feet.

"Bob, Cari, well…this is a first for me," she began. "I have to agree with Bob, though. As long as the minister is good with how we stand?"

The man standing behind Bob and Cari nodded. "Like Bob said, we made it through the basic steps. Why don't you go check on your loved ones? Call me at any time. If we need to postpone, I'll take care of notifying your guests. Don't let this be an added stress right now."

Cari released Bob's hand and stood up. "Dad, I think Joel's car seat is still in your rental car, right?"

"We can drive the kids over to the hospital," Darren said.

"Great," Cari replied. "I'll get a couple things squared away with Bob and meet you there."

Hilary and Joel walked over to Cari's parents and the four of them gathered up their coats, gloves, and hats. Genevieve touched Cari's arm to get her attention.

"Did you have more to add? Something you didn't want the kids to hear?" Cari asked with concern.

Genevieve hesitated. "Let me give you a ride to the hospital so we can talk."

Cari searched Genevieve's face for understanding. "What is it? What are you not telling me?"

"I'll explain in the car, okay?" Genevieve pleaded with her eyes.

Cari looked from her to Bob and back. Genevieve felt sick to her stomach.

"You're coming to the hospital, right, Aunt Cari?" Joel's voice broke the tension.

"I'll be right behind you, buddy," Cari assured him.

"Okay!" he responded and grabbed Darren's hand.

"Grandmother, do you want to go to the hospital too?" Cari asked.

Cari's grandma pushed herself off the pew. "It sounds like there's going to be quite a crowd at the hospital."

Cari's cousin Aaron spoke up. "I'll make sure Grandmother gets where she wants to go."

"Thank you, Aaron," their grandma said. "Give Bea my love."

"I will, Grandmother," Cari said and nodded. "Bob, what are we going to do?"

Bob pulled Cari into a hug. Genevieve could see her shoulders bobbing with each sob. A couple that couldn't be anyone other than Bob's parents joined them.

"Bob, should we call the restaurant and cancel?" his mom asked.

He pursed his lips. "I'm not sure what the right thing to do is. On the one hand, we need to eat. They won't have room for all of us at the hospital. I want to be respectful, though. It would feel weird to have a celebratory dinner while they're at the hospital."

Cari lifted her face from Bob's shoulder. "No, don't cancel. Genevieve said that Bea and Robby only have minor injuries, right?"

Genevieve swallowed. "That's what the paramedics told me."

"I'll call you once I see Bea and let you know what my plan is. I might be late, or I might ask you to place a to-go order for me. Is that okay?" she asked Bob.

"That's fine. Whatever you need, Cari," Bob told her.

Cari kissed Bob on his cheek, then turned to Genevieve and they started to walk away. Bob's mom called out to them.

"Give Bea and Robby our love. We're praying for them," Margie said with her hands clasped at her chest.

"Thanks. I will," Cari responded.

Neither of them spoke until they reached the parking lot. Genevieve unlocked the Expedition with her fob.

216

"What is it that you couldn't say in front of everyone else?" Cari asked with a hint of anger in her voice.

"Cari, I...I feel responsible for all of this," Genevieve confessed as they climbed into the SUV. "I'm so sorry."

"Responsible? What do you mean?" her friend asked.

"If I'd just let this go, Stenoway would still be alive, your sister and Robby wouldn't have gotten hurt...I just had to be right and look what I've done," Genevieve said and felt tears in her eyes again.

"This wasn't just an unfortunate car accident?" Cari asked as Genevieve started the car.

Genevieve shook her head. "No. All this time, I was certain that Stenoway had a partner. I just couldn't figure out who it was. Alex told me to let it go. It had been six months and no one else had died. Case closed."

"But you had doubts. I had doubts too, remember?" Cari asked.

"It's my job to keep people safe. I was reckless. I should have had protection for Robby. I should have realized when Bea told us his car wouldn't start that it wasn't just bad luck. One of the previous victims had a dead car battery. I was so caught up in finding Stenoway's partner, I missed obvious clues and that almost cost your loved ones their lives," Genevieve said and gulped.

Cari was silent for a few moments. Genevieve's stomach flipped and she had to stop herself from gagging. She'd never had a case go this way; never felt like finding the bad guy had come at too great a cost.

"I'm so sorry, Cari," Genevieve said again.

They'd reached the hospital. She pulled into a spot near the entrance and put her car in park.

"I asked you if he was safe," Cari said and wiped tears off her cheeks. "You promised me no one knew about him."

"I…thought he was…protected. His name wasn't on anything. Stenoway confessed, so there was no trial, no discovery phase where we had to turn over all of our findings. No one knew he'd come to us," Genevieve said.

"How did they find him then? How did they know to go after him?" Cari asked.

"Um, I think it was the Beagle's post about your wedding," Genevieve said gently. "Follard saw it and made the connection between you and Bea and of course, Bea and Robby."

"I should go inside," Cari said softly.

"I'll come with you," Genevieve offered and started to turn the car off.

"No, I think you've done enough," Cari told her. "I'll…text you later."

Genevieve watched her friend hurry into the hospital. The wind whipped her curls around, spoiling any effort Cari had made to look her best. Genevieve put the Expedition in reverse and sighed. She didn't know how to make this right.

* * * * *

Cari walked up to the visitor's desk with her ID out. The college student behind the desk smiled and put her hand out to take it.

"Oh, I know you," the young woman said. "You're basically a legend at my school."

Cari smiled, but didn't respond to the woman's statement. She just wanted to see her sister. "I'm here to visit Beatrice Rialto and Robert Rialto. Are they in the same room?"

She typed on the computer keyboard. "Looks like he is getting an MRI, but she is in 315. The elevators are right over there. Here's your visitor badge. Has to be visible at all times. Visiting hours end at eight o'clock."

"Thanks," Cari said and stuck the badge to her coat.

The elevator arrived and Cari pressed the button with the three on it. She remembered the layout from her time visiting another patient a year before. She chewed on the inside of her cheek as the elevator ascended the two floors. Genevieve had seemed sincere when she apologized, but Cari was hurt. She knew what it was like to track down a killer and identify the bad guy. She knew that thrill, but had she ever put someone else's life at risk just to get a story? Maybe she was being unfair to her friend. She couldn't think about that right now. This wasn't how she expected to spend the eve of her wedding day. She shook the thoughts from her head and stepped off the elevator. She needed to see that her sister was okay. She walked down the hallway to Bea's room. She could hear people talking before she reached room 315; their voices sounded joyful, so maybe that was a good sign.

"Knock, knock," she said as she opened the door. "Oh, Bea. I'm so sorry. Are you okay?"

Her sister had a neck brace on and her arm was in a sling. She had two black eyes and her mascara had run down her face, but she was smiling. Joel was sitting in her lap on the bed while Hilary was stroking her hair from her position beside the bed.

Bea's smile broadened. "I'm fine. They should be by any minute to remove this neck brace. I told them my neck was sore from the airbag hitting me in the face. I haven't looked in the mirror, but Joel told me I had the best zombie makeup he's ever seen."

"It's true," Joel said and laughed.

"Genevieve didn't say anything about your arm. What's wrong with it?" Cari asked with concern.

"I dislocated my shoulder. They popped it back in, but I need to wear this sling for a few days while everything tightens back up," Bea said easily. "It's no big deal. Hey, I'm okay. You didn't need to come check on me. I told Genevieve to tell you to go to the rehearsal dinner. It sounded like it was going to be another night of amazing food."

"Are you kidding? I had to come. I needed to see that you're okay," Cari told her.

"I'm completely fine," Bea assured her.

"What about Robby? They said he needed an MRI? That sounds serious," Cari said.

"I think it's standard, but I don't know," Bea remarked. "He hit his head pretty hard. They need to make sure it's just a concussion. He was alert and coherent before we left the scene of the accident, so I'm sure he's fine too."

"I'm so sorry, Bea," Cari said again.

"Why are you sorry? You didn't try to run me off the road," Bea told her.

"But…" Cari paused and looked at Hilary and Joel.

"We're back with ice cream sandwiches!" Darren said as he and Patricia stepped inside the hospital room.

"I want one!" Joel shouted and hopped off the bed.

"Let's go eat them in the visitor's area. Bea doesn't want you to drip ice cream on her bed," Patricia said as she took his hand. "Are you coming, Hilary?"

Hilary looked at her mom. "I don't know. What if Mom needs us?"

"Aunt Cari is here! She's fine. Let's go eat the ice cream!" Joel shouted.

"Go enjoy your treat, sweetheart," Bea encouraged.

The group exited the room with Joel in the lead. Cari stepped closer to her sister's bed.

"I can't believe this happened. I asked Genevieve…she promised me Robby wasn't in danger," Cari said as her eyes filled with tears again.

"Oh, Cari. She didn't see this coming. Robby's boss caused all this. He's a really evil man. Don't be angry at your friend. She was trying to do her job," Bea said and reached for Cari's hand.

"I feel betrayed. I feel like she chose being right and getting the guy over your safety," Cari argued.

"She's stubborn. How many times have you put your job before everything else?" Bea asked softly.

Cari swallowed. "My job description doesn't include the words 'serve and protect' in any way, but you're right, I'm not blameless either. If I hadn't been so focused on trying to find Marjorie's cousin, I could have pushed Gen to get Robby some protection. I hardly gave him a second thought."

"Oh, c'mon, Care-Bear. Look at me. I'm still here. I've dislocated my shoulder before. You know that. It's a repetitive injury. I could have slipped on the ice and had it happen just as easily. And Robby is fine too. I promise. It was scary in the moment. The car was spinning and the guardrail was missing, but Genevieve got there and rushed in to secure our car. She helped us get out safely. You can forgive her," Bea said and squeezed Cari's hand. "Me, on the other hand. She's going to have to carry your train tomorrow. I can't handle all that fabric with one hand. She owes me that much."

Cari raised her eyebrows. "We can postpone the wedding. You were in a car accident. Bob will understand."

"Oh no, we are not postponing this wedding. I have put too much time and energy into making it beautiful the last three days. I am not tying another twenty bows for a wedding until it's Hilary's turn to walk down that aisle. The wedding is happening tomorrow," Bea said pointedly.

"Ok, Queen Bee. I guess I should call Bob and let him know," Cari said and wiped more tears from her cheeks. "We're really getting married tomorrow."

* * * * *

Alex didn't like hospitals. They smelled bad and if you were in one, that meant someone was not doing well. He set down the chair he'd commandeered from the second floor visitor's area. The medical staff wouldn't let him into Follard's room until they were finished cleaning him up. He planned to camp out by the door until he was given the all-clear.

His height allowed him to see into the small window on the door. He tried to peer into it from his seat, but all he could see was the back of the nurse's head. He slumped down in the chair a bit. Dureski said he was coming to the hospital too, but the FBI guy hadn't arrived yet.

Voices at the end of the hallway caught his attention. He squinted and saw a nurse pushing someone in a wheelchair with a large bandage on their head. The elevators were just past Alex's seat in the hallway and he figured that was their destination. The nurse slowed to a stop before she got there. Alex recognized the patient.

"Robby! Good to see you upright, man," Alex said and stood up to shake his hand. Robby was wearing sunglasses.

"Sir, you can't move the chairs," the nurse said ignoring Alex's greeting.

Alex pulled out his badge. "I'm BPD. The patient in this room is under my jurisdiction."

The nurse rolled her eyes.

"How are you, Robby?" Alex asked before the nurse could push him the rest of the way to the elevator.

"Got a pretty bad headache, but they told me it's just a concussion. No brain bleed, so I guess that's good," Robby said. "I did have to get stitches on my forehead, so there goes my chance at modeling. I'm also going to have to wear sunglasses indoors for a day or two—"

"You should do it for a week!" the nurse growled at him.

"Right. Anyway, I've been better, but I could be a lot worse," Robby said. "She's taking me up to see Bea, but I think we're going to get discharged tonight."

The nurse snorted. Alex ignored her. "That's great! I'm glad you're both okay. I can't believe how this played out. We were just one step behind. Genevieve had been telling us for months that we got it wrong. We should have listened sooner."

"She's pretty smart from what I hear. Well, I'd better get moving. See you around," Robby said and the nurse immediately pushed him up to the elevator doors.

When the elevator doors opened, Dureski stepped out. He nodded a hello to Robby before joining Alex outside of Follard's room.

"When will they let us talk to him?" Dureski asked.

"They're cleaning him up. Hopefully, soon. I saw him on the street. He got popped in the mouth by the airbag, but he's fine. Just trying to play victim again," Alex told Dureski.

"I really dropped the ball on this. Follard fooled me and I wouldn't listen to Viacorte when she tried to tell me Stenoway had a partner," Dureski said and shook his head. "Your partner does not let up until she gets the answers she knows are out there. She's relentless."

"It's hard keeping up with her sometimes, but she's a good cop," Alex agreed.

"Is she here too?" Dureski asked.

"No, she's...well, I'm not sure where she ended up. She's a bridesmaid in that reporter's wedding tomorrow," Alex said.

"The Turnlyle woman?" Dureski asked.

"Yeah, Genevieve is friends with her," Alex said and shrugged. "For a reporter, she's not bad."

"She did a lot of the legwork in the Stenoway case. Made me second guess my vow to never trust the press," Dureski said and laughed.

The hospital room door opened and the nurse stuck her head out. "Mr. Follard can speak with you now."

The two men entered the room. Alex brought his chair inside too. He knew the rooms never had adequate seating for visitors.

"Mr. Follard, we meet again," Dureski said.

Follard refused to look at them.

"I don't like being lied to, Mr. Follard," Dureski told him. "You know that's a federal offense, right? Even the crime drama writers know that."

Follard continued to stare at the wall.

"You really pulled the wool over my eyes last summer. I have to hand it to you. Now, I can see much more clearly. Were you the ringleader or was it your college pal, Brensteiner?" Dureski asked him. "See, the way I figure it, you're the smarter one. You have this huge technology company. Everyone wants to use your software. Your company is growing off the charts.

"Brensteiner though? He's nothing more than a fake lawyer. He even has his sister fooled there. She thought he practiced estate law, but he's just a paralegal. Barely scraping by until the two of you hooked up again.

"Yeah, he went to law school. We dug up his graduation records, but he never passed the New York state bar exam. That's a problem when you're trying to practice law. You really need that little piece of paper," Dureski said in a mocking tone. "Brensteiner was the ladies' man though, right? He was the popular one. You knew how to make a good plan and Greg knew how to execute it. And then Stenoway…ah, Stenoway. How many times did you use that guy? He thought of himself as one of the boys, but he wasn't, was he? He was your whipping boy. Was it your idea to kill him? Or was it Brensteiner's? You know, Detective Runimoss, I almost have this whole thing figured out. Follard is some kind of greedy bastard. He figured out how to get new clients and funnel money out of his company into his personal account. His business was getting new clients all the time. Everyone loves NTS. He created a division in the company called 'Expansion and Recruitment' to help funnel new clients into their system. But you know what?" Dureski turned to Alex.

"What?" Alex asked, playing along.

"NTS doesn't have any employees who work on the E and R team. Isn't that odd? That division gets a lot of money every month," Dureski explained. "But the account isn't getting bigger and bigger. It transfers money all over the place. Some goes to an offshore account and a little bit was going to our pal, Anderson Stenoway, but he's dead now, so that will stop. Follard got Brensteiner to take Stenoway out."

"Right. Stenoway knew too much. I think they were giving him money to take the fall. I don't know how they expected him to spend any of it," Alex said and scratched his head. "You can't make withdrawals from a frozen account."

"That's true, and the victim's families are probably filing wrongful death suits, so that could get expensive," Dureski agreed. "Do you think they promised him that money?"

Alex looked at Follard. He didn't seem to be enjoying their charade. "Stop us if we're getting any of this wrong, Follard."

The man just glared at Alex.

"Let's see," Alex said and pretended like he lost his train of thought. "Oh, right, the money and the *new* account you put in Stenoway's name. I think it was Brensteiner's account initially. Did he volunteer to put Stenoway's name on that account or did you tell him he had to? It doesn't matter," Alex replied when Follard remained silent. "You see, my partner has looked at these accounts every day for months. She probably knows them better than you do. She had a hunch that you guys transferred that account into Stenoway's name to hide your role in the scheme, but she couldn't prove it."

"Then, you slipped up and decided to kill Mr. Stenoway. Yeah, it saves you two-k every month, but it put you right back in my crosshairs. I thought you were a victim this whole time. If I hadn't seen you try to force that couple off the road—your own employee! Ruthless…anyway, I might have questioned it, but here we are. You're the only one left, so the buck stops here, Mr. Follard," Dureski growled.

"I want a lawyer," Follard said with his teeth bared. "You can't prove any of this."

"Oh, but we can. You know who keeps really detailed records? Banks. And now that we have proof of your involvement, they're more than happy to turn over all the account details to us. You're done, Follard," Dureski said with a smirk. "Enjoy the freedoms you have within this hospital room because you are getting discharged to my care. And you are not going to enjoy it one bit. As for a lawyer, do you have one on retainer? Or do you need a new lawyer now? Brensteiner went through the windshield, so he can't pretend to defend you."

"I'm really curious about one thing," Alex interjected.

"What's that?" Dureski asked.

"Why do any of this? What happened that made you think these were good life choices?" Alex asked.

Follard didn't say anything, but his eyes grew wide. Alex heard the door open and the sound of high heels clicking on the linoleum. A woman with bleach-blonde hair marched up to the foot of Follard's hospital bed.

"I got a notification that your vehicle was in an accident," she said icily. "Normally, I would have been really worried, but the freaking FBI showed up at our door about ninety minutes before that. They wanted to know where you were and they had a warrant to search our home. Do you know how violating that feels?!"

Dureski grabbed Alex's arm. "We should go."

"Oh, no. I want you to stay. I'm going to file for divorce, so none of this will fall under spousal privilege, Damien. You piece of trash," she snarled at him. "I believed you when you told me NTS was having record quarters. You said our ownership of the company was paying us dividends. Two thousand dollars every month. I'm such an idiot for thinking those would come in monthly. You were embezzling from our company! You're running it into the ground. You refused to form a board of directors and now I know why. They would have seen all the things you were up to. Charging clients a 'setup fee' of two hundred dollars and keeping all of that instead of putting it back into the company."

Follard put up his hands. "I can explain. I thought you liked our lifestyle. Going to the opera and professional sporting events…driving luxury cars…"

"Shut up, Damien," she growled. "The money isn't even the worst of it, you greedy pig. You had people *killed* when they tried to question your methods. You and that no-good Greg Brensteiner. I heard he died in the accident. Good riddance. Just two frat boys who never grew up and never heard the word 'no' from anyone. Well, you're going to hear it now. You disgust me."

Follard's wife slapped him on the face and then marched back out of the room. "You'll be hearing from my lawyer. I'll be sure to give him the number to the prison that I hope you rot in, you coward."

Alex looked at Dureski. "I guess that clears some of it up."

"I want to press charges," Follard said.

"Excuse me?" Dureski asked.

"She hit me. That's assault," Follard whined.

"Shut up, Follard," Dureski replied.

"I'll go track down the nurse and see when we can spring you from here, Mr. Follard. You might want to ask your lawyer to call your dentist too. It looks like you lost a tooth in your battle with the airbag tonight," Alex told him.

He shook Dureksi's hand and exited the room in search of the nurse's station. It was way past the end of his shift. Maybe the feds would offer him some overtime pay. He laughed to himself. Too bad Gen wasn't with him to enjoy that joke.

Chapter 16

The bridal room had a full-length mirror. Cari stood in front of it and stared at herself. She'd grown her hair out for the wedding and her brown curls hung well past her shoulders. Her green eyes were bright with tears. She tried to blink them back. Today was supposed to be a happy day. She *was* happy, thrilled even, to be marrying Bob. She was also overwhelmed with the events of the past week.

Her right hand rubbed her locket. She released it and looked down at her nails. Somehow, they were still flawless. The photographer would be pleased when he took photos later.

"There were times I thought I might never witness this day," her dad's voice broke into her thoughts.

"Daddy," Cari said and turned to face him.

"I'm proud of you, Cari. I know yesterday was a hard day and it felt like everything was spiraling out of control, but we made it to today. It's time to walk in now. Are you ready?" he asked and extended his arm.

She smiled. "I am. Let's do this."

She tucked her hand around his forearm and they walked out of the room. Her train flowed behind her and thankfully, didn't snag on anything. Aspen was standing at the entrance to the sanctuary. She handed Cari her bridal bouquet. Cari held it in her left hand. Aspen pulled open the doors and the organist played the opening bars of the Wedding March. Everyone rose to their feet and turned to look at her. She blinked back another wave of tears and began the procession toward the aisle.

Mr. Ollaman and his wife, along with Michelle and Bryson from the Beagle, sat together in the back row. It looked like most of their guests had positioned themselves near the aisle so they could see better. She smiled at her co-workers and then turned to walk down the aisle.

Bob's face broke into a wide smile when he saw her take the first step in the aisle. She felt her smile stretch across her face as she returned his gaze. For a moment it felt like time froze and then suddenly the minister was speaking.

"Who gives this woman to be wed today?" Pastor Sam asked.

"Her mother and I," her dad responded.

Cari gave Bob the side eye. They'd shared a laugh about the somewhat archaic liturgy the church still used as though she wasn't capable of choosing a husband for herself. Her dad placed her hand into Bob's and she joined him on the landing near the pastor.

The short ceremony continued without a hitch. Cari couldn't stop smiling as the pastor finished with the final words of the liturgy. She had goosebumps on her arms as she realized they were actually married.

"...I now pronounce you man and wife. You may kiss the bride," Pastor Sam announced.

Bob squeezed Cari's hands and they leaned in and shared their first kiss as husband and wife. She felt tears pricking the corners of her eyes as her emotions ran high. Bob released her right hand and they walked down the aisle together as Mr. and Mrs. for the first time. Aspen escorted them to the pastor's office where they were to wait until the guests had emptied from the sanctuary.

"You did it!" Aspen exclaimed. "I wasn't sure we were going to be here today."

"It almost felt like fate was against us getting married," Cari agreed.

The office door opened and Bea, Genevieve, Jordan, and Chad entered with the pastor.

"Who is ready to sign their marriage license?" Pastor Sam asked and clapped his hands together.

Cari and Bob laughed and raised their hands. "We are," they responded in unison.

"A united front. I like that," the pastor said. "I need two witnesses to sign after them."

"The photographer wants a photo. He'll be over in a moment, I'm sure," Aspen reminded them.

"We can stage it again, if necessary," Pastor Sam assured her.

He handed Cari a pen and she signed "Caroline Ann Turnlyle" in the appropriate blank. Bob scratched in "Bobby Gene Hursley" in his spot and then offered the pen to Bea.

"Uh, I'm not a lefty, so..." she looked at Cari and then at Genevieve.

"Of course, I can sign," Genevieve said and took the pen from Bob.

"Thanks, Gen," Cari said and stepped back from the desk.

Genevieve wrote her name above "Witness #1" and then turned to give the pen to Jordan.

"You sure this is valid?" Jordan asked with a grin.

"Just sign your name, man," Bob begged him. "No funny business."

He held up three fingers to his head. "Scout's honor."

"You were never a scout," Bob reminded him.

"It's the thought that counts," Jordan argued. "Okay, okay. No funny business. Jordan David Hursley. Done."

"It's a party in here!" the photographer said from the doorway. "Do you have room for one more?"

"Why don't I take Genevieve and Chad back to the sanctuary? I'm sure Hilary and Joel are looking for their mom, so don't take too long with this photo," Aspen instructed.

The photographer gave them space to exit. "Okay, let's give the bride the pen...yes, and...everyone look at the marriage license...good. Onward to the sanctuary."

They filed out of the pastor's office and back to the sanctuary. Genevieve grabbed Cari's hand in the hallway.

"It was an honor to stand up with you today, Cari," she said as they continued to walk. "I'm glad you still wanted me here."

Cari smiled sheepishly. "Last night, Bea told me I was being pigheaded. Thanks for giving me space to be angry and still agreeing to be a bridesmaid after I stomped away from you at the hospital."

"I'm proud to be your friend, Cari Turnlyle, uh, should I say Hursley now? Anyway, let's go take some photos," Genevieve said. "We should hurry or Alex will have eaten all your food at the reception."

Cari laughed. "He better not. I'm starving! Getting married is hard work."

They entered the sanctuary again and Bob's groomsman Chad rushed up to her with three Hawaiian shirts on hangers.

"Bob said we had to keep wearing our tuxes, but...and hear me out...I think these shirts will complement the bridesmaids' dresses even better. I bought one for all the guys," he said with a big smile.

"Uh, that's Bob's call," Cari said and laughed.

Bob was at the front of the sanctuary shaking his head and slashing his arms in the universal sign for no.

"Chad!" he yelled. "I said no. No means no. You're in the tux for another half hour. Smile nice for the photos and it might be less than that."

Chad frowned. "He's such a rule follower sometimes. You need to work on that."

Cari laughed again. "I'll see what I can do."

The End

Ready for more Cari and friends? Stay tuned for Book 8 in early 2026. A couple is shopping for a used car when they notice something dripping from the trunk of one of the vehicles. Concerned it might be blood, they call the police, who find a dead man inside. Suspicion mounts when the owner of the lot is unable to produce a title for the car. Cari's boss, Mr. Ollaman, knows the car dealer and is certain he wouldn't kill anyone. Ollaman orders Cari to clear his friend's name while Brenington PD's detectives Genevieve and Alex search for clues to the dead man's identity. Cari is still learning to balance married life with work; her typically sharp mind is often distracted. Can she stay focused and unearth the story? Find out in Book 8!

Thank you for reading "Identity Unveiled"! Please leave a review on Goodreads or wherever you obtained your copy. For more information on my books or to subscribe to my e-newsletter, please visit my website at https://leslieapiggott.com.

Acknowledgements

- No book is complete without the amazing skills of my editor, Jennie Rosenblum! Thank you for making every book shine.
- Everyone needs a friend like my friend Desiree. She reads all of my books and blurbs and gives me feedback on how to improve them.
- Congrats to the winner of my review contest, EJ Marino! I hope you enjoyed your character. Thank you again for reviewing my book.
- To all of my readers, thank you so much! I truly appreciate your support of my writing and this series.
- To all of the authors and crew with Indies United Publishing House, you are fantastic! Thank you for your support and encouragement. Best of luck with all of your future books.

About the Author

Leslie A. Piggott lives in the Austin, Texas area with her husband and their two children. She is a scientist-turned-mom who received her doctorate in Biomedical Sciences from the University of Texas Health Science Center at Houston. In addition to writing, she also enjoys running marathons, quilting, knitting, singing in the church choir, and watercolor painting. She has previously published two watercolor and poetry books, both in 2021: *Poems in the Pandemic*, and *Art in Words*. Her first novel, *Rising Pressure* was published in January of 2022. She began publishing her first mystery series with *Chasing the Edge, book 1 of the Cari Turnlyle Series* in July of 2022. To sign up for her newsletter, you can visit her website at https://leslieapiggott.com.

www.ingramcontent.com/pod-product-compliance
Lightning Source LLC
Chambersburg PA
CBHW011514100726
47899CB00010BD/3355